Bus to Corinth

Ladine Housholder

COPPER TEAPOT
PUBLISHING

Charlottesville, Virginia

Bus to Corinth
by Ladine Housholder

Post Office Box 4492
Charlottesville, VA 22905-4492 U.S.A.
monica@copperteapotpub.com
www.copperteapotpub.com

ISBN: Softcover 978-0-9855231-2-1

First Edition

Library of Congress Preassigned Control Number: 2016912826

Cover and bus silhouette art created by Vevonna Kennedy

Maps and sketches drawn by Monica Chappell

For Dr. John Pilch
Friend and Mentor

What People are Saying About
Bus to Corinth

"Weaving solid scholarly historical, archaeological, and cultural information into an engaging narrative of historical fiction, Ladine Housholder's characters rescue Paul the Apostle from centuries of misunderstanding and misrepresentation. Focusing on his activities in Athens and Corinth, the touring group of friends learns Paul's "real" identity as a change agent ministering to expat Judeans scattered across the circum-Mediterranean world. Visits to Delphi, Mykonos, and Delos provide background for understanding the change worked by God in Jesus and preached by Paul. This book casts the Apostle in a new light and leads readers to a better appreciation of him and the relevance of his message for the twenty-first century."

—*Dr. John Pilch, Johns Hopkins University,*
Baltimore, Maryland

"Ladine Housholder's international study group women are on the road again. This time the catalyst is the funeral of one of their number. Two things become apparent as they make their pilgrimage to Corinth: for good or ill, the past is always still alive in the present, and for each of these travelers, taking the risk of choices that move them out of their own 'comfort zones' can open doors to a surprising future. Along the way, they share St. Paul's letters to the Corinthians, experiencing not so much answers to questions as parallels and companionship for their continuing life journeys. This is another meaning-filled book from a gifted author."

—*Rev. Donald A. Cornell,*
Retired Lutheran Paster, Union, Washington

Bus to Corinth is a deep and gentle story, like the quiet conversations I enjoy with my best friends as we walk along the beach in the salt of late September. It explores significant aspects of women's lives, common to all of us, with nary an ounce of preachiness but a bit of instruction through example. I love to begin a story by Ladine Housholder; but I find the ending bittersweet like the knowledge that a cherished friend has gone away for who knows how long. I miss her characters as soon as I close the book. I also find myself wanting to follow their trail, this time from Athens to Corinth with side trips to Delphi and Mykonos as well as from doubt and confusion to lifestyle conclusions that put reason above emotion."

—*Barbara Feeney Abendschein, Writing Instructor,*
Embry-Riddle Aeronautical University,
Daytona Beach, Florida

"Sometimes special journeys take us to places we did not anticipate. That is the experience of the group of friends captured in Ladine Housholder's captivating and relaxed style. Having completed a journey to the Holy Land, they plan another type of pilgrimage to honor one of their companions who passed away shortly after their return from the Middle East. Now, in her honor, they would travel to Greece and find the footsteps of Paul the Apostle. This enticing novel captures the joys, tensions, and lasting impact of travel with close friends, but also subtly rewards the reader with insights about Paul, his times, and his message."

—*Fr. Donald Senior, C.P., Professor of New Testament*
and President Emeritus of Catholic Theological Union,
Chicago, Illinois

"When you 'board' the *Bus to Corinth,* you are in for a delightful trip with a few of the women from Ladine Housholder's successful first novel, *The Well Women: Crossing the Boundaries.* The author skillfully weaves together the colorful Greek culture with inspired word pictures of landscapes and architecture. Her detailed descriptions, along with selected photographs, help the readers feel they are right there, visiting the famous Greek ruins. The trip includes tours through the important museums in various locations. During this trip, each character continues on her personal quest for self-awareness. The bonds of friendship become stronger as they study and learn together how the Apostle Paul witnessed and preached, bringing Christianity to that part of the world. This novel is a great read for women of all ages, but is also an excellent choice for book clubs or Bible study groups. The book is complete with study questions; and Housholder has even provided authentic recipes for some of the delicious Greek foods served to the travelers. Enjoy!"

—Carol Tilley, Interior Designer,
Dallas/Ft. Worth, Texas

"Great read, more than yet another travel novel. Spiritual insights into friendship, life, and love. Inspires me to re-read and re-study St. Paul's letters to the Corinthians and to take a trip to Greece."

—Verlon Stone, Coordinator, Liberian Collections,
Indiana University, Bloomington, Indiana

"In honor of a friend, recently passed away, a group of adventurous women undertake a Bible study trip to Greece, following the paths of St. Paul. This is a road trip on many levels, with a tourist's eye view of the beautiful antiquities of Greece and a revealing look at the personal stories of these close friends. They use the writings of St. Paul to guide them as they work through their life challenges with support from one another. It's a journey of self-discovery where their love for each other and a persistent desire to improve and trust themselves turns out to be a good model for living their lives."

—Sharon Armbrust, Telecommunications Consultant and Senior Analyst, SNL Kagan, Monterey, California

Table of Contents

Preface

Bus to Corinth arrives as a sequel to *The Well Women,* the story of the Samaritan woman at the well and nine contemporary women. Both novels draw from fictionalized accounts of real women who deal with issues lingering from childhood that continue to impact their lives.

Meeting originally in a scripture study group in Rome, these women forged bonds of friendship that enabled them to overcome difficult and painful backgrounds. During travels to biblical lands enlivened by exciting adventures, the women meet the Samaritan woman, Paul the Apostle, and, ultimately, themselves.

On hearing that the *Bus* was on its way, one reader said, "Wonderful. I have missed the 'well women.' They were like friends."

The list found below will serve to introduce the characters to new readers. A list of *The Well Women* characters can be found in the back of the *Bus.*

Since friends often eat together, eleven recipes of foods described in the text are also included in the back of the *Bus.* They are easy to prepare, heart-healthy, and delicious. Enjoy!

Finally, part of the research for the *Bus* included a pilgrimage to Greece, in October, 2015. The purpose was to walk in the footsteps of Saint Paul, and the trip's tour guide was Aliki Pelteki. Aliki is, without a doubt, the best tour guide around. She was everything a guide should be, and more. From ancient Greek history and mythology to modern politics, economics, geography, agriculture, and Greek cuisine, she enhanced the journey with informed commentary along the way. She even knew everyone's name by the third day. Best of all, she was concerned and caring, shepherding her flock back onto the bus with humor and gentleness. Aliki was so delightful that all the *Bus to Corinth's* readers deserve to have this information at the front of the book instead of at the back.

If you are planning a trip to Greece, Aliki is the way to go. She is a free-lance guide and can be contacted at: alikipelteki981@hotmail.com.

Cast of Characters for
Bus to Corinth

Ruth Hanford—By a quirk of fate, Ruth finds herself the leader of a trip to Greece to honor Norma, who always wanted to go but died before she got the chance. Troubled at first by images from her past, Ruth overcomes her self-doubt and brilliantly organizes every detail. She realizes that working outside the box isn't as hard as she thought.

Vicky Bright—Vicky is now retired from her executive position but not from caring for her adult daughter who suffers from lupus. With degrees in church history, Vicky offers background information about Paul the Apostle and a study guide for his Corinthian letters during the Greece trip. A gifted teacher, she clarifies, re-imagines, and encourages new ideas and interpretations about these scriptural treasures. She still hopes to finish her novel about Theodora, last Empress of the declining Eastern Roman Empire.

Beth Cassel—Following two operations, Beth's knees have healed. She is thrilled to be traveling with the group and will be their medic. Alas, the core problems at the center of Beth's marriage have not healed. Growing apart over the years, Beth and her husband ended their marriage peacefully. They are thus surprised and wounded by the unloving and sharp criticism of fellow church members. Beth is now embarked on a new life with a new house, a new job, and a new motorcycle.

Alicia Corrigan—Alicia remains haunted by self-esteem

issues from sexual abuse in her childhood. Incredibly smart, Alicia can deal with so many things, all except her verbally-abusive husband. While serving as art historian for the trip, several profound personal experiences teach her about herself, bringing positive changes that are sure to affect her marriage when she returns home.

Najila Danfi—Najila, a thoroughly-modern Palestinian, reunites with her American friends in Greece after leading them on an earlier tour in her country. Eager to improve her tour-guiding skills by observing their Greek guide, she also seeks advice about marrying a handsome suitor. Her wise and gentle words breathe new light and life into the entire group during the journey.

Minor Characters:
Efie Pappas—Greek tour guide
George Pappas—Efie's husband and driver of the tour bus
Stavros Minos—Man about town

Prologue

April 22, 2012—Tel Aviv, Israel

Dust flying, the old taxi screeched to a halt at the main entrance of Ben Gurion Airport. The taxi's back doors flew open, and Norma Schaffer and Ruth Hanford jumped out. "What a ride!" Norma squealed. "I laughed so hard I was crying. Thank God we made it in one piece . . . and with all those military check points, too."

Ruth thrust two hundred shekels in through the cracked window. "Here, Mr. Yousef. Thanks, I mean . . . *shukran*. No, no, keep the change. You did a great job. Come on, Norma. We've gotta run. Departure time is in an hour."

Cutting it this close defied all of Ruth's principles learned during her years as a flight attendant. Back then she would have been in a crisp uniform, calmly chatting in the crew room several hours early. Yet here she was, standing at the curb in a pair of orange capris and sandals, just fifty-nine minutes before takeoff.

"*Afwan*. Very welcome, Mrs. Ruth," the Palestinian taxi driver said. "You womens safe fly, *insha'allah*."

"Wait, wait," Norma implored. "Let's get a picture of us with Mr. Yousef. Who knows when we'll be back here?" She stepped over to the young Israeli soldier guarding the front entrance and, with a big smile and fluent Arabic, asked him to take a photo of Mr. Yousef,

Ruth, and herself. The handsome soldier looked shocked but agreed. Norma handed him her phone, ran back to the taxi, and she and Ruth stood on either side of Mr. Yousef's window.

"Ah, tip the hat back, Madam," the soldier said to Ruth. "Your face in too much shade." Ruth reached up, whipped off her floppy hat, and ruffled her short, gray hair.

Initiated by her dermatologist, her extensive hat collection was her pride and joy. Her husband, Pete, even teased her about it. Naturally she'd lusted after this sparkly turquoise one she'd seen in Nablus. Whoever had too many hats?

The picture was perfect. Ruth could even see all of Mr. Yousef's gold teeth glistening in the sunlight. She started to give the soldier a small tip but decided against it. She clamped her hat back on and then gave Norma a quick squeeze. "You're too much. I would never have had the nerve to do that."

Norma laughed. "Oh, he was just stunned to hear a red-headed American woman speaking Arabic. It used to happen to me all the time." She turned and waved at Mr. Yousef. "*Shukran,* Mr. Yousef. Good-bye. *Masallamah.*"

Ruth and Norma had been friends since they met in a study group in Rome ten years earlier. Although their professions were different—Norma had been a teacher, while Ruth had worked as a secretary and a flight attendant—their approach to life was the same. Western Pennsylvania girls, both were down-to-earth, practical, and very witty. They could easily light up a room. Now, after a pilgrimage to Samaria in Palestine, they were on their way home.

They hurried up the sidewalk and into the main terminal. "Where's EL AL?" Ruth asked. "Oh, right in front of us. Duh."

They got their boarding passes quickly and then had to endure intimidating stares from three rugged-looking, young Israeli women working the security lines. "No giggling, Norma," Ruth said under her breath. "These girls mean business."

One of the young women scrutinized the photo in Norma's passport. Looking at Norma, she saw a 50-something woman: slender build, medium height, with dark red hair. Yet the woman in the photo appeared a bit heavier with lighter-colored hair. She looked from the picture to Norma and back to the picture.

"I've had chemo three times since that picture was made," Norma explained. "My hair grew back a darker red each time. I actually kind of like it." The young woman's face softened as she returned the passport to Norma.

Ruth set her sandals on the conveyor belt and forced herself not to look at her watch as their luggage was opened and searched. Finally, they walked through the body scanner and set off no alarms. They quickly bought small bottles of cherry brandy at "Duty-Free" before racing to their departure gate.

"Boarding's already started, but we made it. Thank You, Jesus!" Ruth said. A fine sheen of perspiration beaded up on her forehead.

"Thank you is right," Norma whispered. "I can't wait to get on that plane and sit *down*. I might even need a drink. I've been laughing so much and trying not to cough . . . I feel like I'm going to explode. I hope my bladder control is up to the task."

Soon they were airborne, headed towards Frankfurt. When the "Fasten Seat Belts" signs were turned off, flight attendants appeared with the drink carts. Ruth asked for two glasses of white wine for herself; Norma did the same. "We deserve it," Ruth said, as she lifted the first glass. "Here's to a fantastic trip and to our safe trip home."

"And to life—whatever it holds," Norma added as she touched her glass against Ruth's. She took a big sip, coughed a few times, and then pulled out her phone. "We need a selfie, Ruth—something to remember this flight."

Norma took several pictures of them from different angles then smiled up at the flight attendant, whose cart was parked by the next row. "I'm sorry to bother you while you're working, but would you mind taking a photo of us? You're standing up, so you'll get a better view. Thanks so much."

The tall attendant casually smoothed back his wavy blonde hair as he took the phone. "Sure, glad to, no problem. Hold up your glasses. That's it. Super. Arms around each other, maybe a little kissie? No? OK, fine. Big smiles now. Fantastic! Love those earrings. Rome, little shop near the Spanish Steps, I'll bet. Here you go. Shall I top off your glasses as long as I'm here?" He handed Norma's phone back, refilled both their wine glasses, and moved on down the aisle.

Norma chuckled as she leaned her head back in the seat. "What a nice guy. This really *was* the trip of a lifetime, wasn't it? I'm so glad that I came, even though my doctor said I shouldn't. I wouldn't have missed it for anything. I loved every place we visited in Samaria, and I'm so happy that we all shared so much."

She took another sip of wine. "We couldn't have done any of it without Kay. She was so organized and always kept us on task and on time. And Najila was such a good guide, wasn't she? I loved her mom. She was so reluctant at first but then really got into things. Oh, and look what I have," Norma said with a giggle.

She opened her backpack and pulled out a small plastic bag with a wilted red rose curled inside. "I got this as a little souvenir. I picked it up at the well that last night. It was just lying on the ground next to the wall, so it wasn't like I stole it or anything. I'll dry it and then press it in my Bible."

"Oh, Norma, that's beautiful," Ruth said as she set her glass on her tray table. "What a sweet memory for you. Maybe you could even laminate it." She laughed. "My memories will run more to food, I think. Without a shadow of a doubt, I ate my way straight through Palestine. Remember those incredible donuts at the French Corner? I've got those here on my phone plus a whole lot of other stuff." She opened her phone and swiped through the pictures of the donuts, displays of colorful vegetables, fish, platters of *kibbe* and *shish taouk*, baskets of *zaatar* bread, bowls of *hummus* and *labna*, and the delectable sweets for dessert.

"Oh my, yes, all those wonderful foods," Norma said. "Seeing them makes me ravenous. Your mouth will water every time you look at those, Ruth."

Ruth grinned. "I went nuts, didn't I? But who cares? I loved every bite. It wasn't always about food, though. I was blown away by Corinne with her incredible miracle of the cross in the moon. And good old Julia:

proud possessor of the perfect complaint for every occasion. And then there was Inez. Did she ever tell you that when she first went to the States to study she didn't speak a word of English? Now she's amazing."

Norma nibbled on a pretzel. "I know. She's very smart. I spent some time with her in Rome. I also loved everything that Najila told us about Sapha and what she wrote about meeting Jesus at the well. It probably sounds silly, but I feel the same way when I have my little talks with Him. It's amazing that Najila has all this in her grandmother's notebook from her ancestors. I hope she'll follow through and get it published. I'd buy copies for all my friends."

"Oh, hi there," Ruth said to the same blonde attendant who was now coming through the aisle with the meal cart. "Love your uniform—very classy. Let's see . . . the chicken smells really good. I'll have that, please. And you, Norma? Chicken or pasta?"

They finished off with coffee and a cognac. "Jerry will *never* believe I drank this much," Norma said with a faint slur. "I'm a pretty cheap date when it comes to alcohol. With all my medications, I shouldn't drink anything; but I figured tonight was special. After all, we made it from Nablus to Tel Aviv in that hysterical taxi ride; and now I'm getting to sit next to you. I'm glad our plans changed, Ruthie; so we can travel together."

"Aw, thanks, Norma," Ruth said. "I'm happy too. You're a true friend."

Soon the lights and window shades were lowered, and the cabin settled down. Norma stretched her arms and yawned. "Sorry. I hope you don't mind, Ruth; but I think I'll take a nap. I'm a little tired." She covered herself with her blanket and was asleep in an instant.

Poor thing, Ruth thought. Two glasses of wine and a drop of cognac, and she's out. But what a woman she is. She's got a will of iron. Even with two sick lungs, she never missed a beat.

Ruth stretched out her legs and pulled her own blanket around her shoulders. She gave herself a little hug. She felt so happy tonight. At the beginning of this trip, when the group had first arrived in Israel, she'd been so bitter. Her heart had been full of anger and doubt, and she'd been ready to throw away her marriage. Yet, look how things had turned out.

She closed her eyes and let her mind drift back to when they had all first met. Years ago, they'd all been in a ladies' Bible study group at an international church when their husbands had worked in Rome. The years passed, their husbands had retired or been reassigned, one thing led to another, and they'd all gone their separate ways. Most had moved back to the States.

Fortunately, Kay, who always kept track of everything, had stayed in touch with all of them. A few months ago, after a weird dream about the Samaritan woman, Kay felt compelled to go to Palestine and had invited them all to travel with her.

And now it was over.

Ruth and Norma changed planes easily in Frankfurt. Eleven hours, three movies, and two meals later, they were walking out of customs in Atlanta, headed in opposite directions.

Ruth laughed. "Look at you, Norma. How do you *do* it? You're as fresh as a daisy, and I'm a wreck. I feel like hammered crap. My feet are swollen, I've got huge bags under my eyes; and my hair is so greasy, it looks like it was combed with a pork chop. Still, it was a great flight. I've loved every minute of this whole trip with you. I'm really gonna miss you. We've had so much fun together." Tears sprang to her eyes.

She glanced at her watch. "As much as I hate to say goodbye, I'd better get a move on. Pete's meeting me out front, and then we're driving over to Savannah for a few days. He loves that town, and I can get over jet lag there as well as anyplace. I sure hope he's in a better mood than when I left; things were pretty tense between us that last week." She sighed heavily.

"Jerry's picking me up, too," Norma said. "We're stopping to see some of his relatives in Knoxville on our way back to Cincinnati." She gave Ruth a big hug. "Thanks for everything, Ruthie. You're such a dear friend. Let's get together soon. We're not that far from each other. Maybe we could even meet somewhere, like in the middle? Text me, OK?"

"Sure, Norma. I'd love that. Take care of yourself. Eat lots of kielbasa and pierogis. You know, all that stuff we both grew up with. My grandma always said they were good for what ailed you. Oh, and best of luck with your chemo treatments."

"I'll be fine, Ruth. Really. Jesus and I still talk every day. So, whatever happens, I'll be fine."

They shared a quick hug and said goodbye. Ruth took a few steps, then turned and waved to Norma one last time.

But Norma had already disappeared into the crowd.

One

Two years later—March 8, 2014—Louisville, Kentucky

R uth's cell phone played "Memory" three times before she reluctantly gave up on her delicious afternoon nap. Still groggy, she reached for the phone. Tears stung her eyes as she read the text message.

Norma is gone. Please get word to the others from your Rome study group for me. Services at St. Matthew the Apostle Church in Cincinnati March 14, 11:00 AM Mass. More details soon. Jerry

Ruth was stunned. Oh, no, she thought. I can't believe this. I had no idea that Norma was *that* sick.

The tears flowed down her cheeks as Ruth grasped the full meaning of what she'd just read. Jerry was Norma's husband, and he was saying that Norma had died. Ruth remembered that Norma had fought a long and difficult battle against lung cancer. Yet she had never complained. She was always so cheerful, so happy, and so full of laughter and love. No, no, no, no, no! She can't be dead! She can't be!

She was one of the most loving people I've ever known, Ruth thought as she calmed down a bit. I hope it was peaceful for her at the end. And poor Jerry. He worshiped her. He'll be lost without her.

Ruth pulled her sweater around her; she felt cold.

She also felt terribly sad and more than a little guilty. Why didn't I write her more and take the time to go see her more often? How hard would that have been? I *said* I would, but something always got in the way.

Now she's gone.

Slowly, ever so slowly, another feeling started, slithering its way along, deep down inside her stomach. Was it something she'd eaten for lunch? No. She knew what it was. She thought that, after so much time, so many therapy sessions, and all those self-help books, she'd never again have this awful ache in her gut. Yet here it was.

Suddenly she was nine, seeing her mother lying there on the bathroom floor. Ruth *knew* her mother had a bad heart; she *knew* she should help her more. But no: *She* was too busy playing, goofing around, being a kid, and thinking only about how much fun she could have.

Ruth had stood in a dark corner in the hallway, clutching her sides. She had watched as the ambulance people had come and taken her mother away. She was too scared to cry. What would happen to her, her brother, and her little sisters? That whole day she had been frantic, asking all the adults who came to the house: "Who's gonna take care of us?"

She had felt so bad. If only I had been a better kid and helped Mama more, she had thought, this never would have happened. Mama wouldn't have died. It's all my fault.

Now it was happening all over again.

Fresh tears fell. Ruth cried longer this time. Finally, she wiped her eyes and blew her nose.

"Oh, Lord," she whispered, "I've screwed up again.

I've been the wrong person and done the wrong thing so many times in my life. I wasn't there for Norma just like I wasn't there for Mama. Show me how I can be the right person and do the right thing. Give me another chance, Lord. Please. *Please.*"

She heard the big grandfather clock in the hall strike four. Then she slowly stood up and wandered over to the window. She saw the bright pansies in blue ceramic pots on her front porch. They reminded her of what a super gardener Norma had been and how she had loved anything that bloomed.

Ruth smiled a bit when she remembered other legacies that Norma had left: flower petals or little sayings she printed on cards and then sealed with her beloved laminating machine; her idea of placing cotton swabs in a Belleek china pitcher in her bathroom; her profound thoughts on needing and being a well; and, mostly, her absolute indifference to social ranking. To Norma, everybody was equal; and everybody was important.

Ruth sighed. I'm really going to miss her—a lot.

She glanced around her living room and noticed its vibrant colors of green, yellow, apricot, and cherry red. It usually made her think of tropical flowers; today she thought of Norma.

Looking closer, Ruth saw the shelves and end tables were cluttered with Hummel figurines, books, tiny spoons, and a miniature water jar: souvenirs from her travels. And cats. Cats were everywhere. There were cat photos, cat drawings, and cat statues in ceramic, glass, and bronze. What did all these things say about her? That she was eclectic . . . or just a packrat?

I ought to get rid of half this stuff, she thought.

It's taking over my life—all that stupid dusting and cleaning when I should have been visiting my sick friend. Now she's gone, and it's too late.

After she wiped her eyes once more, she folded the yellow fleece throw and placed it across the back of her worn, plush sofa. She loved how the old, brown sofa always had an incredibly peaceful and restful effect on her; but, to be honest, *any* sofa did that to her. Let her get prone, warm, and quiet; and she was out.

Reluctantly, Ruth moved to her desk, slid into her chair, and tapped her track pad. She wondered why Jerry wanted her to pass the word—why he hadn't asked Kay. I'm not a writer, Ruth thought. Is this how Moses felt? 'Could You get somebody else, Lord?'

After she pasted in all the addresses, she typed two brief sentences, then paused to read them. Frustrated, she hit delete and started over. What a mess. What's wrong with me?

Her fingers were shaking, and she craved an espresso. She caught her reflection in the antique mirror on the corner of her desk. After one look at those red eyes, she was bawling again.

From out of nowhere, the face of Miss Elmer, her sixth grade Sunday school teacher, floated into her mind. Ruth remembered her gentle voice admonishing the class: "Students, you are called to be *saints*. In every way, you have been enriched in Him in speech and knowledge of every kind. He will also strengthen you to the end."

Nice, Ruth thought. I always liked the enriched and strengthened bits, but called to be a saint? I doubt it. What's that from, anyway? One of these days, I'll have to look it up.

She squared her shoulders, "Lord, please help me to do this right—for Norma."

The more she typed, the better she felt. Her stomach had stopped hurting.

Two

My Dear Friends,

Norma departed March 8 to the Great Flower Garden in the sky. Funeral in Cincinnati March 14, St. Matthew the Apostle Church, Mass at 11:00 AM. More details coming.

I'll make reservations for us at a good hotel. Let me know soon, OK?

We've got to stick together. Norma was one of us. The best one.

Love you guys,

Ruth

+++++++++

Ruth,

Thanks for BCC'ing me. I couldn't reach Kay, so I knew I could count on you. What you wrote was perfect. The day before she passed, Norma spoke of you. She was very weak—could barely talk; but she laughed softly and whispered, "I love Ruth. She is <u>so</u> funny."

I'll be in touch.

Best, Jerry

+++++++++

Hey Ruth,

This is so sad about Norma, but she's totally well now. What could be better? And think Who she's with.

Count me in for two nights. I'll arrive March 13, leave on the 15th. Bringing pictures.

See ya soon.

Alicia

+++++++++

Hi there, Ruth,

So sorry to hear about Norma. Yes, I'll be there. I'll drive down from Chicago; arrive afternoon of March 13; leave March 15. Can you send Jerry's address? I want to write him a note.

Thanks for letting us all know.

Much love,

Vicky

+++++++++

Dearest Ruth,

Poor Norma. I am very sad to hear she is gone. I am so sorry to miss this; but since I am still teaching my classes, I cannot come for the service. But my spirit will be with you all.

Please send me her husband's address. I will send him flowers.

You are so sweet to inform us, Ruth. Please give my big hugs to everyone.

Missing you,

Inez

+++++++++

In quick succession, Ruth received replies from Corinne, Beth, and Kay; they would all be coming. Kay explained that her computer had been down for three days, which was why Jerry hadn't been able to reach her. She thanked Ruth for writing to everyone.

Ruth started for the kitchen, desperate for that espresso. When her computer beeped once again, she turned back to her desk. She hoped it was Julia.

+++++++++

Dear Ruth,

I am so sorry about Norma, but she'd been ill for such a long time. Let's hope this was a release for her.

If my doctor gives me the green light, I plan to come. I've had so many health challenges lately. My diabetes numbers are all out of whack, and my meds don't seem to be doing the trick. I've been really careful with my food, so I just don't know what's behind all this.

But I want to try. Reserve a room for me, will you? I'll get back to you.

Thanks.

Love,

Julia

PS. Please ask for a room with really good air conditioning. I've got to be cool. A corner room would be nice, away from the elevator.

+++++++++

Ruth smiled as she walked toward the kitchen. Good old Jules. Same as ever.

Late that night, Ruth sat at her desk again.

+++++++++

Dear All,

Everyone's coming except Inez; she has to work. I've made reservations for us at the Silver Rose Hotel in Covington, Kentucky, just across the Ohio River from Cincinnati. Got a good price, since I needed seven rooms. Huda would be happy. Nice views, revolving restaurant. We can sample their "Chocolate Decadence" in Norma's honor.

You can Google for directions depending on your mode of transportation. The hotel is about 20 minutes from the church.

See you on March 13.

Still love you,

Ruth

PS. Julia: The manager assured me the AC is tops. He couldn't guarantee a corner room. I tried.

Three

March 14, 2014—Cincinnati, Ohio

The Church of St. Matthew the Apostle was situated in a quiet, older section of Cincinnati. The main building was constructed of beautiful fieldstone and stained woods. The roof rose to a peak over the main entrance, flanked on either side by large, terra cotta planters holding masses of bright spring flowers. Hand-carved signposts announced directions to the Family Life Center in the rear.

Ruth had slipped out of the funeral service during the organ postlude; she wanted to be sure she was at the luncheon venue in time to greet her friends. Now, inside the Family Life Center, she stood in the doorway of the Hospitality Room where the funeral luncheon would be held. Three rectangular windows opened onto a walkway connecting the Center with the main sanctuary. A flourishing peace lily plant sat on a low wooden table, and green leather armchairs were arranged in conversation groups. Scattered throughout the room were ten round tables, covered in yellow damask cloths with small daffodil plants in the center. The whole effect was warm and inviting.

On the opposite wall a counter held all the necessary service items for the luncheon. A blonde woman with a frilly, white apron arranged silverware while a young girl, probably her daughter, helped her.

Ruth smiled at the woman, then walked across the room to a table near the windows. She draped her jacket on the back of a folding chair, hoping to save a spot so her friends could all sit together. She then went over to check out the food.

A long serving table next to the wall held covered casseroles; platters of many sizes and shapes offered delectable main dishes, breads, salads, and desserts. Ruth stole a chocolate chip cookie from a silver tray. She knew immediately that Norma would have loved them. Just thinking about Norma and cookies made her tear up.

The hall slowly began to fill as people drifted in following the Mass in the sanctuary. Kay Hunter, a small woman in a gray pants suit, hurried toward Ruth. Kay's blue eyes were full of tears.

"Oh, Ruth, I wanted to talk with you earlier; but I arrived a little late. In spite of these sad circumstances, I am *so* happy to see you."

"Me too," Ruth said as she gave Kay a big hug. "I'm sorry for Jerry but happy for Norma because she's with Jesus now, so how can we be sad about *that*? Why don't you take your things to that table where my navy jacket's hanging? I'll stand here by the door and catch the others so that we can all be together."

Ruth couldn't believe what she was doing. Before, it had always been Kay giving the instructions and orders; but now, she, Ruth, was doing it. How did *that* happen?

Like a flash, Ruth was back at her mother's funeral. She saw her nine-year-old self, rigid with shock and fear, trying to corral her baby sister, who was running all over the place in a pink dress and black patent leather shoes.

She jerked herself back to the present. Stop it, she told herself. Forget the Drama Queen. Just don't go there. That was then. You lived through it. This is now. You've changed. Try to act like you know what you're doing—for once.

She arranged her face and managed a smile for Corinne and Julia as they entered the Hospitality Room. Following a few paces behind were Vicky, Alicia, and Beth. They all hugged each other as Ruth directed them to her table. Some of them joined the other guests in the buffet line, but Ruth and Alicia just had coffee. Conversation was subdued.

"Here we are, around a table again. Sure brings back memories, doesn't it, Al?"

"Really. Maybe more than I want right now."

"Beth, how nice that you could make it. How's your knee doing? We missed you on the Samaria trip."

"The service was beautiful, wasn't it, Kay? And all those flowers."

"Thanks, Vicky; my knee is lots better. I'm even back to my dance class now."

"Yes, and I loved the music, Ruth. The organist was wonderful. My, but haven't all these ladies done a marvelous job? I must find the lady in charge and thank her."

"Corinne, as long as you're up, would you get me another napkin, please? I've gotten the tiniest bit of mayo on my slacks. I am such a klutz. I really miss Norma. She would have had the perfect solution."

As the guests finished their lunch, the blonde

woman and her young helper efficiently removed used plates. Ruth could see that they'd done this together many times before. She stood up and walked over to the woman. "Norma Schaffer was a really good friend of ours. She would have been so pleased with this luncheon. You and your little assistant are doing a super job. Thanks so much." Ruth shook the woman's hand and gently palmed a twenty into it.

The woman smiled and wordlessly nodded her thanks. Then she continued her work.

Her friends had finished eating when Ruth returned to her seat. "Ladies, I'm so glad that you could all make it today. The service was a beautiful celebration of Norma's life, wasn't it? It's too bad she's missing all this. She would have loved it and had us all laughing."

Ruth's brown eyes looked sad. "I can't believe it's been two years since we all said goodbye that morning in Nablus. I'm so grateful that we all got to do that trip together." She felt her stomach begin to knot up slightly.

Alicia reached into her handbag and brought out a small album. "I know our photos are all on our phones these days, but I got some of the best ones of our trip printed because they're easier to view that way. Here, Ruth, you can start them around. I'm going to slip out for a cigarette. Yeah, I know I said I was going to quit; but guess what . . . I didn't."

Alicia handed the album to Ruth then hurried out of the Hospitality Room and through the glass doors into the parking lot. She leaned against the hood of her rental car and was soon wreathed in a cloud of smoke.

Ruth watched her go. Something's not right with

Al. I can't put my finger on it, but I know in my gut that she's not OK. Her smile doesn't reach her eyes.

"Wasn't Norma just the sweetest person?" Julia said mournfully. "She was always so kind to me on the Samaria trip, and she was always prepared for every crisis, like when I spilled stuff on my white slacks. And sometimes she'd walk slowly with me when my trick knee was acting up. The best thing was that she always had time to listen. So few people do these days."

"Oh, yes," Kay said, "and she was always so considerate of others. She was a great asset to our trip. How many times did she get us out of close scrapes with her knowledge of Arabic? And how about her instant connection with Huda? Norma had a wonderful gift of diplomacy, yet she often hid it behind a mask of humor. She had such an infectious laugh. I'll miss that."

"I'll always remember Norma's courage in spite of being so sick," Corinne said. "She never let her illness get her down and never missed out on anything. She just kept on walking. Look, Beth," Corinne said as she flipped through the photo album that Ruth had passed to her. "Here's a shot of Norma when she told us her story in Mt. Gerizim National Park. It was amazing."

"I know," Vicky concurred. "I couldn't get over how much Norma loved that trip. She loved traveling of any kind. She had this extraordinary spirit of adventure. If she told me once, she must have told me at least ten times that she wanted to go to Greece, you know, to see the sights and to find out more about St. Paul. She thought he was the greatest. Yet now, she . . ." Vicky's voice caught, and she looked away. A tear spilled down her cheek.

Beth passed Vicky a tissue. "It seems odd to talk

about this now, but I've always wanted to visit Greece, too. But I've just never had the chance. No. That's wrong. The truth is, I did have the chance—several times. I've just never done it."

"Yeah, I hear you," Ruth said. "When I was still working, I flew in and out of Athens every so often but only saw the mountains from the airport hotel's windows. We never took the time. How dumb is that?"

Again, Ruth felt the tightening in her stomach. "But Paul? Nah. Not my kind of guy. I've always thought he was so hard to understand—too complicated. Besides, he really hated women."

"Interesting," Vicky said. "Several of you are saying that you've never taken the time to do something that you'd really *like* to do. That's my middle name: telling myself I'm too busy, that I don't have time, when what I'm *really* saying is that everybody else's needs are more important than mine. Who of us is getting any younger? And Norma's not even . . . here . . . any more." Vicky's voice was choked. She paused and blew her nose. "So why . . ."

Alicia had quietly returned to the table. She swirled the cold coffee in her cup. "So why don't we talk about this later, like maybe tonight over dinner? Tell you what: How 'bout we all get together tonight back at the hotel, say around 7:00? I'll call and reserve a table up in the revolving restaurant. We'll have more time then. Look . . . Jerry's standing up, so we have to stop now anyway." Alicia then turned her chair around to listen to Jerry.

Jerry Schaffer, Norma's husband, now stood next to the table he'd shared with relatives and friends. He cleared his throat several times and then spoke haltingly. "Thank you all so much for coming today. Norma was the . . . the . . . love of my life. She was an incredible woman. She did so many things for so many others—in a quiet way without being asked. She just seemed to know what people needed. I never saw her get angry . . . she was always happy. And she had this great sense of humor; she loved a good story—a good joke."

He touched the daffodil on the table. "She's only been gone a few days." He swallowed hard and cleared his throat again. "I miss her . . . terribly.

"I know lots of you feel the same way. Your being here today tells me how special Norma was to you as well. So if anyone would like to say a word or two about how you knew Norma, what she meant to you in your life, now's the time. Let's keep it light though, OK? We're all sad enough as it is." Jerry looked spent.

Jean Schultz, Norma's older sister, rose first. She spoke about how much fun she'd had when Norma was young. "I'm six years older than Norma; so when she was born, she was like my baby. I even called her Doll Baby. I'd dress her up in little outfits and push her around in a buggy and then, later, in a red coaster wagon out near the barn. Mother was so busy; she would always say, 'The housework needs done, or the grass needs cut.' But I'll tell you: I loved playing with Norma more than housework."

Ruth smiled as she recognized Jean's western Pennsylvania accent.

"You know," Jean went on, "even as a little girl, Norma loved flowers. We'd make tiny dolls out of hollyhocks: a bud for the head and the flower for the skirt. She always wanted me to . . . save them overnight, so we'd float them in a sink full of water in our cellar. But they were always . . . wilted by the next morning. She didn't care, though. She'd just laugh and say, 'More holly dollies, Jeannie.' With all that curly red hair, Norma was . . . oh, my . . . she was like . . . like a ray of sunlight at our house. I can't believe she's gone." Jean's shoulders shook as she blew her nose loudly and then sat down.

An attractive brunette near the door raised her hand as she stood up. "I'm Melanie Allen, and I was Mrs. Schaffer's nurse. I came because I wanted to pay my respects to her. It probably sounds weird to say this, but everybody in the oncology department looked forward to when Mrs. Schaffer would come in for her chemo treatments. When the doctor would talk with her, she would laugh and say, 'Oh, I'm fine. Really. I'm not sick, just a little *part* of me is sick.'

"She was always smiling, always happy, and would always ask how *we* were. Each time she came, she'd give one of us a laminated card with a picture, or a flower, or a little saying. She told me once that her laminating machine was the best present her husband had ever given her."

Jerry's face lit up.

Melanie checked her watch. "I've got to get to work; but I just want to say that of all the patients I've ever had in 20 years of nursing, Mrs. Schaffer was the finest. When she came in, our whole world got brighter. We will all . . . miss her . . . very much." Melanie wiped her eyes, grabbed her coat, and hurried out the door.

An old lady, leaning on an ivory-tipped cane, heaved herself slowly to her feet. She said her name was Mrs. Martins and that she was a resident of the Sunshine

Senior Home. In a raspy voice, she recounted how Norma had always brought a huge bouquet of fresh flowers from her garden for the home's dining room every week.

"All of us over at Sunshine just loved Norma. Once she found a vase for those flowers, she'd stop at our tables and visit with each one of us. She'd tell us a little joke, or how good we looked, or ask our advice about gardening. She made all of us feel so special— not like some of them folks who try to preach at us and tell us about God's love. Oh, I know they mean well; but Norma never preached. She just brought us flowers and laughter. She *was* God's love." Mrs. Martins thumped the floor with her cane and sat down.

"Thank you, Mrs. Martins," Jerry said. "I really appreciate your coming today; I know it was an effort for you. Ah, I forgot this earlier; but I received a letter from Inez Varez. She and Norma were on a trip together a few years ago. Let's see, where is it?" He felt in his jacket pocket. "Ah, here it is. Kay, would you . . . read it, please? I'm not quite up to it."

"Of course, Jerry," Kay said. "I'd be happy to." She walked over to Jerry's table, took the letter from him, and read:

Dear Jerry,

You don't know me, but I feel like I very much know you. Norma told us about you during our trip to Palestine and also before, when our study group met in Rome.

When I first joined the group, I was a stranger

to Rome; and my English was weak. My husband was at his work all day, my daughters were in their school, and I was very lonely at home. During those first hard months, Norma did many special things for me. She took me shopping, introduced me to her hairdresser, and showed me where the best markets were. We visited museums and flower gardens in every corner of Rome.

And we talked and talked. All the time we talked. When I didn't know the right English word, Norma would find a way to use the word so I understood it and then could use it myself. Later she asked me to teach her some Spanish. It made me very happy to be able to do something for her—to teach her my language.

On the trip to Samaria, Norma gave each of us an important gift. She spoke to all of us with the language of love.

So I am most positive that today Norma is in heaven, talking with God about *His* flower gardens. She will speak His language.

Your friend,
Inez Varez

Kay's voice broke several times as she read the last few lines, but she carried on. She then folded the paper and handed it back to Jerry.

"Thanks, Kay."

Other guests related their own Norma stories: how they'd known her in grade school in their little country town near Pittsburgh or were her neighbors in Cincinnati. One man spoke movingly about being in a prayer group with Norma in Washington, D.C.

Norma told us about that prayer group, Ruth thought. I'll bet we know stuff about Norma that no one else in this whole room does. Well, if this guy took the trouble to come all the way out here from DC, the least I can do is add my two cents.

Soon the room grew quiet. Ruth worried that everyone could hear her heart thudding. She twisted her napkin; and then, hesitantly, she stood up.

"I'm Ruth Hanford. All of us at this table knew Norma in a . . . well, uh . . . well . . . a different sort of way. Two years ago, she went with us on a trip to the Holy Land. We visited lots of places in Palestine where the Samaritan woman at the well walked. Norma already had some health problems, but she never let them slow her down. She just kept going. She was so kind and considerate to all of us. She was also a real diplomat. She used her Arabic to make new friends, to explain things to us, and to help our tour guide. And she helped us a *lot* with our shopping."

Ruth paused to let the laughter subside. She was warming to the task. "I remember her telling us that she'd lived in seventeen different places while she and Jerry were in the State Department. But she never bragged—was never in your face about it. She loved all the travel and loved meeting people. During our trip, we shared our personal life stories. Even though she was already sick and had undergone several chemos,

Norma said that being rejected and dumped by her first husband—sorry, Jerry—was much worse than having cancer.

"At that time, I was seriously considering divorcing my husband. Norma's statement changed my life. I know beyond a shadow of a doubt that it stopped me from doing something I would have regretted forever. She also told us about how her talks with Jesus got her through the tough times. In spite of all the bad stuff, she always managed to be so happy. I think I can speak for all of us here at this table: Norma was an amazing lady. She was such an inspiration to us, and we're honored to have been her friends. And I'll bet she's still having her talks with Jesus—only now, they're up close and personal."

Ruth was very red in the face as she took her seat. "I can't *believe* I just said all that," she whispered. "They'll all think I'm nuts!"

Alicia leaned over and gave her a big hug. "No, Ruthie, they'll think you were terrific. The best. I never realized you could speak so eloquently. Who knew?"

Four

At the top floor of the Silver Rose Hotel, as
the elevator door opened, Alicia and Ruth
stepped out onto plush, silver-gray carpet.
They found themselves in the bar next to the hotel
restaurant.

"Uh-oh," Ruth whispered as she grabbed Alicia's
arm. "Are you sure we can afford this place, Al? I
mean, it's got to be a five-star room." The curved bar
was topped with black granite, and indirect lighting
was softly reflected in the mirrored wall above.
Contemporary silver chandeliers hung over the tables.

"We deserve a little splurge after what we've been
through today," Alicia said firmly. "It's going on Jim's
credit card, so I'm not going to sweat the cost. Besides,
it's really not that bad. I checked the menu online
and saw that there's something for everyone's budget.
Anyway, wouldn't Norma have loved all this elegance?"

After seating other guests, the tall, raven-haired
hostess approached them. Chic in red leggings and
a gray, knee-length duster, she might have stepped
directly from the pages of *Vogue*. Ruth explained that
they were waiting for friends, so the hostess graciously
led them to several tables by the windows.

The view was spectacular. Six stories below, they
could see the lights of a long barge snaking its way

down the gently-curving Ohio River. On the opposite bank, Cincinnati's riverside skyscrapers shimmered in the twilight sky.

"This is a super hotel, Ruth. You did a great job in picking it out," Alicia said. "My room is pretty, and this panorama is fabulous. Wonder if I could get a job up here? I'm great at tending bar. Runs in my family. Aw, forget it. I'm here to remember Norma and celebrate her life, not to whine about mine."

Beth, Julia, Vicky, and Corinne were approaching; so Ruth spoke quickly. "Al, let's talk later, OK?"

Kay came in last. When she reached their tables, she stopped and put her hand over her mouth. Tears stood in her eyes. "I don't believe this. You're all wearing the exact same outfits that you had on that night for the dinner at Adnan's. How did you *do* this? Did you plan it? I brought my same caftan along because it was easy to pack. But the rest of you?"

"No, we didn't plan it," Julia said. "I guess it was just an accident. Speaking for myself, I decided it would be a nice way to remember that great dinner; how Norma averted disaster by inviting Najila's relatives to join us; and, and . . . how we all ended up having such a nice time. Maybe the rest of you thought the same thing. I don't know. It just seemed like the right thing to do."

"What a lovely gesture," Kay said gently as she wiped her eyes. "Julia, I can't think of anything that would have pleased Norma more. Many people would say this was just a coincidence, but I believe it's something greater—like a little nudge from God. Perhaps we should toast to this."

Ruth waved to a waitress, who hurried over. When

the drinks arrived, Kay stood and raised her glass. "To Norma, now enjoying eternal life. And to all of us, as we enjoy this earthly life."

What a memory Kay has, Ruth marveled. Those are almost the *exact* words Norma told us that her prayer group always prayed. Amazing.

Soon Ruth's name was called, and they followed the hostess into the spacious restaurant. Alicia patted Julia's shoulder and reassured her that the restaurant revolved *very* slowly and wouldn't cause even the slightest motion sickness. "Well, OK," Julia muttered, "just don't make me sit by a window."

As she was seated, Julia picked up one of the red linen napkins. "Look, there's even a tiny silver rose embroidered in one corner. It fits with the silver vase and roses on the table. Classy. 'Top of the Rose' is the perfect name."

After Ruth placed her order, she sat back in her chair and gazed appreciatively around the table. Who *were* all these women with whom she'd shared so many meals? It seemed like just yesterday that they had gone to Samaria. At the end, she and Norma had shared that crazy taxi ride to Tel Aviv. Now, suddenly, two years had flown by; and here they were, together again, only without Norma.

Most of these women came such a long distance to be here to honor Norma, Ruth thought. But I couldn't even stir myself to drive a measly hundred miles to visit her more. I didn't think she was that sick. I kept putting it off; I thought I'd do it later. Now there is no later. Ruth blinked back the tears.

Ruth had felt hungry when she sat down; but after a few bites of the smoked salmon, she found herself pushing the food around on the plate. Finally, she laid her fork down. She just couldn't shake the feelings of guilt.

Alicia noticed Ruth's face. "You know, I think we're all feeling wiped out, having just been to Norma's funeral and everything; so I'd like to make a proposal. You may think I'm crazy; but instead of just sitting in our sorrow, why don't we turn it into something good, something positive, something different? I don't know . . . maybe do something or go someplace really special . . . in Norma's honor? Maybe someplace like . . . like . . . like Greece. It was something Norma always wanted to do but didn't get the chance, so now we could do it for her. I mean, we could at least *think* about it. We don't have to decide anything tonight.

"But if we do it," Alicia continued thoughtfully, "how would it be if we stayed a little longer, like at least two weeks? There's so much to see there—all that fantastic art. Norma also spoke about wanting to follow in Paul's footsteps. What if we did that? What if we went to a few of the towns where Paul worked . . . um . . . like Corinth? And, of course, it would make sense to start in Athens, wouldn't it?"

"Well," Vicky said, "for sure we'd have to go up to Delphi to see where the famous oracle was. Everything I've read tells me there's something very mystical about that whole area."

Beth leaned forward. "Part of me feels really bad, discussing something like this so soon after Norma's funeral; but, on the other hand, I see that it's the only chance we have to all be together. Somehow I don't think Norma would mind. I like your idea of Corinth, Alicia; I read and studied a lot about Paul's letters and the Acts of the Apostles in my last Bible study class. And as long as we're just dreaming, how about one of those Greek islands, like Santorini or Mykonos? One of my neighbors went to Mykonos and loved it. She said it was so beautiful."

Ruth shook her head; her face clouded. "I can't *believe* you guys. You're really serious, aren't you? We've been back together for only half a day. We've just attended Norma's *funeral,* for heaven's sake; and now you're already planning another adventure? Good *grief!* Can't you show a little respect? I feel like Beth does, or at least did, when she first started talking about it. Isn't this a little premature? I mean, Norma was a very good friend of mine. I need some time to get used to the fact that she's not here."

Ruth's words rang hollow in her ears. She was still conflicted by all that guilt that years of therapy hadn't fixed.

"All the more reason to get going with this," Vicky said earnestly. "How can you better honor somebody than by doing something that she would have *loved* to do? As I said earlier, who of us is getting any younger? Life is so fragile. Are we going to wait until the next one of us dies? Tonight, we're all alive; and we're all together. This seems like a perfect time at least to *talk* about this. Kay, what about you? You're our trip planner." Vicky dug a small calendar out of her handbag and thumbed through it. "How about mid-May? Could we get it together that soon?"

"This whole idea sounds marvelous," Kay said as she folded her napkin, "but I'm sorry to say that I can't go. I'm volunteering twenty hours a week re-vamping our local public library, plus I just started rehearsals for a little theater production that will open in June."

Kay then turned to face Ruth. "But, Ruth, you were a flight attendant; *you're* the professional among us. You could organize everything. I'll help you; I'll send you all my notes. You could also contact Najila and tell her you're thinking of doing this. She would surely have some ideas for you, as well. You'd be wonderful. I know you would."

The group was silent. They all looked expectantly at Ruth.

"What? *What?* Why are you guys all looking at *me?* Ah, no. Hold it right there. I can see what you're thinking, and you can just forget it. The answer is no. Absolutely not. Never. *Nein. Halas. Finito.* No way."

Alicia stroked Ruth's hand. "Come on, Ruth. You can do this. Where's your gusto? Remember when you said, 'If God is for me, who can be against me?' Where's the new Ruth? We'll all help you; and, besides, we don't have to decide everything right this minute. We'll be together tomorrow."

"I'll get you for this, Al," Ruth hissed. "I swear I will. Anyway, I haven't said I'd do it yet."

"You know, Ruth," Corinne said, "my Gran used to tell me that when something just fell into my lap, it was probably the right thing for me to do; but if I had to sweat and strain, I was on the wrong path. She also believed that God would always provide a way. Her job was to get into the boat and steer. God's job was to send the wind. She made it to ninety-seven. Worked for her."

"Aw, thanks, Corinne," Ruth said. "I do have faith. But . . ."

Just then Alicia's mobile phone rang. "Sorry, ladies."

She plucked it off the table and spoke tersely.

"What? Yeah. We're at dinner right now. No. It's just us girls. Look, can I call you back? Give me a sec. Wait." She lowered her voice. "Stop *yelling*! I know she didn't mean it.

"Excuse me, ladies," Alicia said over her shoulder as she rose and hurried toward the foyer. "It's Jim. Minor problem at home. I'll just be a minute."

Minor problem? Ruth thought. Really? Sounds pretty major to me.

Five

In a quiet corner in the ladies' room, Alicia sank into a gray velour armchair. Though she wanted a cigarette in the worst way, she patiently endured her husband's ugly tirade by holding the phone away from her ear for another three minutes.

When he finally paused for breath, she grabbed her chance. "Jim, I've got to go back to the table. They'll wonder what's happened to me. I'll call you tomorrow, OK? It will be fine; I promise. I'll take care of everything when I get home on Thursday. Yeah, I got a second case of Jack Daniels, like you asked. What . . .?" She heard the click, and he was gone.

She leaned her head back against the wall. She felt drained, frustrated, and angry. There was also this niggling feeling that she was being held hostage.

When will he stop drinking? Alicia asked herself. That being said, in spite of his drinking, his timing was perfect. How did he do it? How did Jim *always* manage to intrude in her personal space and ruin things for her? She hadn't even been gone two days. Yet, here he was on the phone, screaming at her that things were falling apart; and it was all *her* fault! Why did *she* always have to be the one to take care of things, not to mention bear the brunt of all his drunken rages? Leaving his job in Rome and moving back to the

States, doing a "geographic cure," should have helped. It didn't. If anything, he'd gotten worse.

He can't even handle a simple matter at home. So what if their daughter, Carrie, had stayed out a little late last night? So what if Carrie had spoken up, Jim called it "talking back," to her dad?

Maybe she's got more guts than I do. She's sure got more guts than my mom did. This all feels so horribly familiar, Alicia thought.

Alicia closed her eyes and sighed heavily. Her brain was racing. How had it come to this? Who *was* it that had rocketed through high school and college in just three years each? Who won the scholarship to study art in fantastic Florence? Who had held the lucrative IT jobs? Who was Mrs. Tennis Queen and otherwise all-round jockette? Who had survived four months of solitary bed rest in an Italian hospital in order to give birth to Kevin? Who had done every last thing her therapist told her? Who had cleaned her mental house, joined study and rosary groups, gardened like a maniac, and thought she was rid of her painful past? What a joke. It certainly wasn't *me*. I thought it was; but, boy, was I wrong. I feel like I'm slipping so fast— away from all the good stuff I know.

Maybe Dad was right. I *am* a bad girl. I deserve all this. No. Stop it. Don't even go there.

The door swung open, and a very pregnant young woman hurried in. "Oh, heavens. I've got to *go!*" She swiveled around when she noticed Alicia in the corner. "Oh, I'm so sorry! I didn't see ya'll sitting there. Hope I didn't disturb ya'll." She squinted at Alicia. "You OK?"

"Yes, thanks. I'm fine," Alicia lied as she pasted a smile on her face. "I'm taking a little rest here, but I'm on my way back to join my friends now."

As soon as the young woman left, Alicia went to the sink. She ran some cool water on the corner of one of the fluffy hand towels that were stacked neatly in a woven silver basket. She dabbed at her face and neck, washed her hands with the lavender scented soap, then dried them with the same towel.

She studied her lined face and haunted eyes in the mirror. For twenty years, she thought, I've tried my best to fix everything myself. I used every ounce of my smarts to balance things and try and make Jim and the kids happy. Now they're gone, and he still isn't happy—and neither am I.

Maybe I need a break—some time away. Maybe this trip would be perfect. When I was in the hospital for those four long months, whenever I asked for God's help, it always came. So I'm asking again, God, this very minute. Is this trip what I need now? Do I just need to get into my boat and hope that You will send the wind? It's so scary to do that. I've always tried to be the one in control of things, and look what it's gotten me. I just don't know. What I do know is that I can't go on like this much longer.

But what's Jim going to say?

She flipped her long blonde hair off her neck, squeezed the used towel into a damp ball, and shot it expertly into the silver wastebasket next to the wall. Then she straightened her beige silk slacks and strode towards the door.

Maybe I don't care, Alicia thought. For once in my life, I just don't care.

+++++++++

Ruth looked worried when Alicia returned to the table. "Geez, Al. Are you OK? I thought you fell in back there or something."

"Nah," Alicia said as she took her seat. "I'm fine, Ruthie. Really. In fact, I may be more than fine. We'll talk later, OK? Let's get the check. I've *got* to get off this foot. It's that old tennis injury, and it's giving me fits. I should ask that surgeon for my money back." She yawned. "I'm ready to hit the sack."

"Can you wait just one more minute, Alicia?" Beth asked. "After the luncheon today, I talked to Jerry and told him how much we had all loved Norma. I said that we were praying for his peace and comfort. Bless his heart; he seemed so pleased. And then, you know what? He suggested that we ought to take a cruise on the Ohio River tomorrow. A company called *B and B Tours* runs river excursions all year long. Jerry and Norma did one just a few months ago, and she loved it. They even had lunch.

"Anyway, here he is, with all that he has on his plate, thinking about us. So if you want, we could all meet there around 10:45 tomorrow morning; the boat landing is close to the bridge. There's a big sign and easy parking, as well. I know it will be cold on the river, so I'm bringing my warm jacket."

"That's a marvelous idea, Beth," Kay said. "It will be a lovely way to all be together and remember Norma. We can share stories and photos from the Samaria trip. I've got some shots of Norma that I forgot to send around to you after I got home. They're really wonderful."

The others concurred; and, as soon as they had settled the bill, Alicia stood up. "I'm off to bed. See you all at breakfast around 8:00 in the coffee shop near the lobby. Ruth, would you stop by my room for a minute?"

"Yeah, sure. But only for one minute. And if you think you're gonna twist my arm about organizing some crazy trip to Greece, you can forget it. Being a flight attendant is one thing, but being a tour leader is a whole different ballgame. Never in my wildest dreams could I do that."

Six

After dinner, Ruth went to Alicia's room; and the one minute turned into ninety. At first, Alicia dithered around, not knowing where to begin; so Ruth started the ball rolling by saying that things had improved between her and Pete. "We've had some long walks and long talks. Now we both understand each other better. We're not totally there yet, but we're moving in the right direction."

She sighed. "The Mass for Norma was really nice, wasn't it? I was impressed that so many people took the time to come here for it. She really affected a lot of people, didn't she? Some people have a talent for art or music, but I think Norma's talent was to make everybody feel that they were the most essential person in her life. I can't put my finger on it, but you know what I mean?

"Meanwhile, there I was, just taking my time, working on my mom's journals, putting together a course for flight attendants, doing a bit part in a little theater play, hanging out with my furry friends at the animal shelter—like all of that was the hottest stuff in the world."

"Hey," Alicia said. "Ease up on yourself, OK? Those things you did *were* all important, and they made you feel good. What's wrong with that? Wish I could say the same. I interviewed for a job in a greenhouse; but when they saw me in person, they told me they'd already filled the position. I know it was the 'age barrier' thing again. Oh well, their loss. I could have done that job with my eyes closed."

Alicia shifted on her bed. "Anyway, we've been pretty tied up getting settled in Orlando. I really like our house. It's only five years old and has lots of designer features, like a gourmet kitchen and a big yard with great possibilities. So I might do some gardening there.

"Then there's Jim. He's still getting used to retirement. He spends hours at the golf course, especially after I ask him to do something around the house. When he doesn't like what I cook, he throws together his own food and makes a huge mess in the kitchen. He also micro-manages my housework and has ever-earlier cocktail hours. You know, the usual 'new retiree' stuff." She twisted a lock of hair around her finger and sighed deeply. "But we're fine. Not too many fights . . . on most days."

After Alicia finished, Ruth looked steadily at her and then said, "Al, we've known each other for years; we're almost like sisters. So I can tell when you're covering up. Sounds to me like Jim is pretty much drifting and drinking. No wonder you look strung out. Cut to the chase, Al. How *are* things? Really?"

And that's when the dam broke and all of Alicia's problems came flooding out. Dry-eyed at first, Alicia told Ruth about the escalation of Jim's drinking, the shouting, the arguments, and the frequent fights over everything from their financial plans to who would feed the dog. By the time she described the extent of all the verbal and emotional abuse, Alicia was sobbing—long, wrenching, choking sobs.

Ruth put her arms around Alicia and held her for a long time. After Alicia calmed down somewhat, Ruth said gently, "Al, I hate to ask this. It's none of my business; but has there been any physical abuse as well? Has he hit you?"

Alicia took a deep breath, bowed her head, and nodded.

"Oh, Al," Ruth said sympathetically, "how awful for you. So, what happened then? What did you do?"

"Oh, you know. We kissed and made up. He said he was sorry and didn't mean it. He said he didn't know what had come over him and that it was just the drink talking. That was the first time."

Ruth's eyes grew wide, but she said nothing. The *first* time? How many times had there been? She didn't want to know.

"You probably think I'm an idiot for staying with him, but I saw my mom hang on for so many years. She thought she was being a good Catholic, doing what the Church told her to do. I guess I'm trying to do the same."

Ruth made a face. "Now I know why all this sounds so familiar. During our trip to Palestine, when you told us your life story, you said that you grew up with this same scenario. You experienced this stuff with your *own* parents, and now you're living it all over again in your own marriage. You poor thing. But haven't you . . . ah . . . well . . . haven't you ever thought about leaving him?"

Alicia shrugged and looked away. "I just keep hoping that things will change and that *he* will change.

And, hey, we're supposed to forgive, aren't we?" Tears leaked out of her eyes as she whispered, "Besides, I love him. Oh, I know it's crazy; but I do."

Ruth held her friend as the tears flowed. The room was quiet while they both digested what had just transpired. Finally, Ruth handed Alicia a tissue and said, "I feel so bad for you. Is there anything I can do to help? Have you talked with your priest? What about counseling? I can tell that you're hurting. You shouldn't have to keep living like this."

Alicia looked shattered. Her hair was a wreck, and her mascara sketched black swirls down her face.

"Here, let me help you," Ruth said. "Take this tissue. You don't want to get that mascara on your dress." Ruth pulled a compact from her purse and held up the mirror.

Alicia stared at herself and began to laugh. Then she straightened up and blew her nose. "Ugh. I *am* a wreck, and everything you said is right. I know I should do something; I'm just not sure what. I've been praying about it—for a long time."

She turned to her friend and managed a shaky smile. "Oh, Ruthie, I'm really sorry that I lost it and dumped all this on you; but talking about it, saying it out loud, has been a huge help. I just hope I'll know what to do soon."

She looked at the clock on the nightstand and sighed. "It's late. We both need to get to bed. Thanks for listening, Ruthie; you're a true friend." They hugged, and then Ruth stood up.

"Are you sure you'll be OK, Al? I mean, I could sit here with you if you need me to."

"Thanks, Ruthie; but I'm fine. See you in the

morning."

But when Alicia got into bed, she couldn't go to sleep. She mulled over ideas—things she could do to help herself. The thought came that she should write Jim a letter. Maybe she'd never mail it, but writing it would be a good way to get everything down on paper and out of the hamster wheel in her head. Years ago, her therapist had urged her to write about all the bad stuff with her dad. It had worked then, so it might work now.

She would tell Jim that she could not go on like this. He was going to have to stop drinking and start growing up, or she'd be gone. She even toyed with the idea of telling him that if he ever laid a finger on her again, she'd call the police; and he'd be gone.

The more she weighed all the pros and cons, the more she thought this Greece trip might just be a very good idea. Being so far from home would give her time for some logical, rational thinking. All her years as a computer analyst ought to be worth *something*.

She slowly began to relax. As she drifted off, an idea fluttered around the edges of her consciousness, but she was too exhausted to grab it.

+++++++++

Despite the short night, Alicia got up early. She took extra care with her hair and face, even though she was emotionally spent. Fake it 'til you make it. That would be her new mantra.

Just before eight, she walked into the coffee shop. She chose a large table with room for the others, and then ordered a poached egg and toast. She was grateful when the waitress set a gleaming silver carafe of coffee near her plate. She drank two cups, needing the caffeine.

She felt a tiny glimmer of hope as she finished her breakfast. The others weren't down yet; so, as Alicia paid her bill, she asked the hostess to please tell the other ladies that she had already eaten and had gone out. "You'll know them because they'll all be together in a group. Thanks a bunch."

She stopped at the front desk, got the address for the nearest mall bookstore from the young receptionist, and hurried out the front door. Though the sun was up, the early morning air was cold. A stiff breeze blew in off the river. Alicia dug in the pockets of her red wool coat and found her fur-lined gloves.

Near the parking lot, she stopped to admire brave, green shoots pushing out of a frosty flowerbed. In a few weeks, brilliant tulips and crocuses would appear.

Look at those little guys, she thought. They tough it out all winter long under the ice and snow; and then, one day—poof! They turn into beautiful flowers—without anybody's yelling and screaming at them. They just do it on their own. All they need is some sun. Maybe that's what I need, too.

After she entered the address into her cell phone's Sat/Nav system, she backed the rental car out of the lot. Then she followed the directions to the shopping mall. She found the bookstore easily. Sales assistants were just opening up as she walked through the doors. A colorful display of gardening books in the front aisle was very tempting. She fingered a book on perennials. No. Not today. Move it.

She checked the store directory and found the travel

section. Several large tables were covered with maps from everywhere on the planet. The U.S. ones took up at least a third of one table, but she soon located the European section. With a little more digging, she found Greece.

No, too small. No, too fat. No, not enough detail. Good grief, I sound like Goldilocks. Ah. Here we are. Hmm, a *National Geographic Adventure Travel Map of Greece* that includes areas, points of interest, and detailed road networks, along with a town location index. It also says the paper is waterproof and tear-resistant. Perfect. And only $11.95? I'm getting two. Now, what else do I need?

She selected a travel book about Greece and one about St. Paul before heading to the cash register. On the way to the parking lot, she congratulated herself.

This was fun, she mused. It's nice to have something positive to focus on for a change. Ruthie and I could make a great team. Now if only she'll agree.

Alicia caught herself humming a bit of "Never on Sunday" as she headed back to the hotel.

Seven

Although she was incredibly tired, Ruth was awake many hours that night, as well. After she and Alicia hugged once more, she went to her own room and got ready for bed; but sleep eluded her. Ruth's heart ached for her friend. She wished she knew how to help her.

All this talk about a trip to Greece bothered Ruth, too. She huddled under the blankets but still felt cold. This is so stupid, she thought. I've done a million flights, so why am I making such a big deal about organizing this trip? It can't be all that hard.

Oh, forget it. No way. I can't do it. I could never make all those arrangements. I'm not like Kay. She's so organized. Geez, I can barely organize my *sock* drawer.

She turned onto her left side and gazed out the window at the night sky. Still, there is my old buddy, Carol. She and I worked flights together for years and even did the Athens run a few times. We used to dream about taking a vacation together to one of the islands. When she retired, she opened her own travel agency. I'll bet she could help me. I could ask her.

Ruth rolled over on her back and stared at the ceiling. Slowly the face of Arlene, her stepmother, appeared in her mind. "Just who do you think you are?" Arlene screamed. "You can't do this! You can't do anything right. You never could, and you can't now. You're just like your dad." Arlene's face seemed contorted with anger and hate. Ruth cringed, just as she had all those years ago. As the frightening image slowly faded away, Ruth heard the sound of Arlene's cruel laugh. "Your dad was a dumb drunk, but you're just dumb. Ha, ha, ha, ha, h-a-a-a- . . .."

Ruth shuddered and covered her ears with the blanket. It was as if Arlene had been standing right next to the bed. Ruth lay there in a cold sweat.

Lie still, she told herself. Relax. Breathe deeply. Let it go. Let her go. She's gone anyway.

Arlene was wrong, Ruth thought as she wiped her eyes with her sleeve. She was wrong. I wasn't dumb then, and I'm not dumb now. I was a great secretary and a great flight attendant. In spite of all my depression, I never missed a trip. I was always ready and always on time. I could leave in an hour if I had to.

Another deep breath, then Ruth shifted onto her right side. Hmm, I could take pictures of those cosmetic bags and the stuff in them and send them to Vicky, Alicia, and Beth. Then they'd know just what to pack. And Carol could book the flights for me through her travel agency. But how would I find decent hotels, a local guide, or a driver?

Well, how did Najila do it? She told us she was new to the business when she did our tour around Samaria, yet everything was great. What if I asked her?

No. I can't. It would never work. The whole thing would be a huge frailure.

Ruth squeezed her eyes shut, willing herself to fall asleep. She heard the clock ticking on the bedside table. Somewhere in the neighborhood, a church bell chimed one, then two. Finally, she sat up and turned on the light. She unwound the blankets, got out of bed, found her tote bag, and pulled out her iPad.

++++++++++

Dear Najila,

How are you? I have been thinking about you. I have some sad news to share with you. Norma passed away on March 8 in Cincinnati, Ohio. All of us, except Inez, are here (March 14) for the funeral. Several of the ladies are now talking about doing a trip to Greece to honor Norma's memory. They want to see the sights and visit a few of the places where St. Paul worked—and maybe an island.

Kay can't come, so they're asking me to organize things. I've never done anything like this before. Can you help me? Your trip was super, and I loved every minute.

Thanks for your help. Hope you are fine.

Lots of love,

Ruth

PS. How is your mom doing? Please tell her we all say hi.

++++++++++

Back in bed, Ruth arranged the covers around her shoulders. She sighed deeply and felt her whole body relax. I did it, she thought. I took the first step and actually wrote to Najila. Hah! Maybe that's what Peter felt like when he got out of the boat. He knew people didn't walk on water, but he got out anyway. Oh sure, he sank a bit; but he didn't go under. A helping hand was there for him.

During the night, Ruth dreamed that she was on a shiny boat speeding towards an island. Whitewashed houses with cobalt blue doors hugged the hillsides in front of her. At the boat dock, an old man smiled at Ruth. He wore scruffy clothes and held a fish net in his left hand. *"Kalimera.* Welcome to Mykonos. I am called Petros."

Eight

March 15, 2014—Cincinnati, Ohio

After her shopping expedition, Alicia hurried back to the hotel, grabbed her alpaca scarf, and then collected Ruth, Vicky, and Beth. Kay and Corinne rode with Julia in her car. Now both cars pulled into the parking lot near the boat ramp.

"Oh, for heaven's sake," Julia exclaimed anxiously as she opened her car door. "Would you look at those clouds? I heard on the news that the forecast is for rain. I hope we don't get drenched. The last thing I need is to get a cold. It took me six weeks to get over my last one. I just couldn't stop coughing."

The women exchanged glances with each other, acknowledging that Julia was being her usual glass-half-empty self.

Ruth patted Julia's shoulder. "Take it easy, Jules. We'll be just fine. I'd be a millionaire if I had a dollar for every time the weather guys were wrong."

"Besides," Beth added with a smile, "now that you've had a bad cold, your immune system is much stronger; so you'll be protected for a good, long while."

Julia sniffed and wrapped her wide, fringed scarf tighter around her neck.

"Ladies," Kay said, as she read the sign by the ticket office, "I see they have a group price. If you'll give me your money, I'll get the tickets for us."

"Thanks, Kay," Vicky said. "You're still taking such good care of us."

While they waited, Ruth said casually, "Oh, by the way, I bit the bullet and sent an email to Najila early this morning. I asked for her help about setting up a trip in Norma's honor."

Alicia gave Ruth a high five and flashed her a big smile.

After Kay bought the group ticket, they all followed her on board. Soon the cruise boat set off down the Ohio River. Recorded announcements pointed out items of interest on both sides of the river.

Corinne and Kay stood on the outer deck in the brisk morning air. "This is just beautiful," Kay said. "Look at all those huge trees on the river bank and those lovely estates coming right down to the water . . . no wonder Norma enjoyed this boat trip."

Corinne nodded. "It must have cost her a lot of energy to get dressed and come out to do this, but it probably made her feel better. That was our Norma— always enjoying life to the fullest."

They chatted a while longer, filling each other in on the past two years. Eventually Corinne said, "Brr! I'm freezing. That wind's like a knife. Let's go inside."

"I'm ready," Kay said. "I could use a hot drink."

They joined the others who were ensconced at a table in the warm lounge. A young crewman brought a pot of coffee and a platter of cookies. Ruth noticed that he winked at Alicia when she thanked him. As he walked away, Ruth rolled her eyes.

Alicia laughed. "Jail bait."

"My, but it feels good in here," Kay exclaimed. "It started out nice on the deck; but when the wind rose, it got so chilly. Still, we had a lovely time catching up with each other."

"We've been doing the same thing," Julia said as she stirred her coffee. "So, Vicky, what's happening in your life? How's your health?"

In her late fifties, Vicky was a petite brunette whose appearance announced that she spent a lot of time at the gym and shopped at designer boutiques. Today she wore a beige cashmere tunic over black leggings. Soft fur edged the tops of her black boots. "I'm fine, thank God. My daughter has enough health problems for the whole family, so I'm grateful that I'm able to help her when she needs me. Of course, I get to have fun with my grandson when I do that.

"What else? Oh, yes. Remember that last night at the well, when I mentioned that I wanted to teach some adult church history classes again? Well, when I got home after the trip, I spoke to my pastor; and he was totally on board with it. So I hustled around and started in September. I've got a really good class going now.

"I still work on my novel . . . now and then. I'd like to finish it. I even brought my green mirror along to inspire me." She opened her purse and pulled out a small, round mirror decorated on one side with concentric circles of diamond-shaped pieces of glass, set in green, enamel circles banded with copper.

"Pretty," Julia said. "Very Byzantine. Wasn't your book supposed to be about some circus dancer chick named Theodora? Didn't she become the last empress of the eastern part of the Roman Empire?"

"Right. Wow, Julia. What a fabulous memory!"

Julia beamed.

As Beth sipped her coffee, she said, "You know, even though I'm so sad about Norma, I feel really blessed to be with you all today. I hated having to miss the trip to Samaria, but my knee just wasn't up for it. I'm happy to say that I'm almost back to normal now."

Ruth glanced at Beth, a graceful woman of medium height. Her shoulder-length white hair brushed the collar of a tan leather jacket. Denim jeans and brown Western boots encased her long legs.

Funny, Ruth thought. I know Beth is close to sixty, but I don't remember all those lines. She's thin as a rake, and she's talking so fast. Wonder what's up?

"Anyway," Beth continued, "Perry, my husband, is about to retire; so I'm looking for a house in New Mexico. I'm renting until I find just the right spot. Once I get settled, I'd like to get a job in a clinic or as a public health consultant." She sighed. "But it's really hard to get hired if your hair is as white as mine. The good news is that I'm back to my passions: learning to fly a small plane and riding my Ducati motorcycle. That probably sounds pretty reckless for somebody my age, but I just love doing both."

During Beth's explanation, Alicia quietly circled the lounge taking photos of the boat and their group and then sent them to Najila.

Alicia pocketed her phone and stood by Ruth. "Great plan, Beth, and an even greater introduction for what I'm about to say. Even though she's denying it, we know that Ruth is a highly-experienced travel professional and will make a great leader for our Greece trip. So, to help her along a bit, I picked up a few things for her this morning." She pulled a gift bag from her big shoulder tote.

"Oohhh, prezzies?" Ruth exclaimed. "I love presents."

Alicia turned to face Ruth. "First, here's a great map of Greece, then a book called *Greece at a Glance*—about the most important sites, and, finally, a book about St. Paul. There were a gazillion books about him on the shelves, but I liked this one: *Paul: His Story*. I skimmed it for a few minutes at the bookstore, and it looks good. I felt like I was reading about a normal guy—you know, an ordinary person—not some holier-than-thou type that I could never relate to. I've read good stuff about the author: Jerome Murphy-O'Connor."

She handed the gift bag to Ruth. "Hold on; let me get our crew guy to take some photos of all of us to send to Inez and Najila."

Tears glistened in Ruth's eyes. "Al, you're too much. It's true that I've been a flight attendant for a lot of years, but that's different than putting a whole trip together like we're talking about. I just got on the planes and followed somebody else's directions. Last night I realized I *could* ask for help, like from my travel agent friend and from Najila. So, like I said, I sent Najila an email and asked for her advice.

"When I finally did fall asleep, I dreamt about seeing a guy named Petros welcoming me to a Greek island. And now, here you are, with these books and a map for me. So if those aren't signposts with neon lights, I don't know what they are.

"The best thing is that those of you who are going can all help me. Alicia, you get to be the art historian; Vicky, you can handle the background stuff about Paul; and, Beth, you'll be our nurse. Ha-ha. And you thought *I'd* be doing all the work. We'll make a great team."

"Hey," Alicia said as she held up her phone, "I just got an answer from Najila. Get this: Not only did she say she'll help Ruth, but she wants to improve her tour-guiding skills by observing our guide. She's going to join us in Athens. How cool is *that*? Now all we need are some dates."

"Incredible," Vicky said. "I can't believe how all the pieces are falling together. You know, I think maybe Norma's helping us with this. I can almost feel her presence. I used to think people were crazy when they told me things like that; but, now, well, all I can say is that something really amazing is going on."

Nine

March 20, 2014—Louisville, Kentucky

Dear All,

What an emotional roller coaster Norma's funeral was, at least for me. She would have been happy that we were back together. Somehow, I think she knew it.

Najila says she's free in early May, so how does something like May 5-20 sound? I know that's not much prep time, but you guys are all pros.

Here's what I'm thinking:

Meet in Atlanta, fly to Athens; sightsee for a few days

Corinth–2 days.

Delphi—2 days

Back to Pireaus harbor; hydrofoil to island of Mykonos–2 days

Athens for one last day

Good prices at that time of year, as it's not high season. I've found some fun hotels.

Check your calendars, and let me know ASAP if these dates work for you. Flight details will then follow, and we'll be on our way.

Norma would have loved this.

Happy trails,

Ruth

PS. Read First and Second Corinthians. Alicia and Vicky, start your homework. Beth, bring a small medical kit. I'll pack the whisk broom. You never know.

PPS. Najila, I'm so glad that you'll be coming. It will be wonderful to have you with us.

Ruth got up from her computer and walked to her sofa. She kicked off her fuzzy cat slippers, leaned back on the squishy, brown pillows, and hugged herself.

This is not really me, she thought. It's somebody who looks like Ruth, but it can't really be me. I cannot *believe* I am doing this. Earlier this week I got up the nerve to speak at Norma's funeral lunch. Now I'm blasting out trip plans like I know what I'm doing. What's happening to me?

Maybe what Norma said two years ago is right: Each tiny step we take gives us courage for the next one. Maybe that's what made her so happy; she just kept taking those little steps and trusting that God would really be there for her. Will that work for me? Can I crawl out of my comfort zone and into the boat that Corinne was talking about? This is all so scary.

Maybe it would help if I read what Paul wrote to those Corinthians—to sort of get a feel for what he had to deal with and what kind of guy he was. That would be a little step.

Ruth reached over to the end table and picked up her Bible. As she hunted for the letters to the Corinthians, a small orange card fluttered to the floor. She picked it up and read:

"If an Arab in the desert were suddenly
to discover a spring in his tent, and so would
always be able to have water in abundance,

how fortunate he would consider himself—
so too, when a man as a physical being is
always turned toward the outside, thinking
that his happiness lies outside him, finally
turns inward and discovers that the source is
within him, not to mention his discovery that
the source is his relation to God."

She saw that the author was Kierkegaard. She also
saw that the card was laminated. Ruth's eyes filled
with tears.

Oh, Norma, you just keep popping up.

Ten

March 21, 2014—Nablus, Palestine

Najila Danfi turned off her TV set. She still hadn't purchased a new model, although her brother told her repeatedly he would shop with her. Why bother, she reasoned, when the news is so distressing? Besides, the local Palestinian station often had interruptions and was frequently off the air.

She walked out to her balcony, watered her lemon tree, and picked a handful of dead leaves from her grapevines and red hibiscus bush, now in full bloom. The planters were old petroleum cans, but everything was thriving. Perhaps it was the oil residue.

After she had disposed of the leaves in an old basket, she climbed the rickety ladder up to her roof. She walked over to the wooden deck chair her mother had given her for her birthday and pulled off the plastic tablecloth. She fluffed up the pillows and sat down. She needed to think; her rooftop retreat was the perfect place.

She felt confused. She wasn't sure she had done the right thing by replying to Alicia and telling her that she would meet the American ladies in Athens. She had been in Athens once, years ago with Kanaan, her husband, when he had gone for a medical conference. She remembered thinking how the antiquities were very beautiful and the museums were most interesting; but the modern city was loud, frantic, and full of noisy traffic. It was worse than Jerusalem, if that was possible.

But the thought of seeing those wonderful women again was very enticing. She was so glad they had stayed in touch after their trip to Nablus and their pilgrimage to the well in Samaria. They were all so nice, so honest, and, most importantly, so caring. Their culture was very different; she envied the fact that they were able to speak their feelings openly.

Maybe they would even have some ideas for her. She knew she could not discuss her problems with her mother, much less with her Auntie Rania. She was certain what *their* answers would be. Although Mama and Rania were very modern in how they dressed, they were firmly set in the old, traditional ways of thinking about what women should and should not do.

A light breeze lifted her dark curls. The night air was cool on the open roof. She tucked an old navy sweater around her shoulders and pulled a tattered blanket around her legs. She loved it up here, but she didn't love being cold.

In front of her, the lights of Nablus began to glow; while above her, a sea of diamonds glittered in the inky sky. So many stars were out tonight. That was surely a good omen. The constellations always gave her such a feeling of security and comfort. No matter how jangled the details of her life might be, the timeless stars were always there, secure in their same places as they moved across the heavens, always lighting the way. She knew that her ancestor, Sapha, had seen these same stars.

Perhaps I could allow myself to think of this trip as a small vacation, Najila mused. I have been very busy these past two years. I have guided many groups, not only to the sites of the Samaritan woman, but also all over Palestine. Fortunately, business has been very good; but now, with the renewed fighting, tourists will not come. Who can blame them with things so unsettled? Two thousand years separate Sapha and me, yet the same peoples fight over the same lands. So many people die. And for what? Will this ever stop?

She pulled herself back to the present. Only one small group was booked for early May. Perhaps Mama would be willing to guide them on her own. She will complain that she cannot—that her English is not good; but she will be fine. Truthfully, I think she loves doing it. Her friends now regard her differently. "You, a business woman, Huda? At *your* age?" I have seen how proud she is. And the shopping and bargaining? These are her passions.

But what of Sami? He is such a nice man, and he has such beautiful eyes. I like him very much, perhaps may even love him a bit. When he kissed me that first time, it was so thrilling.

But just because he has taken tea with me and invited me to dinner a few times does not mean I want to marry him, as handsome as he is. Auntie Rania thinks I am foolish for not flying into his arms. She thinks I should marry him next week.

On the other hand, I notice that Rania has remained a widow, even though she has had many suitors. She enjoys her single life and her travels: jetting off to London when she needs a new hat or going to an art exhibition in Paris or an opera in Milan. She spends her departed husband's money just as she pleases. I heard her tell Mama once that she had earned it. I wonder how Uncle Mahmoud really treated her.

Ah, well. Rania has a good heart; she sees how simply I live and believes I could have a society life, if I just tried harder. Hah. I know she would truly enjoy telling people that her niece is married to a leading internist, a university lecturer, and all that. Claiming prestige is very necessary to Rania.

The truth is, I like my life. At forty-seven, I have done things that many women in my country only dream of. Why should I change that just to get married? Will I be any happier?

There are still several things I want to do, like publishing Gran Najet's notebook—making Sapha's story more widely known—and becoming a better tour guide.

These would be difficult if I had the responsibility of running a big house, entertaining, and all the many jobs that would go with marriage to an important doctor such as Sami Ayed. I might have more security, but I would lose my freedom. And I would always stand in his shadow. I am not a fresh-eyed girl of twenty; I can see what lies ahead.

And what example would I show to young girls, like Hani's daughter, my niece? That a woman is only complete if she has a man? That she can do nothing on her own? That was the way of the past. Now things are changing.

Still, Sami is so handsome, kind, and generous, plus he was a dear friend to my Kanaan. Would I ever find anyone else like him? It would hurt his feelings if I said no.

Would it hurt my future if I said yes?

Aiyee! What is the right thing to do? I do not know. What I do know, though, is that I could join those strong American women in Greece, hear their ideas, see some of that country with them, observe and learn from their tour guide, and very much enjoy a trip that I am not leading. So I will do that.

Najila stood up, covered the wooden chair with the plastic tablecloth, and anchored it with a rock. As she climbed carefully back down the ladder, she looked up at the stars once more and saw a meteor shower flash across the night sky.

Her heart filled with wonder. Is that a sign for me? Sapha, is that you?

She lingered on the ladder a few moments more, then came back down into her small living room. She studied her reflection in the mirror by the door. If I make this trip, I will have to buy a few new things, she decided. These jeans are old and frayed. And this loose shirt? No. Greek women are more fashionable. And my hair? It is fuzzy and unruly. I must get it trimmed. Mama will be pleased.

A glance at her watch told her that it was only 8:00 PM. Good. I will call Mama and tell her of my plans. I will see if she can do the small tour in May. It is possible that she will actually enjoy doing one alone. Perhaps Maher, her new husband, might even join her.

Najila smiled as she picked up her mobile phone. What would Sapha think: me, a Samaritan Palestinian, making a trip to Greece with my American friends?

I think she would be happy.

Eleven

March 21, 2014—Louisville, Kentucky

A red pencil stuck behind her ear, Ruth made herself a large cappuccino and then sat down at her kitchen table. Tilly, her white Angora, was stretched out next to her chair. Ruth unfolded the map of Greece that Alicia had given her and smoothed it out in front of her. Several pieces of blank paper lay next to the map as well as a packet of colored stickers. Her laptop rested on a bar stool near her. She sipped the frothy drink while she drummed a rapid tattoo with the red pencil.

OK, let's see, she thought as she began to jot down notes. I'll leave from Louisville, Alicia from Orlando, Vicky from Dallas, and Beth from Albuquerque. Najila will fly from Tel Aviv; she'll do her own reservations. I've already told Carol, my travel agent, the main flight dates and that we want to meet in Atlanta, fly to Munich, and then to Athens. We can get a good price from Delta on that route. I still need to ask her to find a Greek tour guide.

Ruth peeled off four colored stickers and attached them to the map at the four cities she'd chosen: Athens, Corinth, Delphi, and Mykonos. Using the map app on her laptop, she calculated the distances between each town. She saw that it was possible to do the route she had in mind and not be too hectic. She'd have to factor in stops for coffee, lunch, and shopping. They'd need naps, of course, because, except for Najila, they'd all be dealing with jet lag.

She took one of the pieces of blank paper and sketched a simple itinerary:

Day 1: Arrival in Athens, check into hotel, unpack, and freshen up. Maybe short walk in Syntagma Square, National Gardens. Dinner at hotel. Early night.

Days 2-4: Acropolis. Acropolis Museum (Lunch in museum restaurant. Make a reservation.) Areopagus (where Paul spoke to the Athenians). Other museums. Roman market (*agora*.) Lycabettus Hill. *Attica* department store. Dinners in *taverna*; list in Greece book.

Days 5-7: Drive from Athens to Corinth. See old city. Corinth Canal boat ride—another reservation. Discuss Paul's time in Corinth; letters he wrote to the Corinthians.

Days 8-9: Drive from Corinth to Delphi. Visit ruins; site of the oracle. Other religious beliefs that preceded Judaism and Christianity? (Vicky?) Need hotel.

Days 10-11: Drive from Delphi to Pireaus harbor. Hydrofoil to island of Mykonos. Fun in the sun. Maybe ferry to Delos: birthplace of Apollo. Need hotel.

Day 12: Afternoon hydrofoil back to Pireaus; drive to Athens—same hotel. *Taverna* for drinks and dinner.

Day 13: Last Athens sights, souvenir shopping in Monastiraki. Dinner and Greek music at restaurant in that area. Same hotel.

Day 14: Packing, check out of hotel, afternoon flights home.

Ruth finished the now cold cappuccino, then sat back and reviewed her efforts. That looks like a lot of stuff, she thought. But we might as well go for all the gusto we can. We can always dump a few things if we're tired.

Now I'll find at least three hotels in each town and send my choices to Carol; she'll get the best deals. And I still need to choose sailing times for the Corinth Canal cruise boat and for the hydrofoils to and from Mykonos. Museum opening times are in that travel book of Greece.

What else? Oh, yeah, the photos of the cosmetic bags. Never mind. I'll do them tomorrow. I'll stick them in an email along with a packing list. Now maybe I ought to get serious and finish reading Paul's letters to the Corinthians that I started the other day before I got sidetracked.

She picked up her Bible from the table where she'd laid it, stretched out on her sofa, and began to read. Two hours and four pages of notes later, she sat up, refreshed and invigorated.

I've got a whole different picture about Paul now, she thought. I've heard lots of these famous one-liners all my life; but when you read these letters all the way through, you can really see who he was, the people he was dealing with, and all their issues.

And from the sound of it, he couldn't have picked a tougher place than Corinth turned out to be. He worked so hard, loved those people so much, but had so much opposition and criticism. He went through hell and high water for them. Well, probably not just them, but for all the other groups he preached to, as well. Yet he just kept on. He believed he was right, that he had a job to do. Talk about commitment. Do we all have our own "Corinth?"

A word he used over and over was "called." In First Corinthians, he used it six times in Chapter 1 and nine times in Chapter 7. This was a really big deal for him. He felt that he was *called* to tell these people that Jesus was the Messiah, and they were *called* to live like they believed it.

She scratched her ear. On the Samaria trip, I remember telling Julia that she could get a new calling, could try to change, to listen to what her husband was telling her, and not keep letting the old critical injunctions from her mom and all her female relatives drag her down. I wonder if it's working for her?

What's my call? Back in the day, I used to think I was called to work for the Campus Challengers and, later, to be the best flight attendant I could be. But that was then. Has my calling changed? What am I being called to do *now*? Is it something as easy as organizing this trip to Greece? Funny. Trip Planning 101. Well, why not? Paul said that whatever we do, we should do everything for the glory of God. I'm up for that.

She felt pleased with herself. This isn't as hard as I thought. I guess I have learned some stuff. Arlene was wrong. Why did I waste all those years, letting her nasty, hateful words affect me so much? It was like I was schlepping around this five-hundred-pound bag of garbage.

But I wasn't the one with the problem. It was Arlene. I am *not* dumb. I can do this. I am doing it. Woo-hoo!

+++++++++

March 21, 2014

Dear All,

I'm almost done with the trip plans. I've made a tentative itinerary and sent our flight needs to Carol, my travel agent. I have also asked her to find us a good tour guide. I sent her a list of possible hotels in each town; she'll pick nice places at good prices.

Before we confirm those, I need to run something by you. What would you say to the four of us splitting the cost of Najila's hotel rooms? She runs on a pretty tight budget, and this will be a little surprise for her. I mean, she did so much extra stuff for us in Samaria.

Let me know.

Love you,
Ruth

PS. The mailman just delivered an envelope from Jerry. It's probably for all of us. I'll stick it in my suitcase and bring it along. It feels like a card.

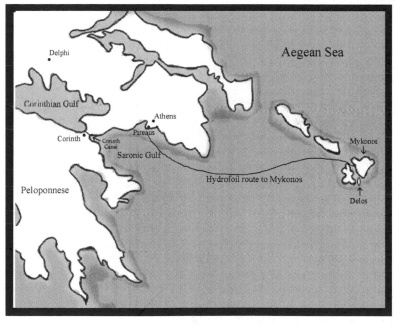

Map of cities the ladies will visit

Twelve

March 22, 2014

Hi Gang,

Super itinerary, Ruthie. I knew you could do this. Fine with me about covering Najila's hotels.

I also want to put in an early request for some time at the National Archeological Museum. This place houses many of the things that the famous archaeologist, Heinrich Schliemann, found: all kinds of sculptures, pots, and figures of every sort. The really big deals are the amazing artifacts, especially a fantastic mask, maybe of Agamemnon, all in hammered gold.

Schliemann was amazing, as well. Born in Germany in 1822, he worked in Amsterdam, Russia, and California and learned twenty languages along the way. When he was forty, he made a huge career change and switched into science and research. He went to college at the Sorbonne in Paris, traveled around the world, sold off all his assets (sixty-five million in today's dollars), and went to Turkey to search for Troy. He excavated a lot of really important artifacts and changed the way archeology was done.

This guy really followed his passion. Maybe there's a lesson for me.

Love ya,
Alicia

PS. Pack good walking shoes. The ground around the

Acropolis and in Corinth is very rocky. Save the party sandals for dinner.

++++++++

March 23, 2014

Al -

Will all this stuff be on the quiz? Geez!

Ruth

++++++++

March 25, 2014

Hi there,

Now that Ruth and Alicia have done so much work, I decided I'd better get busy as well. I wanted to get something to you before this; but my daughter's been sick again—in and out of the hospital with more lupus complications. I help her as much as I can.

You all know that my degrees were in theology and church history, not scripture study; so I'm working outside of my comfort zone here. That said, I've come up with a plan of how we can pool our knowledge and share insights about Paul and his letters to the Corinthians.

There are sixteen chapters in I Corinthians and thirteen in II Corinthians. So how about if I take I Cor. 1-6; Beth, you cover I Cor. 7-16; Ruth, you do II Cor. 1-6; and, Alicia, you finish up with II Cor. 7-13? It will be like what Kay asked us to do with the Samaritan woman's story in John 4: 1-42, only a bit longer.

Read both letters first before you zero in on your particular chapters. You might also want to skim through the Acts of the Apostles, particularly Chapter 18, since that's when Paul comes to Corinth. Then read through your texts, jot down your general impressions, and maybe make a little synopsis. Make a note of any passage or any concept that really jumps out at you. What was Paul trying to say in that section?

What does Paul tell us about himself? Who were some of the people, or at least, the kinds of people in his Corinthian group? What were some of their questions and issues? What's relevant for us today? You might even write down two or three questions for discussion. It will be just like our Rome study group.

(Author's Note: These suggestions are listed in the back of the book as Study Guides.)

Meanwhile, I'll get going with some background material about Corinth and Paul. In the books I've already read, each author has his own concepts, his own agenda, and tends to discount other scholars. Imagine that! So my thought is that if we study his letters, we can form our own ideas of what he was trying to do. I've never been a big fan of Paul's, but all this reading is changing my mind.

This won't be a heavy-duty theology or scripture study. It will just be well-traveled, smart, talented (and beautiful) friends sharing their ideas. In my book club, one of the things I like best is that everybody sees things differently. That adds so much to the discussion.

The same thing might happen with us. Because we all come from different family, educational, and church backgrounds, we'll each have our particular take on things. Who knows? We may turn out to be a lot like the original Corinthians!

Love you,
Vicky

++++++++

March 25, 2014

Ladies -

Thanks to Ruth, Alicia, and Vicky for all of your super information. You'll make us the best-prepared group ever. I know you've all done lots of traveling, but I want to pass along a few things.

First, no shots are required for Greece. However, you might want to update your tetanus immunization. Of course, bring your insurance card. Athens has several international pharmacies. The other towns we'll be visiting might have small pharmacies, but they'll be pretty basic. Therefore, bring an adequate supply of any prescription meds.

Be sure to bring your sunglasses and a good sunscreen or block. Greek sun can be very strong. Pack a few band aids, your most effective diarrhea remedy, and maybe something for headaches and colds. I'll bring a few more essentials.

Don't forget your favorite water bottle. You'll need to drink a lot, but go easy on the beer and wine. Alcohol dehydrates.

As Alicia said, good walking shoes that you have already broken in are a must. Wearing new shoes on a trip is a recipe for disaster. And if you don't already, start walking a lot in these next few weeks. Get in shape. Your legs and back will thank you, and you'll enjoy the trip much more.

I'm excited about going to Greece with you. I'd love to bring my Ducati, but a motorcycle is too big for my suitcase. I'm going to travel light. It will be so nice just to relax and not have anything to worry about. I am so ready for that.

See you soon.
Love, Beth

Thirteen

May 5, 2014—Atlanta, Georgia & Athens, Greece

When they all met for a quick lunch in the Atlanta airport food court, Vicky gave each of them a thin folder. Inside were copies of the texts of First and Second Corinthians complete with study guides. "For your inflight reading pleasure," she said, "to keep things fresh in your mind. This is easier than hauling a big Bible around. You can just stick this folder in your tote or backpack."

"Thanks, Vicky," Beth said. "I did read both of Paul's letters to the Corinthians, but it's been several weeks ago. So it will be good to review it all. And you gave me my very favorite chapter: First Corinthians 13. It's the one about love. Those verses are so precious to me. Sometimes I don't do all the things he says, but I know I should."

"Yeah, this is really good," Ruth added as she flipped through the folder. "Now if I can just find where I stashed the notes I made when I first read my part...."

"Very handy, Vicky," Alicia said. "Thanks for putting all this together. Now, why don't I take some photos to send to Kay and the rest of the gang? Scrunch together at the table a bit, OK? Fine. Ruth, would you take one of me with the others? Perfect. Oh, and I'll send these to Najila, as well. I wonder what she's doing today?"

++++++++

The flight from Atlanta to Munich was smooth. The Delta 767 jet was only two-thirds full, so they had room to stretch out. "Gotta love this!" Ruth whispered as they all quickly laid claim to their own row two minutes before the 5:30 takeoff.

When dinner was served an hour later, Ruth remembered the inflight dinner with Norma when they flew from Tel Aviv back to the States two years before. How fun that was, she thought. We laughed our brains out. Maybe that's another thing I could do to honor Norma—lighten up and laugh more. It worked for her.

Ruth lifted her wine glass from her dinner tray and said softly, "To Norma. I'll always remember you with love and laughter."

They dropped through the clouds early the next morning. As they approached Munich, the flaming red and gold of the sunrise blazed a brilliant contrast to the verdant forests and farmlands surrounding Franz Josef Strauss Airport.

During the three-hour layover, they used the time to stretch their legs, do a little shopping in Duty Free, and sample the local specialties at Dallmayr's café. Beth and Alicia ordered coffee and a pastry, but Ruth and Vicky had a Weissbier and a pretzel.

Alicia shook her head. "Are you guys nuts? It's only 6:30 in the *morning!*"

"Hey, we're in Germany," Ruth said with a smile. "Lots of these folks drink this wheat beer for breakfast every day. Liquid bread. Al, take a photo of us, would you? Pete will never believe this."

They were in the air again by 10:00. After some turbulence over the Alps, things settled down when they crossed into northern Greece; and the landing in Athens was smooth. Ruth noticed the mountainous terrain near the airport resembled the landscape around Salt Lake City where she'd been based as a flight attendant.

The group disembarked and walked into the Arrivals' Hall of the modern Eleutherios Venizelos Airport, located at Spata, thirty miles from Athens.

"This terminal is fantastic," Ruth said. "it's light-years better than the old place that I used to fly in and out of back in the day."

Beth looked puzzled. "Hmm. All the signs say Spata. Here all this time, I thought this airport was in *Sparta*. Is there some mistake?"

"Spata is correct," Ruth said. "I thought the same thing until I looked it up. The town of Sparta is over in the Peloponnese, about seventy-five miles from Athens. Not to worry; we're in the right place."

After passport control, they found the baggage claim area. All of them had chosen to pull their own carry-on—all except Alicia who had checked her bag at her first departure in Orlando.

The others now stood with her at the baggage carousel as she waited. And waited. And waited. The area around their carousel was almost deserted. Everyone from their flight had collected their bags and left—all except Alicia whose grim expression didn't match her stylish Chico's outfit.

"I knew this would happen," she said angrily. "I

just *knew* it. I have a perfectly good carry-on—not too big and with great wheels. I wanted to pull it on board; but, no, Jim tells me I should check it because it would be less bother that way. He thinks he knows everything. We had a huge scene about it just before I left home." Fighting back tears, she sighed heavily as she flipped her long blonde hair off her neck. "Why do I always let him do this to me?"

"Hey, take it easy, Al," Ruth said as she laid her arm on Alicia's shoulders. "It's OK. Don't beat yourself up about it. Listen, we'll go to the baggage office guys and tell them what happened. You fill out this form, give them your name, hotel, blah, blah; and they'll see that it gets delivered. It happens all the time. Anyway, you're wearing your jacket and your walking shoes; and you've got your passport, glasses, money, and meds in your backpack. Those are your most important items. We'll get you some stuff to tide you over. This way, you don't have to schlep your suitcase yourself. It will be brought right to the hotel."

Ruth's face broke into a huge smile. "Besides, Al, this might mean a trip to that *Attica* department store. A mandatory expedition? Five-star shopping? What's not to like? Shopping trumps jet lag any day."

Fortunately, an accommodating agent at the lost baggage window who spoke perfect English assured Alicia her bag would be delivered as soon as it arrived. While Ruth and Alicia were arranging that, Beth had spotted an airport pharmacy a short distance down the concourse.

As they entered the pharmacy, Ruth said, "Al, don't bother about shampoo, shower gel, or body lotion. The hotel will have those. Stuff might cost more here than it would in town, but never mind. Don't even look at the prices. We're here, you need them, and you're getting them. Done. Now we won't have to hunt for a drugstore the minute we get to the hotel. As soon as you've paid, we'll be all set; and we can go out and find the bus."

They located the express bus station directly in front of the airport main entrance. "The Metro's quicker. It takes only thirty minutes to our hotel," Ruth explained, "but I figured we'd see a lot more from the bus because we'll be above ground the whole time. The bus will stop fifty yards from our hotel door. Anyway, this is a perfect spot to people watch. Look, down by that Olympic Airways bus . . . don't you love those new crew uniforms? Great colors."

Beth was enchanted with the powerful motorcycles that roared through the pick-up zone in front of them. "I've counted at least seven different makes, just since we got here. I sure miss my Ducati," she said wistfully.

Vicky took several quick photos with her phone. "These Athenian women are gor-ge-o-so. They're all so *thin*. They must never eat."

Alicia dabbed at her eyes, held her backpack tightly on one shoulder, and said nothing. She loved her old backpack; it had been all over Italy with her when she was a student. Today it offered a small measure of comfort.

"OK, ladies," Ruth said as she patted Alicia's arm. "Here comes the bus. I've got enough euros for the tickets. Just be sure you stamp them in that little orange machine."

They stowed their bags in a luggage area in the center of the bus and collapsed into four empty seats.

Vicky put her arm around Alicia. "Just think: you don't have to mess with your suitcase on this bus. Yours will be hand delivered to your room, you lucky dog."

"Luck has nothing to do with it," Alicia muttered darkly. "More like stupidity. This whole thing was bad karma from the beginning."

"Aw, come on, Al. Lighten up," Ruth said. "We're in golden Greece. It's not raining, and this is gonna turn out to be a fine day. You'll see. And besides, Jim is 8,000 miles away!"

As their comfortable bus sped along the highway, Beth captured the scenery on her phone. "See those vineyards and pine trees over there? I read that grapes have been grown around here since ancient times. They still make retsina the same way today: by adding pine resin to the grapes."

Vicky was reading her map but glanced up just in time to see the familiar IKEA sign flash by. "Hey, if we get bored in Athens, we can always come back and pick up a few fun things at IKEA. I just love their stuff."

As they drew closer to Athens, blocks of elegant, commercial establishments began to appear, followed by areas of fashionable houses. Ruth noted the U.S. Embassy, bristling with pointed metal fences and rooftop antennae. A little further on, they passed the War Museum and the Byzantine and Benaki Museums. Soon they were slowing down and turning into Syntagma Square.

Alicia straightened up and rubbed her eyes. "Are we here already? I must have slept the whole way." She looked down. "What's this? Did you put your sweater over me, Ruth? Aww, thanks."

"Don't mention it. I figured you needed to chill . . .

but not literally. Naps are great."

The bus stopped in Syntagma Square, very close to the *Amelika* Hotel where Ruth's travel agent, Carol, had booked their rooms. They checked in just after two o'clock and now stood in the lobby, artfully decorated in a neo-classical style. To the left, a long entry table with a gold leaf base held a large arrangement of fresh flowers and palm fronds. The floor was gleaming black marble with the Greek key design in gold near the walls and in front of the door.

Ruth looked at her watch. "OK, ladies. You're free for the rest of the afternoon. We could meet over there in that little bar, say around five, for a drink and then figure out what we want to do for dinner. We can go out and find a *taverna*; or, if you're too tired, we can eat right here in the hotel restaurant. Actually, maybe we should eat here, since Najila is supposed to arrive around 8:30. So how about we clean up a bit and then head out to *Attica*?"

"Gosh, Ruth, I'd love to go with you," Vicky said, "but I've got to get some sleep. I'll set my alarm and meet you down here at five."

"Me, too," Beth said. "After all those hours on the plane, my knees need to unbend and stretch out flat for awhile."

Alicia looked slightly more relaxed; the nap on the bus into town had done her good. "Sure, fine, Ruthie. I just need a few clothes and maybe some sandals. I'll meet you down here in forty minutes."

The attractive young woman at the hotel reception desk then spoke to Alicia. "Excuse me, Madam, but I see you come without luggage. There is some problem?"

"Yes, you could say that," Alicia answered. "I

checked my suitcase in Orlando, Florida, in America; and it didn't get here when I did. We filled out a form at the airport, and the agent assured me that my bag would be delivered here whenever it arrives. My friend and I want to go to the *Attica* store to get a few things for me to wear this evening."

The young woman's dark eyes showed her concern. "Oh, I am most sorry. That is annoying. *Attica* is very close by to us. I will prepare a small map for you. You may pick it up whenever you are ready."

Ruth linked arms with Alicia as they headed to the elevator. "See, Al? I told you it was going to be a fine day. You either fly by faith or you don't. If God is for us, who can be against us?"

Fourteen

Forty-five minutes later, Ruth and Alicia met in the lobby. They both looked considerably refreshed. As they stepped out onto the crowded sidewalk, Ruth held the map that the hotel receptionist had given her. "Let's see. She said to stay on this side of the street, walk along in front of the Parliament building, then cross at the Grand Bretagne and walk along the right side of that hotel 'til we get to their pub called GB Corner. Take a left there, and then walk along that busy street until we come to the store. She said we can't miss it. C'mon, Al. Let's go."

Inside the main entrance of *Attica*, giant marble columns crowned with carved acanthus leaves towered over their heads. Dark mahogany counters shimmered under subdued lighting. Ruth noticed that the sales assistants were attired as stylishly as the customers. "This place is fabulous. It could rival *Harrod's* or *Neiman Marcus.*"

"Come on," Alicia said impatiently. "Stop gawking. I need some lotion; there wasn't any in my room. Then I'll see about the other stuff. Where's the store directory? Oh, there it is, by the escalator."

They located the cosmetics department and began browsing through the international brands. A slender, elegant woman, garbed in an exquisite, black silk suit, approached them. "How may I help you ladies?" With raised eyebrows, her frosty glance swept over Alicia's slightly rumpled clothes; but she said nothing.

Alicia looked directly at the lady in black, deliberately twisted a wide gold bangle on her arm, and then smiled sweetly.

Ruth tried not to laugh. They're like two cats sizing each other up, she thought. And they're both pros at this game.

"We just arrived from America," Alicia explained, "but my luggage didn't. So I need some lotion, some lingerie, and a few clothes for this evening. I'd like a small bottle of the Biotherm Eau d'Energie. That's the orange one."

"Certainly, Madam." The woman paused for a long beat, as if coming to a decision. Then she flashed them a big smile. "You know, the same thing happened to me when I went to New York a few years ago; so I understand how most irritating that can be. If you ladies will just wait a moment, I will collect some small items together for you."

Soon the woman returned, carrying two fashionable tote bags loaded with small sizes of makeup, creams, lotions, potions, perfumes and even colorful, silk print scarves. "These are samples our suppliers give us. I want you ladies to have them, with our compliments, of course. And if you are free later this afternoon around five, I would also like to offer you a complimentary makeover. I will have our girls fix you up very pretty for tonight."

Tears welled in Alicia's eyes. "This is all so nice, but . . . but . . . we have two other lady friends back at the hotel. We promised that we'd meet them for a drink around five."

"No problem," the woman said. "Bring them along. We can make all four of you beautiful this night. It will be good training for my girls. Now, I call my friend, Elena, in Ladies' Fashions. She will assist you with some clothes."

"Thank you so much," Ruth said happily. Below the counter, she gave Alicia the thumbs up sign.

The woman smiled again. "When this happened to me in New York, the ladies there helped me. Now I just pass along to you." She turned, picked up her cell phone, and spoke in rapid Greek. "Ah, Ellie, a lady here needs some clothes. Her suitcase did not arrive on the same airplane. We will take care of her. Fine. She is tall, very blonde, and very tan. I will send her and her friend up to you. Two minutes. We will do a makeover down here for them this afternoon also." The woman then turned back to Ruth and Alicia.

"Please, ladies: take the escalator just over there, get off on second floor, walk straight along to Ladies' Fashions. When you come back to me later this afternoon, please to wear the clothes you will wear this night. Then there will be no rush back to hotel to change before dinner. We will take our time, make this relaxing for you. You can go out to dinner directly from here, and you will look beautiful!"

As Alicia paid for the lotion, Ruth punched her lightly in the arm. "What'd I tell ya, Al? A fine day or not?"

"I just . . . I mean . . . I can't believe this," Alicia stammered as they left the cosmetics department. "I don't . . . I mean . . . what did I do to deserve this?"

Ruth clucked her tongue. "Girl, your '*deserve* level'

is way too low. Some people might think that what's happening here is just a coincidence. I think it's a total God deal. After all, don't you like to do nice stuff for *your* kids? I rest my case. Just relax and enjoy all this attention."

Elena was waiting when they arrived in her department. She assisted them very well indeed. "Welcome to Ladies' Fashions, madams. I am Elena, friend of Liana in Cosmetics."

She took a few steps back and cast a long look at Alicia. "Hmm . . . let me see. Yes, good. I have perfect things: perhaps a light, cream top with some little sparkles and, oh, yes, some bronze, silk balloon pants with little ties on legs. And a soft shawl in pale aqua for when evening becomes cool. Not too expensive, either. All from spring sales. Come with me, ladies."

When Alicia tried on the clothes and stepped out of the dressing room, Elena clapped her hands.

"Yes, yes. Perfect, Madam. They are very right for you. Your gold hoop earrings so nice, Madam. And your blonde hair very long. Is it not hot for you?"

"Yes, it is," Alicia admitted, "but my husband likes it long." Ruth rolled her eyes.

Alicia shrugged, then opened her wallet. "Can you take a credit card, Elena? It's international."

Elena quickly completed the transaction. "I make you some extra discount, too." She winked at them. "I want you should enjoy your stay in Athens."

After they thanked her profusely, Elena said, "Please, after you have makeover, come up and find me. I want to see you finished."

They made a quick stop in the lingerie department and were soon back on the street, heading up to the hotel. Alicia suddenly slapped her forehead. "Sandals! I forgot to buy sandals."

"I saw a shop," Ruth said, "really more like a hole in the wall, just before we crossed by the Grand Bretagne. Let's see if we can find it." They retraced their steps, located the shop, and did a little bargaining; and, soon, Alicia was the proud possessor of a pair of tan leather sandals. "These are actually comfortable, too," she said. "For ten euros, how can you go wrong?"

"Huda would be proud of you, Al," Ruth said with a laugh. "Now let's get back. I've got to have a nap. I'm fading fast."

At four-thirty, Ruth called Vicky and Beth to alert them of the changes. Shortly before five, Alicia and Ruth were introducing them to Liana. Four young, smiling assistants in white smocks stood behind her.

"We are most happy to welcome you ladies to our Cosmetics Department here at *Attica*," Liana said. "Because you are four, we have arranged places in our Facial Salon for you. The chairs are most comfortable there, and it is more quiet. Please, come along with me."

Vicky's eyes widened as they entered the salon. Soft lighting shone from alabaster wall sconces, while serene music surrounded them like a silken shawl. The air was scented with the fragrance of rosemary and lavender candles lit at each station. A young attendant passed among them, offering glasses of champagne.

Ruth laughed. "Am I in heaven? This is fantastic— beyond my wildest dreams!"

After the women were seated in padded, reclining chairs, their makeup was carefully removed; and warm towels were wrapped around their faces and necks.

Once they were covered, the head assistant spoke to them. "Anna is my name. First we do small facial and then little making up. Please, you ladies close all your eyes. Do not open until we finish, yes?" Anna giggled. "You get big surprise. We make you very beautiful for this night. Who knows? Maybe you meet cute Greek guy." Everyone laughed, and then the four assistants set to work.

When Alicia opened her eyes, she gasped. Her hair had been swept back and fastened with a burnished gold clip on one side. Her skin glowed from the facial and gentle massage. Deftly applied makeup concealed her tiny laugh lines and left her with a soft, natural look. Her long lashes were brushed with gold-toned mascara, and her beautiful eyes were highlighted with iridescent shades of bronze and aqua.

"Wow, Alicia," Beth exclaimed. "You look gorgeous! It's a whole new you. Jim wouldn't recognize you."

"Thanks, Beth." Alicia smiled at herself in the mirror next to her chair. She turned her head from side to side. Is this me? Really?

She felt like a new person. For the first time in months, she felt wonderful.

Make that awesome.

Fifteen

Ruth and Beth purchased the lip gloss and blushes that their assistants had chosen for them; Alicia and Vicky bought the same eye shadow and mascara. "I'll probably never be able to duplicate this look again," Ruth said, "but it'll be fun to try. Gosh, I wish Norma had been here. Wouldn't she have loved this? Wait. Let's ask one of the assistants to take a few pictures. Then we can send them around to everyone."

After their relaxing session in the luxurious salon, they went up to show Elena the finished product. "Look at you!" she exclaimed. "All you ladies be, ah, how you say, sunning. No, that is not right. All very beautiful."

"Maybe you mean *stunning*," Vicky said. "But we'll take the compliment and thank you for it." The other women smiled.

"Ladies, we deserve a celebration," Ruth said, as they all walked towards the escalator. She consulted her notebook and found a nearby *taverna*. "We're all too sexy to eat in the hotel restaurant," she declared. "We'll save that for later."

Shortly before nine, satiated with *moussaka*, fried zucchini, and salad, they returned to the hotel, just in time to see a taxi pulling up beside them. "It's Najila," Vicky squealed. "She's here!"

The driver opened the rear door, and Najila Danfi

stepped out onto the curb. "*Marhaba*, ah, hello, everyone," she said with a big smile. "It is so good to see you all again."

"Hi, Najila," Ruth said. "Welcome to Athens. Oh, don't bother. I've got the taxi." After some haggling, Ruth paid the taxi driver who then sped off into the night.

"My mother would be most proud of your bargaining skills," Najila said. Her eyes twinkled.

The women all talked at once as they hugged Najila. When they finally moved from the sidewalk into the hotel lobby, Ruth introduced her properly to Beth.

"I am most happy to meet you, Beth," Najila said. "I hope your knees are better. Your letter was very wonderful and so honest, and your hair is now longer than in the photo you sent from the Roman Coliseum."

Beth looked surprised. "Bless your heart, Najila. What a memory you have. All that happened two years ago."

"Let's go sit in the bar where we can relax," Alicia said. "That table in the corner looks good. Najila, have you eaten?" She noted that Najila looked thinner and was dressed in the same white polo shirt, olive safari jacket, and brown sandals she'd often worn in Nablus. Alicia recalled Najila saying that her wardrobe was small because she donated so many things to the camps in Palestine.

She walks the walk, Alicia thought.

"Yes, thanks Alicia. I am sorry that I am so late," Najila apologized as she settled herself into a comfortable chair. "I would have been here sooner on the Metro, but Sami made me promise to take a taxi in from the airport. I had to wait for one. I told him I was perfectly cap . . . uh . . . cape . . ."

"*Capable?*" Beth offered.

"Yes, thanks. 'Capable' is what I meant. You can see I have not spoken much English since you left. Anyway, Sami insisted I take a taxi since I was arriving in the night; and, before I forget, I also bring you best greetings from Mama. She is happy that I am meeting you and wishes she could be with us."

Najila smiled. "Mama is running my tour business while I am here. She becomes quite good. She even bought my ticket for this flight on Aegean Air. She called the agent so often that he finally gave her a big discount, just so she would leave him in one piece."

"That's our Huda," Vicky said, laughing. "Always going for the best price. I love it."

Alicia had a word with the bartender, who quickly brought glasses, a large pitcher of Greek white wine, and a dish of nuts to their table. "So how was your flight, Najila?" Alicia asked as she resumed her seat.

"It was fine, thanks God. We had to sit some minutes on the running way at Ben Gurion before we took off, as there was much traffic. The distance is short—only seven hundred and forty miles—so the flight was just one hour and a half. We had some bumping before we landed in Athens. I think the winds were blowing in from the sea. But I was so excited to see you that it did not bother me. You all look so fresh and wonderful. Alicia, I very much like your hair to the side. You look . . . somehow . . . very . . . ah . . . different. Much younger."

Alicia flashed her a grateful smile.

"Oh, and I want to say how sorry I am about Norma's passing. She was a special woman, having much strength and courage. Her light was always most bright."

Ruth then briefly told Najila about the funeral service, about what people had said about Norma, including Inez' note, and about how many lives Norma had affected. Ruth also mentioned the letter that Jerry had sent her just before she'd left for Athens. "I haven't read it yet because I figured it was for all of us. It's in my suitcase. I'll read it along our way."

Vicky reached for a handful of nuts. "And how are you, Najila? You look great. Tell us about this Sami. Is he just an old friend or someone special?"

"Thank you for your sweet words. I am fine, thanks God. Business was very good until the fighting began four months ago. Now there are few tourists. That gives me some little free time to come and see you.

"Dr. Sami Ayed is a . . ." Najila colored slightly, "a . . . very nice, old friend. He was a colleague of my husband. We have gone out some little bit these past few months. He has taken me to tea and for dinner. We have also met each other's families and friends. Tonight we took dinner before he drove me to the airport. He was very kind but acted like I had never traveled or done anything on my own. He is that way with his mother and sisters. Here is a photo." She took out her phone and passed it around the table.

"He's a knock out!" Beth exclaimed. "And he's a doctor? Super. Any plans? Oh, sorry. That's none of my business."

"Your question is fine, Beth," Najila said as she put her phone away. "My answer is that I do not know. Auntie Rania thinks I should rush into his arms. But I am not sure. He is a very nice man and full of attraction. I might even love him. He is kind and generous. But I fear I would lost, no, sorry, *lose* my freedoms. My time would not be my own. On the other hand, I do not wish to hurt his feelings. I could never do that. Ah, it is hard to know."

She frowned a bit. "Since my husband, Kanaan, died, I make my own decisions, especially about my time. I am more independent than many women in my country. Perhaps that makes little problem for Sami."

Really? Ruth thought. And for you, too, my dear.

Najila took a sip of her wine. "You see, there are many things that I wish to do. I want to think about this during our trip these next days. Perhaps you can help me know the best solution. You are all such strong women. You do many things on your own. It is very different in my country." Najila sighed. "Many, no, wait, *much* more difficult."

"You've done the right thing, Najila," Ruth said firmly. "Getting ideas from my friends here helped me a bunch when I had a hard decision to make. Somebody will come up with something."

She stifled a yawn. "Oh, gosh. Excuse me. Ladies, I think we should call it a night. It's almost ten, and Najila hasn't even been up to her room yet. We've all had a long day, and tomorrow will be busy. Efie, our guide, will meet us here at 8:30—right after breakfast. The Acropolis will be our first stop. Efie said it's not far, so we'll walk down. It gets crowded later, so she wants to take us there early."

Just then, the front door of the hotel opened; and a small man hurried to the reception desk. He was carrying a piece of luggage and looked very tired. "I have a suitcase from the airport for Mrs. Corrigan."

Although she didn't understand the man's Greek, when she heard her name, Alicia jumped up and ran over to the desk. "I'm Mrs. Corrigan. Thank you so much." She took her passport from her purse and showed him her identification. Then she reached into her pocket, found a few euros, and handed them to him. He nodded and then hurried back out to continue with his deliveries.

"It's here, ladies," Alicia said excitedly. "It made it, and no worse for wear. Oh, yay! Thank You, Jesus."

"What did I tell you, Al?" Ruth said. "I predicted this was going to be a fine day, and it was. Come on, Najila. Let's get your key, then we'll find your room." She paid the bartender and then led Najila to the reception desk. The others gathered their things and headed to the elevator.

Back in her own room, Ruth heaved a huge sigh of relief. So far, so good, she thought. Take *that*, Arlene. I'll show you dumb. Suitcase lost; suitcase returned. Amazing help from everybody we've met—from the luggage guys to the hotel receptionist to the women at *Attica*. We're all doing fine. Looks like Al and Najila may have a lot to discuss. I'm also thinking that Najila will never marry Dr. Sami. She's way too independent for him.

As Ruth got ready for bed, she realized how much she had learned and accomplished in planning this trip. She felt really proud of herself. Their flights and the first day had been great. Except for Alicia's suitcase, everything had gone like clockwork—beyond her wildest dreams. Was this all part of her new calling?

Before she turned off the light, she read a few more

chapters in Second Corinthians. She now understood better what Paul had gone through trying to tell these people about Jesus. She realized that Paul was one tough guy. In spite of so many obstacles, he kept on going; and the best thing he did was to *write* about it in his letters.

I've got to make sure I keep up with my journal, she told herself. Who knows? Maybe someday there will be First and Second Ruthie.

Funny.

Sixteen

May 6, 2014—Athens, Greece

At 7:30 the next morning, most of the women were in the hotel breakfast room; Vicky joined them at 7:45. "Sorry I'm late," she said apologetically. "I had a really hard time getting up this morning. I'll try to be on time from now on."

A huge bowl of creamy yogurt sat in the middle of the buffet table; a smaller bowl of thick, amber-colored honey stood next to it. Trays of fresh fruit and baskets of warm rolls and crusty breads were on either ends of the table. Back in the kitchen, a radio played cheerful Greek folk songs.

Beth and Ruth observed the other guests for a minute and then helped themselves to a bowl of the yogurt. They made an indentation in the middle, and then they spooned a scoop of honey into this "well."

"That Greek travel book said that eating the local yogurt is good for your flora and fauna," Ruth said. "It protects against stomach issues. I'm for that. Hey, are these baklava? For *breakfast*?" She pointed to a platter with small pastries. "Whatever—they look scrumptious. I'm getting one."

Back at their table, Ruth poured steaming coffee from the silver thermos pot. "Man, you could skate mice on this stuff. It's like syrup! I'll be awake 'til Christmas."

She bit into the pastry. "Oh, yum. I know what this is. It's not baklava; it's a *tiropeta*. It's a mixture of feta cheese and eggs in phyllo dough. I had one when I was still flying here ages ago. It's to die for. I might have to get another one, since—ha, ha—they're so small. Norma would have loved these. I'll just get another one and eat it in her honor."

Alicia and Vicky sat with Najila. They were just finishing off their pastries when Ruth stood up. "Don't mean to rush you, ladies; but it's 8:15. Efie was always really quick to answer my emails, so I have the feeling that she'll be right on time. I'm gonna run up and finish getting ready; I'll be down in the lobby by 8:25. Don't forget your sunscreen, hats, and water bottles. The TV weather said it will be hot today."

During their correspondence, Efie had told Ruth that she'd worked in England and Canada before getting into the tour business in Greece with her husband, George. She'd said that her full name was Efemia, but everyone called her Efie. Her photo had shown a plain, middle-aged matron.

Ruth returned to the lobby just as a blue and white Volkswagen bus pulled up to the curb. A slight, fifty-something woman with curly red hair got out. She turned and spoke in Greek to the driver. "Thanks, George. Around four? Fine." Then she walked into the hotel.

"*Kalimera*. Good morning. I am Efie Pappas. And you must be Ruth, eh?"

Ruth was astonished at this beautiful woman who extended her hand. Efie was wearing pink designer jeans, a white ruffled blouse, and low-heeled cowboy boots. Her earrings and necklace were gold disks with the profile of Alexander the Great; each piece swung on a thin gold chain. A pink umbrella was stuffed into a gray leather handbag slung across her shoulder.

Note to self, Ruth thought. Ask for a recent photo. I would *never* have recognized her. What a change!

"Ah, yes, I'm Ruth Hanford. And here's the rest of our group." The other women had come down and assembled behind Ruth. She introduced them to Efie. "We're all from America except for Najila Danfi here," Ruth explained. "She flew over last night from Tel Aviv."

Najila and Efie kissed each other on both cheeks. "I am most happy to meet you, Mrs. Pappas," Najila said. "For several years I had, no, sorry, I have a small tour business in Palestine. Not many women give tours there. I wish to improve what I do. So I hope you will not mind if I watch you and maybe ask some small question here and there."

"I am very happy to help you, Najila," Efie said. "I am flattered that you wish to observe me. You can walk with me as we go, eh?" Efie then turned to face the rest of the group. "Please call me Efie, all of you. I hope to learn your names soon as well. Now then, we will walk over to the Acropolis. It should take only twenty or thirty minutes. There are some nice shops along the way, but please do not stop now. We will have time on our way back this afternoon.

"Here are some small maps showing you how the Acropolis used to look. There were many more temples up there in the ancient times. Built between 447 and 432 BC, the Parthenon is the biggest building remaining from the early days. It was dedicated to the goddess Athena, the patroness of Athens, and is surely the most famous monument in Greece.

"I say all this to you now because sometimes it is very crowded on the top, and you will not hear me. As we go along, I will tell you more." She handed the maps to Ruth who passed them around.

Efie moved towards the door. "Everybody ready? Sun hats? Water? Oh, yes, half way up the hill, there are clean public restrooms. There are none on top. All right, eh? Now we go."

Ruth was the last one out. "Business must be good this year," she whispered as she caught up with Alicia. "Sharp outfit. And that jewelry!"

"Yeah, classy stuff," Alicia said. "Wait, I'm getting a text." She took out her phone and then smiled.

Dear Friends,

Good luck on your first day of sightseeing. I know you'll have a marvelous time. Take lots of photos. Watch your step on the Acropolis. When I was there five years ago, I was so busy being a typical tourist that I tripped over a chunk of marble and went flying. I miss you and am sending you bushels of love.

Kay

"What a sweetheart," Alicia said. "Still looking after us. But hey, we're all agile. Who's going to fall?"

Ruth linked arms with Alicia as they followed the other women. "You sure sound better than yesterday, Al. Even the tone of your voice is different."

"Thanks, Ruthie. I feel different. Can't put my finger on it exactly. Maybe it was the makeover or getting my suitcase back. Or maybe it's just having a little time by myself. Last night, before bed, I did some serious praying. I asked God to help me—to show me what to do about Jim. And then I went right to sleep. Just like that. No jet lag at all. This morning, I feel pretty good. This is gonna sound dumb, but it was like . . . like my new face could be the beginning of a new me." She shrugged. "I don't want to get my hopes up. I don't have any answers yet; but, yeah. I feel better."

"Well, I'd say that's an answer," Ruth said. "What do you want—an airplane with a banner out the back? We get what we need for the day. God's never failed me. He won't fail you either. Hey, let's move it. Efie's way ahead of us."

+++++++++

Efie led them through a series of winding side streets in the bustling *Plaka* district. They passed boutiques whose sparkling windows were filled with elegant clothes and jewelry, a decided contrast to those of a grimy auto repair shop a few doors down. Obviously the Planning and Zoning Commission was a bit flexible here, Alicia thought.

As they walked further away from the hotel and closer to the Acropolis, Beth took photos of the street signs at each intersection. "Just in case I have to come back by myself."

Vicky laughed. "What are you doing? Taking photo bread crumbs, like Hansel and Gretel? Actually that's a great idea. Who knew?"

They soon arrived at the tree-lined road next to the walkway that led up to the Acropolis. Opposite the walkway, a quartet of musicians in black leather jackets was playing lively Greek music.

Beth also saw that many tourists along the road were on crutches or using walkers. There were even a few in wheelchairs. Her heart went out to them. She knew that those people would have a tough time getting up that path. She looked down at her own recovered knees and said a silent prayer of thanks.

Efie stopped them under an olive tree. "Before we go up, I will tell you a few things. The word 'Acropolis' comes from two Greek words: *acro*, meaning 'above' or 'up,' and *polis*, meaning 'city.' Through the ages, people have sought out high places for worship. The Acropolis has been such a place for over 3,000 years. The first temple was built there in the 6th century before Christ.

"The biggest building is the Parthenon. Right now, it is being repaired; so you will see machines, metal scaffolding, and many workmen. Do not go too close to this building. You can see it better if you stand back a little. Please watch where you walk, as there are many large pieces of marble on the ground.

"Now we will make our way up the hill. Please stay close to me. You see there are already many other groups here." She raised her pink umbrella and began to walk up the hill. A chain divided the path. Those going up walked on the right; going down was on the left. "This chain has not always been here," Efie told them. "Some years back, everyone just tried to get up and down the same way. It sometimes got very crowded and confusing. This is much better."

They followed Efie up a series of steps cut into the side of the hill and onto a wooden walkway between many columns. Alicia consulted the map and saw that they were actually passing through the ruins of the Propylaia. She saw that, according to the map, propylaia must mean "gateway." It was slow going because there were so many people in front of them.

As they finally emerged on the top, Efie turned and pointed in the distance. "Down behind those trees is a big rock called the Areopagus. It is where St. Paul spoke to the Athenians. We will stop there after lunch."

Alicia tapped her map. "Look how many buildings were on the Acropolis in ancient times but how few are still here. What happened?"

Efie then described the three major sources of destruction to the buildings. "In the late 1500s, travelers wrote about seeing many temples up here; but in the mid-1600s, the Parthenon was blown up by gunpowder stored inside. Cannon fire during the Venetian war destroyed more temples. The second problem was from careless renovation work in the 19th century. The last problem is the worst: Acid rain from millions of autos in Athens causes great damage to the grooved columns, the statues slowly lose their faces, and so on."

Alicia shook her head. "Unbelievable. Three thousand years of incredible beauty—trashed by war, stupidity, and cars. What are people thinking of?"

"They aren't," Ruth answered. "Dumb, dumber, and dumbest."

Tourists from all over the world filed slowly past the women as they stood with Efie. "Can you believe how many different people we're seeing here?" Beth asked quietly. "There are so many nationalities, each with their own language. Lots of these people probably come from countries who are at war with each other;

yet up here, bless their hearts, everybody's helping each other, waiting their turn, being polite, and getting along. Nobody's fighting. What does that tell you?"

"In former times," Najila said, "it was the same in my country. Sometimes I think they now enjoy to fight."

Efie then stepped away from the Parthenon and pointed to a smaller temple. "Over there is the Erectheion. It was built between 421 and 406 BC. On the porch on this side are copies of the Caryatids, the six maidens who hold up the roof with their heads. Five of the original statues are in the Acropolis Museum. They were taken to England in the early 1800s but have been returned to us from the British Museum.

"Now you have some time to walk about and take photos. Please meet me here at 11:00, eh? You will find my pink umbrella. Ah, Najila, some other guides are just over there. I am sure they would like to meet you—a woman guide from Palestine."

Najila's eyes shone. "Oh, yes, Efie."

The other women walked closer to the Caryatids. "Look at those big things on their heads," Ruth said. "They're like stone crowns. If they wore those in real life, I'll bet they had the headache of the century."

"Hey, ladies," Alicia said. "If you stand just there, I can take a photo that looks like you're right next to those statues. Pose yourselves to look like they do. Yeah, like that. Perfect. Wait, let me back up a sec."

Alicia swiveled around, saw the big column fragment next to her foot, and tried to step over it. She was fast.

But not fast enough.

Her phone flew out of her hand, and she was on the

ground on all fours. "Oh, good grief!"

As she hauled herself up, a thin line of bright red blood began to trickle down her knee. She reached down and picked a tiny stone out of the wound. "If this didn't hurt so much, I'd have to laugh. I was the one who thought nobody would fall up here. Serves me right. What a klutz!"

Beth was at her side instantly. She took Alicia by the arm and helped her to a larger fragment a few steps away. "Sit here, Alicia. I've got the perfect stuff for you." Beth opened her backpack, pulled out a packet of antiseptic wipes, cleaned the wound, and then applied some tea tree oil on a cotton swab.

"Ow! Ow! That stuff really stings!" Alicia yelled as she bit her lip.

Ruth hurried over, gave Alicia some tissues, and rubbed the back of her neck. "You'll be OK, Al. You're tough."

Meanwhile, Vicky retrieved Alicia's phone. "Maybe those stone maidens will have to wait 'til another day, Alicia."

Beth pushed up the pant leg of Alicia's denim capris, placed a large bandage over the wound, and taped it firmly in place. "I'm sorry I hurt you with that oil, Alicia; but it's the absolute best stuff. Tonight after you take your shower, I'll apply a new bandage. You won't get any infection. You'll see. Now, are you OK?" She looked at her watch. "Maybe we should get over to our meeting point. Efie and Najila are probably already there."

"Here, Al," Ruth said solicitously. "Lean on me. I'll help you."

"Oh, will you *stop*?" Alicia said with a little laugh.

"I'm not an invalid, for heaven's sake. I didn't break my *leg*; I just dinged up my knee. I've had worse injuries than this sliding into third base. Come on, let's go. I'm getting hungry. And don't . . . I mean, DO NOT say anything about this to Efie. Please! I'll be fine, and I want to do the rest of the stuff today."

After they met up with Efie and Najila, they slowly worked their way down the hill and over to the new Acropolis Museum. Efie and Najila sat together near the main entrance and chatted about their work. Beth and Ruth wandered through the Parthenon Gallery while Alicia and Vicky viewed the original Caryatids, still elegant in their stone silence.

"Look at them," Vicky said. "All that beautiful drapery on their robes. And their hair is so realistic. They seem like they could step down and start talking to us. Imagine—they've been standing like that for 2,500 years."

"Yeah," Alicia said. "You know, I feel like that at the post office sometimes. But you're right. They're amazing, especially when you think how long ago they were sculpted. Let's go find the others. I'm starving. I also need to sit down for a minute and take one of those pain relievers Beth gave me. She thought of everything in her meds kit."

Efie had reserved a round table on the balcony of the museum's restaurant on the second floor, giving them a panoramic view of the Acropolis and much of downtown Athens. After lunch, they finished off with tiny cups of strong Greek coffee and some sweets.

"Ladies," Efie announced, "you have just enough time to visit the museum shops. There is one on this level and one on the main level next to the café. Many visitors like to have an owl from Athens. The owl is our symbol of wisdom, and the shops have them in everything from tiny earrings to beautiful diamond pendants. Please meet me at the main desk in twenty minutes, and then we will walk to the Areopagus."

"Gift shop?" Ruth exclaimed. "Say no more. Let's go."

The twenty minutes flew by; but everyone managed to purchase post cards, book marks, and, of course, an owl. Alicia and Ruth bought gold owl earrings; Vicky got a blue glass owl pendant for her daughter, and Beth chose a silver charm bracelet with nine miniature owls. Najila found a small brooch made of malachite. "Mama will love this. She is crazy about green, and the owl has such big eyes."

They left the museum and walked ten minutes over to the Areopagus. Vicky stopped in front of the huge rock, laid her hands on it, and closed her eyes. "This is *earth-shattering*," she breathed reverently. "It's the Bible coming alive! And we're a part of it! I can't *believe* I'm actually getting to touch something that the apostle Paul touched! Look, I've got goose bumps."

"The name 'Areopagus' means 'Hill of Ares,'" Efie explained, "but also refers to the Athenian Council of Elders that met here five hundred years before the time of Paul. He would have been here in about 50 AD."

"Yes," Vicky said, "he had come into Macedonia, like maybe in the summer of 48, went to Philippi, met Lydia and her riverside prayer group, was imprisoned, released, then went to Thessaloniki and Veria before arriving in Athens." She paused, her face very red. "Oh, I'm *sorry*, Efie. I got carried away. I didn't mean to step on your toes. *You're* supposed to say all this."

"And I am very thankful to you," Efie said graciously. "Will you come to work for me? I need someone just like you on all my tours. What else can you tell us?"

Vicky's eyes lit up with her love of biblical history. "Well, Paul came here hoping to convert lots of Athenians. He spoke to them at what he thought was their high intellectual level. You know, maybe it would be better to let Paul tell us himself. I was hoping we'd get to see this place, so I brought along a copy of his speech to the Athenians from the Acts of the Apostles, Chapter 17. Najila, would you read it for us? It's not very long. Your accent is better than mine." Vicky opened her tote bag, pulled out a sheet of paper, and handed it to Najila.

"Oh, but," Najila sputtered, "I . . . ah, my English is not . . ."

"You'll be perfect," Ruth said reassuringly. "Pretend you're on the stage back in that Roman theater in Samaria. Remember? You told us it was your favorite place."

Najila smiled, took a deep, calming breath, and started reading slowly:

"Athenians, I see how extremely religious you are in every way. For as I went through the city and looked carefully at the objects of your worship, I found among them an altar with the inscription, 'To an unknown god.' What therefore you worship as unknown, this I proclaim to you. The God who made the world and everything in it, he who is Lord of heaven and earth, does not live in shrines made by human hands, nor is he served by human hands, as though he needed anything, since he himself gives to all mortals life and breath and all things. From one ancestor he made all nations to inhabit the whole earth, and he allotted the times of their existence and the boundaries of the places where they would live, so that they would search for God and perhaps grope for him and find him—though indeed he is not far from each one of us. For 'In him we live and move and have our being'; as even some of your own poets have said, 'For we too are his offspring.'

Since we are God's offspring, we ought not to think that the deity is like gold, or silver, or stone, an image formed by the art and imagination of mortals. While God has overlooked the times of human ignorance, now he commands all people everywhere to repent, because he has fixed a day on which he will have the world judged to righteousness by a man whom he has appointed, and of this he has given assurance to all by raising him from the dead."

When they heard of the resurrection of the dead, some scoffed; but others said, 'We will hear you again about this.' At that point Paul left them. But some of them joined him and became believers, including Dionysius the Areopagite and a woman named Damaris, and others with them."

When she finished reading, Najila handed the paper back to Vicky; while the rest of the ladies applauded warmly.

"Thanks, Najila," Vicky said. "You were terrific. Whenever I hear these verses, I marvel at how Paul spoke to those Athenians in such philosophical terms. He was trying so hard, wanting to be on their same wavelength. Sadly, not many of them were interested. They just yawned, checked their sundials, and wandered off.

"Later, in other places, when Paul decided to share only his personal story, people believed. After his encounter with Jesus, Paul was *so* excited about what had happened to him that his words must have been really convincing. Oh, gosh. Here I am, getting carried away again. And I never even used to *like* Paul; but after I've read more about him—and now, being here and seeing these places where he actually *stood*—I'm changing my opinion. Anyway, thanks for letting me spout off, Efie. You're very kind. And now, I'll bet you're ready to go. I know you've got a schedule to keep."

Everyone was tired as they walked back to the hotel. In the front, Vicky chatted with Efie and Najila about what they'd just seen. Beth helped Alicia, whose knee was now slightly swollen.

Ruth was pensive as she brought up the rear. I wonder how many people I've turned off, she thought, being like Paul when he spoke to the Athenians— spouting out pious platitudes, sounding holier-than-thou. From the heart might be better. Besides, actions trump words any day. She said a quick prayer. "God, help me think before I speak."

She caught up with Efie and Najila. "There's a *taverna* just ahead under those trees over there—the one with the brown checked tablecloths. How about we stop for something to drink, like some bottled water or a glass of wine? My treat."

Parthenon on the Acropolis in Athens

The Caryatids on the Acropolis in Athens

Seventeen

At the sidewalk *taverna*, Efie chose a shaded table. She sat down, pulled her cell phone from her shoulder bag, and then called George and arranged for him to pick her up at the hotel at 4:45. "This is a fine idea," she said as she stretched her legs out in front of her. "It feels good to sit. These new boots pinch my feet."

Alicia's knee was throbbing, but she was not about to mention it. She ordered bottled water, swallowed another pain reliever, and distracted herself by breathing in the heady fragrance from the yellow roses twined on a trellis behind them. She took a close up of one perfect rose to send to Jerry in honor of Norma. He'd like that.

The stop at the *taverna* was a welcome break; they all enjoyed themselves immensely. As they sampled dishes of tiny black and green olives and shared several bottles of sparkling water, Ruth raised her glass. "Ladies, here we are, doing the 'new wine in new wine skins' thing. This is what it's all about. It's the Bible in real life again."

Alicia rolled her eyes and laughed. "Yeah, well, it feels like *old* wine skins today; but maybe that's just me."

After Ruth paid the *taverna* owner, they walked

back to the hotel, then said goodbye to Efie. She and George would pick them up early the next morning.

"Let's meet here for dinner in two hours," Ruth said as they stood in the lobby near the hotel restaurant. "That will give us time to clean up and have a nap. I'm still pretty jet-lagged."

They agreed and went up to their rooms. In her room, Najila sat down at the small desk. During the day, she had done a lot of thinking about Sami. Now she was eager to write out these thoughts. She knew her mother was very favorably impressed that Sami had gone to all the best schools, and he was now the assistant medical director at a large clinic. He also dressed very well and had beautiful manners. Najila was attracted to him. He was so handsome: all that black, wavy hair and those dark eyes. Aiyee, those eyes.

She thought back to when she had met Kanaan, her husband. There had never been any doubt, no need for a list. From the beginning, she knew she loved him. But she was very young then—just out of university. Now she was older and a little wiser. She had been on her own for a long time.

Sami had taken her for drives and dinners; she had met all his family. She knew his mama liked her. There was no question that her mama really liked him. Family was very important in her culture, as were friends. Once, at a reception, one of his medical colleagues had whispered to her, "Sami needs a good woman like you, Naji. Ever since his Eva died, he has not been happy. With you, he smiles again."

But was all that enough? Could she think with her head as well as her heart? Would they get along?

Would he accept her for what she was now—a female entrepreneur successfully running her own tour business? Could she be like her American friends and have a life with Sami and still run her business, or would he be like most traditional Palestinian men? Would she have to give up her independence?

With so many questions in her head, she took a piece of hotel stationary and drew a line down the center of the paper. She labeled one column, "Reasons To" and the other column, "Reasons Not To." She wrote quickly, listing the many pros and cons. Alas, both columns were almost equal in length. Frustrated with the results, she laid her pen down, rose from her chair, and went to the window.

Making lists is helpful, she thought; but I still have no answer. I need to talk with some of the other women. Perhaps Beth might have some ideas. She has been married many years and has worked a lot, as well. Yes, I will ask her, Najila decided. She walked back to the desk, folded the paper, and tucked it into her suitcase. After she set the alarm on her phone, she removed her shoes and then stretched out on the bed. A short sleep would be refreshing.

+++++++++

Tantalizing aromas greeted Ruth as she entered the hotel restaurant. Since it was early by Greek standards, only a few other diners were there. While she waited, she leaned over and sniffed the white lilacs arranged in a tall vase on the sideboard.

The others arrived and were quickly seated. Although the menu was extensive, most chose the house specialty, called *pastichio*: a casserole of sautéed beef and ziti topped with a creamy white sauce. They enjoyed the meal but were all tired from their first big outing.

"Everything was so delica . . . delight . . . no . . . oh, what am I trying to say?" Najila said as she sipped her coffee.

"*Delicious*?" Alicia offered.

"Yes, thanks," Najila said. "That is the word: *delicious*. Greek foods are similar to Arab dishes but with some small differences, mostly in the spices. Oh, yes, I had a most interesting talk with the other tour guides this morning. They were surprised to meet me. They did not know women did such work in Palestine." Her cheeks grew pink as she lowered her eyes. "They had even bigger surprise when I told them I had my own business."

"I'm really happy for you, Najila," Alicia said enthusiastically. "It's terrific that you've been able to do that, especially in your country. Working for oneself seems a good way to go. Then age doesn't matter. When I got turned down for that greenhouse job, I know they thought I was too old. Hah! I've forgotten more about plants and gardening than most of those kids know."

"Well, you could always try volunteering," Vicky said. "Every organization I've ever been involved with ran on volunteer power. Age is no barrier there. Volunteers are people with time, talent, and passion. They're the ones who make things happen."

Beth looked worried. "Oh, gosh, I want to find some kind of part-time nursing job, maybe in a small clinic or a hospice. I've experienced the same thing. Lots of times people don't even look at my face. All they see is my white hair, and it's over—no matter what I'm trying to do. Once I even had somebody at the mall ask me if I needed a wheelchair. Honestly!"

"What a hoot," Ruth said, laughing. "Speaking of people with a passion who made things happen, Vick, you just gave me an idea. This afternoon at the Areopagus, you said that when Paul tried to talk to the Athenians, not many of them were interested. They just said 'see ya' and left. And to think, here we are, just a few blocks from where that happened—maybe even near the house where he stayed. How cool is that?

"Do you ladies realize," Ruth went on, "that we're leaving for Corinth the day after tomorrow? Paul went to Corinth from Athens, as well. How do you suppose he felt two nights before *he* left? Was he totally bummed at being brushed off? Or was he anxious to try a new place? You know, did he want to shake the dust off his sandals and go find some new fertile soil to till? Compared to stodgy, academic Athens, Corinth was wide open—a happening town. Think New Orleans, or San Francisco, or New York.

"Or maybe he just needed work and thought there would be better chances in a port city like Corinth where there were lots of travelers and merchants, all wanting tents. Or was he so on fire after his Damascus road experience that he felt compelled—he uses the word 'called'—to tell expat Judeans everywhere that Jesus really was the Messiah?

"I can just see him now, trudging down that dusty road, maybe with Timothy and Silas, heading towards Corinth. Back then, a guy could walk twenty miles in a normal day; but they probably did close to thirty that first day."

Alicia's eyes widened. "Wow, Ruthie. How do you know all that? Where did you get those facts?"

"Oh, from the Jerome Murphy-O'Connor book you gave me," Ruth answered. "It's the best. I've learned so much from it. Now I've got a much different picture of the kind of guy Paul was. I'll bet he was pretty excited to be going to Corinth. I sure am." She looked at her watch. "I think I'll call it a day. I'm still really jet-lagged, and I know we'll do a lot of walking tomorrow. See you all at breakfast."

Soon Ruth was ensconced in her bed, the Murphy-O'Connor volume in her hands. Despite her heavy eyes, she started a new chapter anyway. She managed to read, "Paul must have recognized rather quickly that it had been a mistake to come to Athens."

Raising her eyes from the text, she reflected on what the ladies had seen that day: the climb up to the Acropolis, the Areopagus rock below where Paul had spoken, and then part of the market or *agora* nearby. How did Paul feel after he'd been such a failure there? What gave him the courage to go on? Ruth tried to form a picture in her mind of what the area would have looked like back in Paul's day, but she was so sleepy.

Three minutes later, she lifted the book off her face, laid it on the bedside table, and turned out the light.

Eighteen

March, 50 AD—Athens, Greece

"Come, my friends. Let us sit under this olive tree. This small grove is away from the dust and flies of the animal pens. My old bones are aching and in need of a rest. The day grows late; see how low the sun is. I am surprised that shops are still open, that so many people still linger here in the agora. Do they have nothing else to occupy them other than to converse with friends? What? Oh, yes, Sylvanus, a cup of wine would be refreshing, perhaps a bit of bread as well. I have eaten nothing since that hard cheese this morning. Here, take these coins. Perhaps food and drink will lift my spirits. Today at the Areopagus was difficult."

Paulos gathered his coarse robe around him as he lowered himself to a stone bench beneath leafy olive branches bright with spring growth. A short, balding man in his early forties, he was strongly built with the sinewy arms and rough hands of a tentmaker. The furrows on his forehead deepened as he pondered the day's events.

"Well, Timothy, what do you think? What

chance have we here in Athens?"

His young assistant considered his response carefully, aware that Paulos' towering intellect concealed a sensitive nature.

Timothy cleared his throat. "Your speech was most forceful, Paulos. As I stood at the edge of the crowd, I could see that many learned people—Epicureans, Stoics, and other philosophers—were gathered. You spoke in their terms, praising them for their spirituality, commenting on the many statues of gods you have observed here. But when you talked of the divine not being found in images of gold, silver, or stone, and then mentioned ignorance and the need for repentance, I saw angry faces. When, finally, you discoursed on the Resurrection, some whispered about a goddess called Anastasis, who had to do with resurrection. They did not understand that you meant the Resurrection of Jesus. Sadly, a few even scoffed at your poor robe and dusty sandals. They wagged their heads and said that you were like all other common street preachers. Many drifted away.

"Our innkeeper told me this morning," Timothy continued, "that Athenians think they are still the center of the world—of culture, philosophy, and learning—and they laugh and make jests about other towns, like Corinth, that are growing rich from much industry and business, especially in shipping and hosting the Isthmian Games. He said that Athenians boast proudly that they discuss the latest new idea, but he thinks they are only happy when they are preserving their old ways."

"Ah, good," Paulos said, "Sylvanus returns." Sylvanus handed him the wine and a large chunk of bread. "Thank you, my son." Paulos nodded as he took a long drink of the wine and then broke off a piece of bread. "You are most perceptive, Timothy. I am grateful for your eyes and ears. Actually, a few did show interest—Dionysius, a council member, a woman named Damaris, and others." He sighed. "But it was just a few. I am saddened that there were not more. How can these people not want to know Jesus is Messiah?"

Sylvanus finished his own wine and then wiped his mouth on his sleeve. "You are the teacher, of course, Paulos; and you know best. But . . . but . . . perhaps if you spoke less like a scholar and, instead, shared your own experiences with Jesus—as you did in Thessaloniki—and told how you have been changed, more people would listen, wanting that for themselves." He lowered his head and then spoke softly. "That is why I followed you."

Paulos straightened his shoulders, set down the wine cup, and stood up. His face was visibly relaxed, and his eyes shone. "Sylvanus, your words gladden my heart. Tomorrow we will make our preparations, and the next day we will start for Corinth. With you two men at my side, how can I possibly fail?"

Nineteen

Alicia was exhausted. Armed with a plastic bag of ice from the hotel kitchen, she propped her injured leg on the bed and tried to relax in an armchair.

What a day, she thought. Up to the Acropolis, down on my knee, to the museum for lunch and shopping, hearing Najila read Paul's speech, a stop at a *taverna*, and then a quiet dinner here. The good news is that I didn't think about Jim. Not once.

But I've got to. I've got to find some resolution. I am so tired of this whole thing—always feeling like a failure.

Alicia sat back and reflected on verses she remembered from Second Corinthians. Paul related what the Lord said to him: "My grace is sufficient for you, for power is made perfect in weakness." Then, further on, Paul himself said: "Mend your ways, encourage one another, agree with one another, live in peace, and the God of love and peace will be with you."

She began to pray. "God, I really need Your grace and Your power in all this. I'm so confused. I can't keep going on like this—like I have for so many years—always saying yes to Jim, always swallowing my feelings, never standing up for myself. At his age,

I can't change him; so maybe I'm the one who needs to change. But how?"

Soft at first, her voice grew stronger. "Does he still love me? How the heck would I know? He doesn't even *talk* to me anymore. I'm sick to death of our lives now. God . . . please . . . help us to . . . to talk to one another . . . without getting into a shouting match. I just want to sit down and visit with him, and have him really listen to me, without having to always pour himself another drink. Tell me what to say: what subjects to bring up . . . give me the words to speak . . . because I flat don't know what to say to him anymore."

She moved to the bed and lay down but kept talking. "Does that mean that I don't love him? Sometimes I can't even *stand* him! He gets on my nerves so much. I feel better just . . . just walking out of the room. Does that say that I've fallen out of love? Can you still love someone that . . . that you . . . you don't even *like* anymore?"

She was crying now, and her pillow was wet.

"God, I just hate this not knowing," she sobbed, "I hate it. What should I do? Can't You give me a sign? Something? *Please?*"

She felt awful. She waited but nothing happened. There was no answer.

Discouraged, she sat up and blew her nose. As she got ready for bed, she looked at herself in the mirror and prayed once more, "OK, God. I'm on my very last nerve. I can't go on like this. So I'm begging You . . . help me . . . please. I'm so tired of feeling like this: of Jim's taking over my life in every way. Even here in Greece, where I'm a million miles away from him, he's still ruining my peace. Show me what's best for our family . . . for Jim . . . and for me. Please."

As she climbed into bed, she felt a warmth, a presence, fill her. Her muscles began to unwind just a bit, and she began to breathe easier. She was almost asleep, but she could have sworn she heard that funny little laugh.

Oh, Norma. It's you, isn't it?

Twenty

May 7, 2014—Athens, Greece

The blue and white Volkswagen bus pulled up to the hotel shortly before nine. Soon they were driving along the main streets of Athens. "George will go slowly, so you can see," Efie said as she adjusted her microphone, "but he has to keep up with traffic. Athens drivers are a little crazy."

Najila laughed heartily. "These cars are nothing. You must come to Jerusalem. There, the drivers are a lot crazy. But where are all the donkey carts?"

"George, how do I do this? Where is the connection? Ah, there it is. I see it. Can you all hear me?" Efie turned around to face the other women. "We just got this new microphone system installed last week, and today is the first time I am using it. I hope it works, and you can hear me over the traffic. I think it will be better than my shouting. Let me know if I should turn it louder, please."

Najila made a mental note to ask her brother, Hani, if he could arrange such a microphone in her old van.

"There on the right," Efie said, as she pointed, "are the National Gardens. Originally Queen Amalia, wife of King Otto of Bavaria, ordered 15,000 plants from Italy: palms and agaves and many others. Sadly, today, the Queen and her money are gone. It is a bit of a jungle in there. Still, there is a little duck pond, a playground, and some small cafés."

They passed by the Arch of Hadrian and saw the Temple of the Olympic Zeus just behind it. George slowed by the Stadium and the National Gallery and then turned onto Vasilis Sofias Street. Efie pointed out the Byzantine, Cycladic, and Benaki Museums before they drove by the University and the National Library. Soon George pulled up near the National Archaeological Museum.

Efie removed her headset, started to open her door, and then turned back to the women. "Ladies, while we are sitting here, I will tell you a few things. This museum was first opened in 1889 and is the most important in all Greece. It is one of the ten best museums in the world. It houses treasures from many parts of our past—from the Neolithic Era up to the last years of the Roman period. Fortunately, during World War II, most of the pieces were put into special boxes and buried to avoid looting or destruction.

"Once we are in the museum, we will have a guided tour at 10:15. Only licensed, professional guides are allowed to give tours in this museum. Our guide today is my friend, Evangelia; and she is very good. I have asked her to show you not only the most famous highlights, but also some things of special interest to women."

Her face aglow, Alicia nudged Ruth. "This is the place I wrote to you about. I'm so excited to see all this stuff. Thanks for setting this up, Ruthie."

Ruth grinned at Alicia. "Sure. What are friends for?"

"The tour will take about an hour," Efie continued,

"maybe a bit longer, depending on how many other groups are there. After the tour is over, you will have free time to view other things. Of course, there is a very nice gift shop. I will meet you at the café in the sculpture garden at 12:30, where we will have our lunch. Najila, perhaps you would like to come to the café around 12:00? Then you can meet some more guides." Najila nodded gratefully.

"All right, ladies," Efie said. "Are you all ready? Then we go in." She got out and quickly led the way into the museum.

Evangelia was as engaging as Efie had promised. They started in the prehistoric collection with the Neolithic Era, then moved into the Cycladic section. "Get a load of those terra-cotta figurines," Vicky whispered to Beth. "Their hips are as big as mine. I was born 4,000 years too late. If art reflects reality, I would have fit right in with those girls."

They viewed glassware and jewelry from the Mycenaean section and golden funeral masks in the Heinrich Schliemann room. In the Egyptian rooms, Evangelia showed them mummies, including one with a wooden body tag; intact bird eggs; and even a 3,000-year-old loaf of bread with a bite taken out of it.

"Some kid probably dropped it on his way home from the store," Ruth said. "I'll bet his mom whopped him good."

Although they walked through a maze of large statues in marble and bronze, Evangelia directed their attention to the cases of small household items, jewelry, glassware, family groupings on grave markers, and even theater masks. Each piece was beautiful beyond belief.

I love being here, Alicia thought. My stomach isn't in knots like it was last night, and I don't feel like I'm constantly walking on eggshells. Maybe I really did need this trip. Evangelia is a super guide. She really knows her stuff, yet she didn't drown us in details.

After the tour ended, during their free time, Alicia went to the lower level. Near the ladies' room, she passed several offices. Signs on the doors were in Greek and English and read: "Special Events," "Graphic Design," and "Public Affairs."

She took quick photos of each sign, so she wouldn't forget. She could feel her pulse racing. Now those are things I could get into, she thought. I could do any of those jobs. Oh, forget it. Get a grip. Who am I kidding? Even if I went back to college, I'd still be too old to get hired. But maybe I *could* be a docent. I'll have to check on that.

Excited, she hurried back to the main level and joined the others in the sculpture garden. Rustling palm trees provided background music as they lunched, surrounded by elegant marble statues.

After she finished her bowl of *avgolemeno*, a chicken soup laced with egg-lemon sauce, Efie said, "Ruth has told me that she, Beth, and Najila want to go to *Attica* for some shopping this afternoon, while Alicia and Vicky wish to visit the Byzantine and Benaki Museums. If you like, George can drop you at these places. When you are done, it is not too far to walk back to your hotel from *Attica* or the museums.

"Then we will pick you up at the hotel at 7:30 to take you to our favorite *taverna* tonight. The food there is excellent, and the music is even better. You might even want to take part in the folk dancing. George is a very good dancer."

George, who had joined them for lunch, shrugged and looked down at his plate.

Soon they were back in the VW bus. George sped down the busy main streets and stopped at *Attica*. "Here you are, ladies," Efie said as Beth, Ruth, and Najila got out. "Enjoy the shopping. Evangelia told me there are sales in the shoe department. It is good that I am not there today. I am weak around shoes."

+++++++++

Five minutes later, George halted at the Cycladic Museum. Before Alicia and Vicky got out, Efie said, "Just across the street from here is the Byzantine Museum. Two blocks down on the right is the Benaki Museum. You both have your street maps, eh? Good. Then we will see you this evening. *Adio*."

Alicia waved at Efie as the van pulled away and then checked her watch. "It's almost 2:00, Vick. Let's meet back here at 3:30. Then we'll decide what we want to do, OK?"

"Sounds like a plan," Vicky said. "See you then." She started to dart between the speeding traffic but thought better of it. She walked to the nearest traffic light, waited for the green, looked carefully both ways, and then crossed.

Smart girl, Alicia thought. I would hate for her to get smashed by some nutso motorcyclist. Alicia then turned right and walked to the Benaki Museum. Last night's sleep had done her knee a world of good.

She entered the stately old mansion that, until 1931, had been the home of the wealthy Benaki family.

It now housed exhibits on the history of ancient and modern Greece. As she worked her way through the various periods and collections, she observed exquisite pieces everywhere she looked: sculptures, paintings, icons, and jewelry.

But it was the third floor that really grabbed her. Here she saw the heroes of the Greek Revolution and the birth of the modern state of Greece. She stood for a long time in front of two large paintings, studying the people depicted, particularly their faces and hands.

Those people were done being dominated, she thought. So they decided to change things. It probably cost them a bunch of time and agony, but they did it. They were over being stepped on, yelled at, and pushed around. They'd had enough.

Can I do the same thing? Dear God, give me the fearlessness that these people had.

She looked at her watch, realized it was already after three, and then hurried down the steps of the grand staircase and into the gift shop. From the bookrack, she selected a paperback called *Flowers of Greece: Yesterday and Today*. The blooms on the cover made her think of Norma. She was very tempted by some reproductions of the gold jewelry she'd just viewed but opted instead for a small watercolor of the freedom fighters. She might need a reminder of their courage.

A few minutes later, Alicia arrived at their meeting place. Vicky was already there, pacing back and forth under a palm tree and waving a book. "Look what I found! This book has marvelous pictures of most of the things I just saw. There was this huge mosaic of Theodora and Justinian. The colors were so bright you'd have thought it had been made last week instead of 1,500 years ago. Then there were all these jewel-encrusted pieces, like chalices and crosses, and, of course, tons of embroidered church vestments. They were really into gorgeous brocades with golden threads running through the fabric. And now . . ."

"And now, you're going to have a heart attack," Alicia said dryly. "Good grief, Vick. Get a hold of yourself. Slow down. I take it you enjoyed the Byzantine Museum."

"Yes, oh yes," Vicky exclaimed after taking a deep breath. "I got so inspired there, not to mention getting all kinds of ideas about how I can work out the plotting for my book about Theodora."

She reached in her pocket and pulled out her green mirror. The glass diamonds winked in the sunlight. "When I showed this on the river cruise, Julia thought it looked Byzantine. Today, on a whim, I brought it with me. It was sort of like a rabbit's foot. I think it helped."

"Well, yay for you," Alicia said. "So why don't we celebrate this? We can walk over to the funicular—you know, that little car on rails that runs up Lycabettus Hill. According to my map, it's only about six blocks from here. It's the highest point in Athens and will have a good view of the city. We can look at the St. George Chapel and then maybe have a drink at the St. George Hotel. That's supposed to be very posh."

"You know," Vicky said, "normally, I'd do that in a heartbeat; but I have so much stuff running around inside my head now that if I don't go back and write it down, it'll all fall out. I'll forget it. I've been dead in the water on this book for so long. Now I can't wait to get going on these things. You won't mind?"

Alicia laughed. "Hey, relax. It's totally fine. I understand, and I'm excited for you. I think I'll go up there anyway. It's just twenty to four; and, if I get a move on, I should be there in about fifteen minutes. You go on back and write your brains out. See you for dinner."

They hugged and then went in opposite directions. As she strode along, Alicia thought about the precious works of art she'd seen in the two museums today. She had studied art and pottery making right after college, so she knew a little something. On the other hand, she had also grown to love gardening as well. For fun, she had taken a botany course in Rome ten years ago. She had even compiled a detailed brochure on the local plants for her garden group. She was anxious to read the little book she'd just bought.

On her way, Alicia passed by exclusive walled villas. She glimpsed terraces filled with lemon trees and climbing roses. Pink and purple bougainvillea vines cascaded over fences and balconies. Lamborghinis and Maseratis were parked casually on the narrow streets. Big money was evident everywhere.

From the foot of Lycabettus Hill, the funicular carried Alicia through a tunnel up the steep hill to the top. She stepped out and breathed in the piney air. Feeling like she was in a different world, she walked to the jewel-like Chapel of St. George, directly opposite the platform. Inside it was cool and peaceful. She sniffed the faint smell of incense combined with lemon oil furniture polish. After she examined the beautiful icons and brass hangings, she sat down to rest, drinking in the calmness. She felt herself totally relax.

Refreshed, a few minutes later she walked outside and up a winding path. Off to the left, she saw the St. George Lycabettus Hotel tucked under a canopy of tall pine trees. When she entered the elegant lobby, she knew the prices would be stiff. Never mind. How much can a coffee be? She moved past the restaurant, choosing the terrace instead. Jasmine vines, dotted with delicate white blossoms, spiraled up trellises on the walls.

She sat at a table near the wrought-iron railing and viewed the city below. She ordered coffee and a small bottle of Perrier water from the tuxedo-suited waiter, flashing him a brilliant smile. Not amused, he tossed his head and minced off to get her drinks.

She argued with herself, sighed, gave in, and lit a cigarette. When she opened the flower book, after the first few pages, she could tell it was going to be good. The flowers were portrayed in intricate detail. She was browsing through the colorful illustrations in the second chapter when a man appeared at her side, carrying a tray with the coffee and water.

But he wasn't wearing a tux, and he wasn't the waiter.

Her gaze traveled up the length of his black jeans, to a burgundy polo shirt, to his tanned face. She suddenly found herself staring into the deepest, bluest eyes she had ever seen.

Her heart did a little lurch.

"And why is a beautiful angel like you sitting alone up here, reading a dry botanical treatise, for God's sake? I sent Konstantinos away on an errand. Until he returns, I am your waiter; and I will care for your *every* desire. May I join you?"

He set the tray on the table and pulled a chair close to her.

"My name is Stavros."

Twenty-one

As Ruth, Beth, and Najila walked into *Attica*, Liana recognized them and waved from her cosmetics counter. After Ruth introduced Najila, Liana asked them to wait. She quickly assembled a flowered tote bag full of samples and presented it to Najila.

"Welcome to Athens," Liana said graciously.

"*Shukran*, oh, I mean, thank you," Najila said. "You are so generous. This store is most beautiful. You must be happy to work here. I, ah, I will buy the small Guerlain perfume over there, yes, the Pamplelune. It is a favorite of my mama. Now if you can just direct me to the shoes?"

Ruth and Beth went to Ladies' Fashions while Najila found the shoe department. From the sale rack, she chose two pairs of the same walking shoes: one in black/white, one in brown/white. She thought her mother would enjoy being twins when they led a tour together.

An hour later, when they met back at the front entrance, Ruth said, "Your mom will love those, Najila. She'll also love the good price. So, what do you ladies think? Is it too far out?" She held up a white peasant blouse with flowers embroidered in bright yarns.

"No, it's perfect," Beth said. "It has all your fave

colors, so it will go with everything you have."

"Yeah," Ruth said. "I think Norma would have liked it, too. Same kind of Polish designs that she and I grew up with. So what did you get, Beth?"

"Well, I saw this killer tan, suede jacket. It could work with leggings and a short skirt for dinner or with jeans on my Ducati. But it was soooo expensive. I'll have to think about it. Let's go, OK? If we're going dancing tonight, I need a nap."

When they were back in the hotel lobby, Ruth laid her hand on Najila's arm and then waved to Beth as she disappeared into the elevator. "Najila, I have to tell you something. This is going to sound really dumb, but I've had the craziest thing happen. I had a dream about Paul—well, I *think* it was a dream—it might have been just my imagination. Anyway, last night I dreamt that, after his talk at the Areopagus fell flat, Paul was really sad. But then Silas and Timothy cheered him up, and they took off for Corinth."

Najila turned to Ruth and gave her a big hug. "Oh, Ruth. That is most exciting. My Gran Najet always told me that dreams are little seeds from God, given to special people. The seeds are to be planted so they will grow into more love around us. Remember Kay's three dreams about the Samaritan woman? Those were her seeds. They led her to organize the trip to Palestine; she asked me to be your guide; I told you about Sapha and her story of meeting Jesus; and now, here we are, all together again. No, no, you are not crazy. You are chosen." Najila's eyes grew wide.

"You have been touched by *God*."

+++++++++

Efie picked them up at the hotel promptly at 7:30. "George is outside in the bus. We are taking you to the *Tsekouras*. I hope you will like it."

While they were being seated at the *taverna*, Efie said, "Shall I order for us? We'll start out with *mezze*—a selection of appetizers. Next, we should try their specialty, beef *stifado*, a thick, beef stew with a sauce of onions, tomatoes, cinnamon, and shallots. And then, um, I think cabbage rolls would be nice. Of course, bread comes as well. I'll get a bottle of *Xinomayro*. It is very good; it's a red wine made from a grape native to Macedonia."

Spotting two empty seats, Alicia grabbed Ruth's arm excitedly and propelled her to the far end of their long table. "Ruthie, you'll *never* guess what happened this afternoon. After I finished at the Benaki, I took the funicular to the top of Lycabettus Hill and had a coffee at the St. George Hotel up there. I was sitting outside, minding my own business, starting a book I'd just bought, when this guy comes up to me, acting like he was the waiter—only he wasn't. But he *was* incredibly good looking. I mean, we're talking drop-dead gorgeous! He asked me why I was reading a book about flowers and if he could sit down. He said his name was Stavros.

"Naturally, I thought he was just some slick gigolo preying on American women tourists. My first impulse was to brush him off with 'Actually, no. I was just leaving.' But he seemed harmless enough, so we started talking. He asked about my knee bandage and then about the book I had. He said he knew something about flowers since he was an ethnobotanist."

Ruth laughed. "A what? An *ethnobotanist?* What's

that? Sounds like a racial statement about dandelions!"

"Oh, cut it out," Alicia retorted. "It's actually quite a sophisticated profession. He studies both wild and domesticated plants. Many disciplines are involved: anthropology, archaeology, botany, chemistry, folklore, medicine, pharmacology—especially how chemicals affect plants—and," she took a deep breath, "religious studies. His specialty is researching lentils and their use in the ancient and modern Near East."

"*Lentils?*" Ruth scoffed. "Riveting. I have one question. How did you *ever* remember all those subjects?"

"Easy. I just put them in alphabetical order. Anyone can do it."

"Oh, sure. I see. Nothing to it. Al, you are something else."

Alicia chattered on. "We had a really nice conversation. He divides his time between fieldwork and university library research. That's why he's in Athens right now. He's involved with the impact of civilization and modern human societies on traditional cultures and natural habitats. In a nutshell, it's basically about how plants and animals are being screwed over and how the changes or losses of many plants affect the people who have lived off them."

She smiled. "Then he asked about me. I told him a little—not everything, of course—but some. I think he was impressed by my knowledge of plants and flowers. He even envied my computer skills when I mentioned that handbook I'd put together for the Rome garden club. Best of all, he seemed genuinely interested in what I had to say."

Alicia's eyes shone. "Ruthie, I haven't talked about

stuff like this in ages! Jim just grunts about the weather, the kids, the bills, and the state of the liquor cabinet." She paused. "I told Stavros about our travels and where we're going next."

"WHAT?" Ruth hissed. "You did *what*? What's the matter with you? He could follow us and kill us all in our sleep!"

Ignoring Ruth's anxiety, Alicia said, "When he brought me a Coke, his hand sort of brushed mine. Oh, Ruthie. His blue eyes were so gorgeous. I felt myself melting. I thought I'd die! Thank God I happened to glance at my watch and saw that it was almost 6:00. I jumped up and said, 'I've got to run. I'm meeting people for dinner. No, I'll take a taxi. But thanks.'"

Ruth's face relaxed a bit. "My, my. Didn't we have a busy afternoon?" She laid her hand on her friend's arm. "Al, do you realize what you sound like?"

"No. What?"

"Like some ditzy, teen-aged girl who's delirious about her first boyfriend, not to mention somebody who loved every *minute* of the attention. But really! What were you *thinking* of? Who knows what kind of scam this guy is running?"

"Knock it off. We just chatted over a soft drink. Big deal. What's wrong with that?"

"Nothing, I guess," Ruth said, warily, "as long as you know what you're doing. So, did you lose your shoe when you were dashing out of that hotel?"

"What? Oh, ha, ha. Very funny. My fat foot would never fit into her tiny glass slipper."

The arrival of their food brought an end to Alicia's revelations—but not to Ruth's worries. Lord, help us, she thought. Like we really needed this. I hope Al can keep her head on straight.

The beef *stifado* was as good as Efie had said; they all had seconds. Close to nine, a bouzouki player and a man with an accordion came through the kitchen door, followed by a clarinetist. They set up near an illuminated fig tree, and the music began. As tables were cleared and people got up to dance, Beth said, "Look around us, ladies. Besides Greek, I'm hearing English, French, German, Italian, and Japanese here tonight. We're a regular United Nations."

"Yes," Najila said wistfully. "In my country, if we could just eat and dance together, perhaps the fighting would stop. Our foods, our music—all same same."

George downed his wine and then, with a flourish, invited each woman at the table to join his dance circle. He waved to the bouzouki player, who started an up-tempo folk tune.

"This is a very popular dance called a *kalamatiano*," Efie informed them. "The rhythm is a bit unusual, sort of uneven. But it is much fun."

George demonstrated a few steps; and, quickly, the women got the swing of it. Normally quiet and reserved, George gave vent to his emotions on the dance floor.

"Wow," Vicky whispered. "George really gets into it, doesn't he? Like total abandon."

When the music modulated to a new key, George pulled Najila from the circle. Soon they were alone on the dance floor, matching each other with intricate steps in time to the plaintive wails of the clarinet. Faster and faster they whirled, accompanied by the steady clapping of the other dancers, now watching from the sidelines. When the accordion player rippled through his final chord, the whole crowd broke into wild applause.

Beth and Ruth yelled, "You go, *Najila!*"

As he led her from the floor, George kissed Najila on both cheeks and gave her a big hug. "*Efharisto,* Miss Najila. You most magnificent. A born dancer."

Najila's cheeks were flaming. "Oh, so much fun I have not had in many years. I love to dance. Unfortunately, Kanaan had no time; and Sami cares not for it. I will do this again . . . but not for some minutes. I must sit down for breathing."

As they all returned to their table, Alicia glanced at her phone and saw a text from Jim. "Oh, great," she muttered.

The washing machine is broken and the dryer doesn't work. You should have gotten those things fixed before you left. What am I supposed to do now?

Before she lost her nerve, she replied:

Try Mr. Schneider, the repair guy. His number is next to the kitchen phone. I'm 8,000 miles away. You'll have to deal with it, Jim. Sorry.

Alicia reread the text, deleted "Sorry," and then firmly pressed SEND. She couldn't believe what she had just done.

Her mood was light, and she smiled to herself as she stuck the phone into her pocket. Her thoughts returned to her afternoon encounter.

Stavros seemed more attractive by the minute.

Twenty-two

May 8, 2014—Athens, Greece

R uth raised one eyelid and sniffed. Rain. She opened the other eye and saw puddles growing on the windowsill from the steady downpour. She tried to get out of bed, but she sat down quickly and put her hand to her throbbing head. Rain or red wine? She knew the answer.

She grabbed a towel, wiped off the sill, closed the window, and started to dive back under the covers when the bedside phone rang.

"*Kalimera,* Ruth. Efie here. We will need to change our plan a bit for today. The rain will make the *agora,* sorry, the ancient market, too muddy. What can we substitute: some other museums, a visit to the Greek Women's Institute, or just having an easy morning?"

"Uh, those all sound like good ideas, Efie. Let me take a poll at breakfast, OK? I'll call you back, say, in about an hour? Yes. Fine. *Ef* . . . uh . . . *efha* . . . ah . . . *efharisto.* There. Did I get it right?"

"Perfect, Ruth. Soon you will speak Greek as a native. *Adio.*"

Ruth dragged herself out of bed, took two aspirins, and headed to the shower. That third glass of wine had gone down so easily. Lesson learned.

The others were already in the breakfast room

when Ruth arrived. After she poured herself a cup of coffee, she said, "Efie called me about an hour ago. She said the old market area was out because it's too muddy there. Her options are more museums, the Greek Women's Institute, or back to bed. And your pleasure is?"

"Back to bed for me," Alicia said. "That way, I'll do what I should and stay off this stupid knee for awhile. It's still puffy. I want to be up for all the walking once we hit Corinth."

"I'd like to find a laundromat," Beth said. "I need to do a few things."

Najila saw her chance to talk alone with Beth. "Oh, may I go with you? I brought not many clothes, so a washing time would be good. And you, Ruth?"

"Nah, I'm fine. Thanks. I'll go to the drugstore; and, after that, I think the Greek Women's shop might be fun."

"OK if I tag along with you, Ruth?" Vicky said as she licked the last bit of yogurt from her spoon. "I'd like to stop at both of those places. By the way, ladies, we're supposed to meet Efie and George at 5:00 this afternoon to drive out to Cape Sounion, so maybe we could get together earlier to have a little reflection about Paul's first letter to the Corinthians. It would be good prep for the trip down to Corinth tomorrow. How about if we meet in the back corner of the lobby, say around 3:30? Would that work?"

They all nodded their agreement. "Sounds like a plan to me," Ruth said. "I'll call Efie and tell her all this and also that you and I will meet her around 10:30, Vick. Let's head out to the drugstore in about half an hour."

After she called Efie, Ruth checked her cosmetic bags. She wrote out a quick list, and then she returned the bags to her suitcase. She saw Norma's letter, pulled it out, and held it up to the light. She could see only a folded piece of paper. I must remember to read this to the others soon, she thought. Maybe Delphi or Mykonos would be a good place.

In her room, Alicia got busy on her iPad. She typed in "Museums in Orlando" and was surprised when ten came up. One was a Smithsonian affiliate; but it was in Daytona Beach, an hour away. Too far. Two others looked very attractive: Orlando Museum of Art and the Harry P. Leu Gardens. Both boasted of active volunteer programs.

Why haven't I heard about these places before, she wondered. These Gardens look terrific. It would be fun to dig in the dirt again . . . with nobody yelling at me. But will they take me? What the heck? It won't hurt to ask. She filled out the volunteer form and hit SEND.

+++++++++

Armed with hotel umbrellas, Beth and Najila rode the Metro from Syntagma Square to the stop near the Acropolis; and then they got off and walked two blocks to the *Athens Washateria* on Veikou Street. The attendant there was pleasant and spoke enough English to show them how to operate the machines. While their clothes were washing and then drying, they sat in two scarred, white plastic chairs.

After some preliminary chit-chat about the weather, Najila came to the point. "Beth, I am glad to have this chance to speak with you. I know you are many years

married and have also worked at your jobs. So what is
your thought? Should I marry Sami? I find myself very
attractive, no, sorry, *attracted* to him." She blushed. "I
may even love him a little. He is a wonderful man. He
is kind, considerate, and has a very important position
in a big clinic. And, my mama likes him."

She inclined her head. "But he is a man of my
country, used to being in charge, always the one
making the decisions. And since I am alone for many
years now, I make my own decisions. I decide what
I want to do with my time and my life. I know I have
much luck; most women in my country cannot do this.
They have little freedom. I have fears that, if I marry
Sami, I will lose my freedom. Yesterday, I made lists of
reasons why to marry Sami would be good or bad. But
I still do not know an answer."

Beth considered her response. "Well, there are
always two sides to this kind of thing, aren't there?
When we were at Norma's funeral, I saw that Kay
was so happy in a new relationship with a man
she'd known back in high school. They had married
other people, then lost their spouses, and, now, have
found each other again after many years. Bless her
heart; Kay was ecstatic. So this is definitely the right
arrangement for her.

"On the other hand, I may be the wrong person to
ask. You see, Perry and I divorced last year."

Najila's eyes widened. "But . . . what . . . what
happened? When Ruth read your letter to us in
Samaria two years ago, you seemed most happy in
your marriage."

"Early on, we were. We married right out of college."
Beth chuckled. "Oh, my. We were so young and had so

many stars in our eyes. We were also very immature. Part of the problem was that we came from different types of upbringing. I had been given a lot of freedom but also a great deal of responsibility at a very young age, while Perry had been sheltered and protected— he was a momma's boy. In the beginning, that didn't matter. Everything was rosy and wonderful, and we sure thought we knew everything. Things were pretty good while we were raising our children.

"Slowly we changed. We grew at different rates and in different directions. We have both tried very hard for the past several years to keep things going and to stay together because we believe in biblical marriage and God's plan for us to stay married."

She sighed. "But it wasn't working. We were both unable to 'be as Christ loves the church' to each other. There was no fighting; we had just grown apart and were living separate lives in the same house. I was waiting for him to retire so we could handle things quietly, leave Rome together, and not make a big fuss.

"Unfortunately, it didn't happen quite like that. You see, we had both been very active in our church group there. I had been a worship leader and a Sunday school teacher; Perry had been an officer on the church council. So we were very involved and very visible.

"We talked things over a lot with our pastor; he was really supportive and understanding. Finally, though, we agreed that our marriage was dead. It had probably *been* dead for several years, but we just didn't want to admit it.

"So when the news broke that we were divorcing, it came as a huge shock to many in our church family. Some couples that were having trouble with their own marriages thought that if Perry and I couldn't make it, what hope did *they* have?

"Then there were others who were upset and even angry because *they* hadn't known what was going on, and *they* thought I should have trusted them enough to tell them. I mean, we just didn't want any picking and prying. Goodness knows, in a small community like ours was in Rome, there's enough dirty laundry flying around any day of the week. We didn't want to add more. Anyway, it's nobody else's business, is it?"

Najila's dark eyes were full of concern. "Oh, how terrible for you, Beth. That sounds so hard, no, wait, I mean *harsh*. Why did they think only for themselves? Why did they not help you during such a heavy time?"

"Why, indeed?" Beth asked. "It was pretty hypocritical. They called themselves good Christians and yet were so unloving and mean spirited. There was so much talk and gossip for months. It really got me down. It hurt a lot." She heaved a big sigh. "Whatever. Eventually I got through it. Things weren't easy; I sought counseling, prayed constantly, etc. It occurred to me later that some of them might have been jealous of our courage to end our marriage with honesty, you know, and let each other move on."

"Divorce is very hard for Samaritans as well," Najila said slowly. "Very few couples are able to do it. Personally, I think that when two people have changed so much and would end up hating each other and having a terrible life—becoming bitter, or even ill, if they stayed together—then it is better for everyone if they slice the ties and separate. People do not speak this idea out loud at home, but I think many share it."

Both dryers buzzed at once, so they removed their

clothes and began folding them on a battered metal table. They smiled as a young man pulled his warm clothes from a dryer, stuffed them into his backpack, and left.

"It may come as a surprise," Beth said as she smoothed the wrinkles out of a pair of jeans, "but I'm actually fine with everything. Perry got remarried in the fall. My daughter and I even went to the wedding."

"Aiyee," Najila whispered. "Did that not make . . . make . . . pain for you?"

Beth shrugged. "My daughter's not a baby; she's a smart and capable young professional. She wanted to meet the woman her father was marrying. She asked me to go with her, so I did. I was surprised at how happy and content I felt. I suppose that's because our marriage had really been dead for years. Oh, sure, when I saw them at the altar, I got a little teary eyed and had a few fleeting memories about how that had once been us.

"But things changed. I've accepted that now. I'm trying to make a new life for myself. We both are. Perry and his new wife are still working in Rome. He wasn't ready to retire, after all."

She folded up the pair of jeans. "I'm in New Mexico now, in a new house; and I'm making new friends. I've joined a ladies' biker club, and I'm putting my name around for just the right nursing job. It was hard at first, but I remembered that Norma had done almost the same thing. I will say that I'm taking my time finding a new church."

"I am full of admiring for you," Najila said. "You seem truly happy with your new life. You are looking forward to finding a new job and making fun with your hobbies . . . all on your own. And, I see that, although you and Perry divorced, Perry was the one who soon remarried. Perhaps he enjoys to have a wife who can be a housekeeper, a cook, a laundress, a secretary, and a social director."

Beth nodded. "A friend told me once that a lot of guys need a nurse with a purse."

"Aiyee," Najila said, her eyes twinkling, "many men are like this. They want someone to do all these things for them. They cannot, or do not want to, live alone. Perhaps they do not know how. Many go directly from the house of their mama to the house of their wife. Women seem to be more strong and manage these things quite well on their own. Rania does. And I do. I am most happy with my life."

Najila matched the last pair of socks and smiled. "That is my answer. Sami will be my friend but not my husband. There. Thank you, Beth. I am better already. Ah, but if only he were not so handsome."

Twenty-three

A fitful spring breeze blew the rain clouds away by mid-morning, as Efie, Ruth, and Vicky walked to the Greek Women's Institute, an attractive shop in the bustling Monastiraki district.

"All the pieces here," Efie explained as she showed them around, "have been handmade by women from the Greek islands. They often do not have the opportunity to earn much money; but they are very gifted in handwork: sewing, knitting, weaving, and the like. My friend, Tanya, who runs this shop, works very hard to make contacts with these women. She brings in their creations several times a year. Today you are helping to support them."

"I'm for that," Ruth said. "And, hey, they're helping me. These woven tablecloths are beautiful. I'll get one for Jerry as well; I'm positive Norma would have brought one home for their house."

After Vicky selected several chic scarves, they were back on the street. A few doors down, they smelled the fragrant scents of a spice shop.

"Wait, Efie," Ruth said. "Could we stop here for a minute? Norma was crazy about the smell of spice souks. Do you suppose I could take a photo? I'll send that to Jerry right now. Also, I'd love to buy some frankincense."

Efie spoke with the owner who nodded and invited them to come in. Efie took several photos of Ruth and Vicky with the smiling proprietor between them.

"You are very kind to think of your friend's husband," Efie said. "These pictures will please him."

As they left the shop, Ruth grinned. "You know, I'll bet Paul stopped at a place *just* like this the day before he left for Corinth. There he was, haggling over little bags of sunflower seeds and dried apricots—some munchies for the road—while Timothy and Silas were nagging at him to get a move on. I can see it now."

"Ruth, you do have a flair for the drama," Efie said with a laugh. "Smelling all those spices has made me hungry. Shall we stop for a small lunch? There is a good market just ahead. They have no seating, so we will stand at a table outside, if that is all right with you."

"Perfect," Vicky said. "The better to people watch."

As she finished her gyro, Ruth asked Efie about her life—what jobs she had done before. "I don't mean to be nosy, Efie, but I'd love to know what you did to transform yourself from that photo you sent me to now. You look *so* different."

"Of course," Efie said. "I am happy to tell you. Twenty years ago, I decided I wanted to see the world and meet new people. So I took small jobs: as an *au pair* for a Greek family and then as a waitress in Greek restaurants in London. Later I worked in the Greek embassy in Toronto. After some years, I needed something more. I had saved up my earnings, so I returned to Greece and enrolled in a work-study tourism program at the University of Athens. I love to travel and thought to help other people have nice trips. I decided to make money doing it."

"So what was your plan?" Vicky asked as she sipped her tea.

"During my apprenticeship," Efie replied, "I observed other guides and saw that, to be successful, one must look the part and also have a bit of flair to stand out from the rest. I realized I needed to change my image; so I lost weight, changed my hair color, and bought more trendy clothes. My friend, Fotini, is a hairdresser; so she gave me a new hairstyle. Several shop owners were happy to advise me and even called me before their sales. Of course, they like it when I tell my clients where I shop.

"Another friend, Marisa, who runs a little boutique at the Hilton Hotel, introduced me to her brother, George, who was a detective for the Athens police department. We saw each other for three years and then married when he retired. He loves to drive the van for me. It is also very nice to have his eyes watching the crowds when I do tours, and he knows *everyone* in town. It was a big change for me, but we are very happy together. I see now that I must change my photos, too, eh?"

"Beyond a shadow of a doubt," Ruth answered. "You don't look *anything* like that photo. You have really transformed yourself. I see that if I want to give courses to flight attendants, even as a volunteer, I need to update my style. I've got to wow that thirty-something gate-keeper girl at the front desk before I'll *ever* get in to see the training director."

Efie shrugged. "My mother let herself go. She was unhappy and looked old at forty-eight. I will not do that. One must always step forward."

+++++++++

Later that afternoon, the women met in a back corner of the hotel lobby. "This won't be a class or anything," Vicky explained as she distributed some handouts. "It's just that when I was in Chicago a few months ago, I attended a lecture by Dr. John Pilch; and I took a lot of notes. When he was done, he gave us a handout as well. He called it a 'road map' and said we were welcome to use it. When I knew we were going to do this trip, I revised it for you ladies."

She adjusted her gold-rimmed reading glasses. "Most scholars think Paul was born around 6 BC, had the vision of Jesus on the road to Damascus around 33 AD, started his missionary travels around 45/46 AD, then visited Antioch, Galatia, Macedonia, and arrived in Corinth in the spring of 50 AD.

"Like most of the other people that Paul spoke to around the Mediterranean, his Corinthians were expat Judeans who'd moved there looking for work, adventure, or whatever. These early believers were Judeans; later translations use the word *Jews*. Paul started out speaking *only* to these people.

"Here's the thing. After his Damascus road experience, Paul himself was really, really changed— like *completely*. Dr. Pilch told us that, from then on, Paul saw himself as a change agent—somebody to whom God had given something new and different to share. He said Paul was the agent between God and those who needed the change. He was on a mission and felt called to do this work. He told the Corinthians they were also called.

"He stayed in Corinth for eighteen months, living and making tents with Priscilla and Aquila. It's possible that they were believers even before Paul was. They were a married couple who helped Paul a great deal in several other cities, as well. People would come to their workshop to hear about Jesus.

"Later, when Paul was in Ephesus, around 54 or 55 AD, he learned from the messengers of a woman named Chloe that all wasn't going smoothly in Corinth; so he wrote a letter back to the Corinthians, addressing his concerns and answering their questions.

"That was always a big problem for him. He'd visit a place, start a new group, and then he'd leave. When troubles arose, he wrote letters back to these people; but he wasn't there personally. He was out of touch when they needed him most." She made a little face. "Hmm, my mom was just like that when I was little. Sorry. I digress.

"Anyway, here's the part I covered: the first six chapters of First Corinthians. Paul opens the letter in his usual way. He identifies himself and gives the standard compliments; but after only nine verses, he gets right down to business. He wants them to agree and be united with the same mind and purpose. He's heard they have gotten themselves into all kinds of weird stuff: divisions and spats about who their leaders are and about who's got wisdom and who doesn't."

Alicia laughed. "Sounds like a lot of church groups today, doesn't it?"

"For sure," Vicky replied. "Paul then says, 'Cool it. Who is powerful? Who has wisdom? Not you guys. Only God. The cross is a paradox. Everything is totally

upside down. Try to get over yourselves and get this.'
And then he laid out the even bigger problems he'd
heard about: sexual license, even incest, or hauling
each other into civil courts instead of dealing with
their own difficulties themselves. Twice he tells them
that their bodies are temples of the Holy Spirit, and
they should behave like they believed that."

Vicky removed her gold glasses. "That's actually
pretty hard for me today. It's easy to say that I believe
that, but do I really live it? Anyway, I know you all read
these chapters before this trip; so does anyone have
anything to add? Maybe you'd like to share something
that really spoke to you?"

Ruth tapped a pencil on the table. "Paul really
impressed me. I think he was one *really* smart guy who
tried his darndest to get this mixed bag of people, who
weren't exactly rocket scientists, to believe that Jesus
was the *real* Messiah. To help them, he used the kind
of imagery he thought they'd pick up on. He talked a
lot about buildings and temples—stuff they saw every
day. I'll bet it made him totally *crazy* to think that he'd
been with these people for eighteen months, teaching
them, helping them, and trying to get them to live a
new way, only to hear later by the grapevine that they
were into all kinds of bad news behavior."

"There was also another small problem," Najila
said. "Paul was growing up in Tarsus. He was then
long years a Pharisee in Jerusalem. Possibly many of
the Judeans in Corinth had lived there some time and
spoke more like the local people. By his accent, they
could tell Paul was not from Corinth. He was not from
around there. He was a *stranger*. In ancient times,
people did not welcome strangers, especially one who

had been persecuting early Christians. He might preach to them, but why should they believe this man who had done so much harming?"

"Thanks, Najila, "Vicky said. "That's an important point. Anybody else?"

Alicia absently twirled a strand of her blonde hair around her finger. "I know all about being a stranger in a new place—been there, done that many times as a kid. Paul knew these Corinthians, as well. He loved them, but they were not loving each other. He realized it must have been an uphill battle for them to believe what he had taught. He knew their potential for misunderstanding and juvenile, immature behavior and even for their falling apart completely. He must have worried that all his hard work was going down the drain."

"But he just kept on caring, didn't he?" Beth observed softly. "Here he was, gone from Corinth for four or five years already. He could have just blown them off, saying, 'Oh well, they'll have to look after themselves now.' Yet he was so concerned, and he wrote so many beautiful words to them. His example is sure a lesson for me."

Vicky surveyed the group. She never knew what to expect from these women. They could come up with some incredible insights. Or they could say nothing. Today they had said a lot.

She allowed a few moments to pass and then said, "Thanks, everyone. You're amazing. I know we could all talk longer, but we'd better stop. We're meeting Efie soon."

Ruth stood up. "Thanks, Vick. That was really super. I love how we all contributed something. Now

I'm gonna run up and change. I'll see you all in the lobby in a half hour, OK? I'm excited to see Cape Sounion."

+++++++++

As George drove through the outskirts of Athens, they passed by the exclusive suburbs and resorts of Glyfada and Vouliagmeni that bordered on the Saronic Gulf. Efie explained that their destination, Cape Sounion, was a very popular tourist spot. "In the warm months, people go there to spend the day, to swim and picnic, and then to watch the sunset. Today it is a bit cool to swim, but we will see the ruins of the beautiful temple of Poseidon as the sun goes down. Then we will have dinner at a beach hotel."

After George parked the bus, Efie led them to the site of the temple on a cliff overlooking the sea. "A legend says that this place is where Aegeus, ancient king of Athens, believing that his son, Theseus, was dead, was overcome in grief and jumped off the cliff. Thus, he gave his name to the Aegean Sea.

"Another legend says that sailors offered a last sacrifice to appease Poseidon, the mighty sea god, at this temple, built 2,500 years ago. They would ask Poseidon's protection on their journey before leaving the calm waters of the Saronic Gulf for the open and deeper waters of the Aegean Sea.

"While I don't believe in Poseidon," Efie said, "this is still a very special place for me. When I am about to start something difficult or have a problem, I like to come here to think. Ah, I see some empty benches over there. Shall we sit for a little while?"

The slanting rays of the late afternoon sun warmed their faces, as they relaxed on two stone benches. Silently, each woman considered her personal application of what they'd discussed with Vicky and what Efie had just told them.

As Najila put on her sunglasses, she contemplated her next tour booking and wondered if being a tour guide was *her* calling. It was such a simple thing and so much fun for her. She knew she was good at it. She certainly did *not* feel called to marry Sami.

From where she sat on the end of the bench, Vicky debated about finishing her book. Was it a good use of her time to write a historical novel about the last days of the Roman Empire? Big deal. Who'd benefit from that? Was that a *calling* . . . or just another menopausal fantasy?

Alicia bit her lower lip and worried about the next deep waters and open seas in her life. The main dilemma was Jim. Could she really do something about their marriage? Like what?

What will happen to us? She sighed. She'd really need God's help here. No way could she sort all this out on her own.

Two seagulls swooped down and skidded to a halt in the dirt next to Beth. They squawked loudly as they fought over a bit of bread. Beth smiled. Was that a sign? Was she being called to use her experiences with her husband, Perry, to help other unhappy, quarrelling couples? And then, was she *really* a temple of the Holy Spirit? What did that mean?

"You know," Ruth said, "I used to feel that my work as a secretary for the College Challengers evangelist group was my calling . . . until I left them. Later, I was *sure* that being a flight attendant was my call; but then I retired. Now what? I've prayed a million times asking what my new call is. I hope I get an answer soon. I wonder if I'm missing something, or maybe God's put me on hold."

She felt her pocket vibrate. "Hey, this is it! It's my answer. No, wait. It's not God. It's just a text from Julia. She says,

You all must be having so much fun on all your travels. Meanwhile, I'm just worn out, running from one doc to the next, trying to get my bum knee going. But I have started an exercise program. It feels good to get outside again. Beth, I hope your knees are holding up. How I wish I were there with you all. I'll bet the baklava is to die for. Be safe.

Love, Julia

"How nice that your friend wrote to you, Ruth," Efie said as she glanced at her watch. "Now I think we must move on. We will walk to the Seaside Hotel to take our dinner. The hotel is just over there, beyond those palm trees."

"Sounds good to me," Ruth said. "C'mon, Al. Race you to the bar. Loser buys!"

Twenty-four

May 9, 2014—Corinth, Greece

The next morning, George and Efie picked them up at the *Amelika* shortly before ten. After stowing their luggage in the back of George's bus, they left Athens and headed down the E94. They passed the exit for the port of Piraeus, then veered left and south along the coast.

"The distance from Athens to Corinth is only about 72 kilometers," Efie told them, "and with this traffic, it should take about one and a half hours. We ought to arrive in time for lunch."

"That's forty-two miles," Alicia whispered.

"We're on our way!" Ruth exclaimed gleefully. "We're actually going to Corinth." She began to sing the chorus of Willie Nelson's "On the Road Again." Beth joined her, harmonizing the alto line.

"Good grief," Vicky whispered. "Keep it down. Efie will think we're all nitwits. She'll never do a trip with any Americans again."

Ruth laughed. "Oh Vick, lighten up, will ya? We're just having a little fun. Meanwhile, who wants some snacks? I've got trail mix, cheese crackers, and the dried fruit I bought in that market. There are water bottles in the back when you need them."

The roadway was lined with stately palms, pines,

and fruit orchards. Tidy, three-story, red tile-roofed apartment buildings were interspersed with strip shopping areas and busy truck stops.

"Athens is not too careful with zoning down here," Efie remarked drily.

Off to the left, a few rusty ships listed at anchor in the sparkling waters of the Saronic Gulf.

"Just think," Ruth said. "Paul and his buddies saw that *same* water and the island of Salamis over there when they walked this way 2,000 years ago. Is that cool or what?"

"All that blue, blue water . . ." Alicia said dreamily.

In the back seat, beside Alicia, Ruth knew what she was thinking. She patted Alicia's hand and whispered, "Get over it, Al. Forget those blue eyes. You've already got enough man troubles in your life. You sure don't need any more."

Najila looked at both of them but said nothing.

As they drove along, Efie spoke into her microphone. "We will be much outside at the ruins this afternoon, so I will tell you a few bits now. Corinth lies in the northeast corner of the Peloponnesus, near the east end of the Gulf of Corinth. The ancient city was very important because it was situated on the Isthmus of Corinth, the shortest route from the Adriatic to the Aegean Sea. In other words, the shortest route from Europe to Asia. The city was destroyed by the Romans in 146 BC. The Corinth that Paul would have seen was rebuilt by Julius Caesar in 44 BC."

"Good old Julius," quipped Alicia. "Always had his eye on the best real estate."

"It was a gateway city," Efie continued, "since Corinth sits between its two ports: Lechaeon on the

Gulf of Corinth and Cenchreae on the Saronic Gulf. In the early days, cargo was offloaded from ships on one side, put onto wagons, and then pulled on rollers to the other side. Or, small ships themselves could be set on the wooden rollers and hauled to the other side, about six and a half kilometers."

"Four miles," Alicia said.

"Clever," Vicky observed. "No matter the obstacles, they figured out a way to bring their stuff to market. Money always talks, doesn't it?"

"Yes," Efie said, "those early traders were resourceful. The city attracted a large and diverse population from the East; in fact, most of the citizens were *not* Greek. The commercial importance of Corinth between East and West in New Testament times was very great; extensive ship traffic guaranteed lots of business and money changing hands. Corinth was also the seat of the Isthmian Games, so that brought in many tourists as well.

"Ancient writers, especially a traveler named Pausanias, who visited in about 155 AD, testified to the splendor of Corinth's buildings, confirmed by remains which have been uncovered. Besides the big temple to Apollo, there were many temples to other gods, as well.

"There were also public baths, fountains, two theaters, one seating 18,000, and an amphitheater. On the south side of the *agora*, Greek for market, were council chambers and the rostrum for speakers, called a *bema*. It was where Paul was tried by Gallio. I will show you this afternoon."

Efie glanced in the rear view mirror and switched off her microphone. George looked over at her. "What's wrong, sweetheart?"

Efie jerked her chin towards the back seats. "Look at them. All asleep, poor things. Listen: Someone even snores a little." She stifled a laugh. "I see I must shorten my descriptions."

A few miles from the Corinth Canal, groves of salt pines, scrubby grass, and clusters of modest houses came into view. "Perhaps you should open the windows, George, to wake them gently. It *is* warm in here." Efie turned around in her seat. "Ah, Vicky, you had a nice nap, eh? Would you like to say anything about St. Paul before we get to the Canal?"

"Oh, Efie. I'm so embarrassed," Vicky said as she sat up and rubbed her eyes. "I must have dozed off. It was the smooth ride, and the sun, and . . ."

". . . and the wine from last night," Ruth added. "That stuff is dangerous. C'mon, Vick; tell us about Paul."

Sitting behind Efie, Vicky covered a yawn and took the microphone. "Let's see . . . what can I say? Well, I think it's interesting that Corinth already had a thriving Jewish colony and synagogue by 50 AD. Many Jews went there from the East and the West to find jobs or a better life. Some had been displaced by the Emperor Claudius' expulsion of Jews from Rome. Of course, some came against their will, as slaves.

"Corinth had the best and worst of a busy international city. For some people, there were the high ideals of Greek civilization; they were drawn to the spirituality, the culture, and the aesthetics. At the other end of the spectrum were the *hottest* in pagan playtimes. Corinth had a reputation all over the Mediterranean for being a big, brawling port. We're talking a serious party town. With a mixed and mobile population, it was a center for pleasure and vice: girls, gambling, and guzzling. You name it, they sold it. Pick your poison. Pay the price."

Beth laughed. "Can you spell Miami? Or San Francisco? So what's new?"

"Right," Vicky said. "Then, too, Corinth was a religious melting pot for Jewish, Roman, and Greek practices, plus other Eastern religions coming in with all the sailors. Paul couldn't have *chosen* a tougher place for evangelization. His two letters to the people in Corinth show that he had to deal with a wide range of problems—troubles that didn't occur in other communities.

"But he had to eat, didn't he? Luckily for him, with all that shipping and all the people involved with the Isthmian Games, there would have been plenty of business for tentmakers. Paul lived with Priscilla and Aquila. He worked with them and preached in the synagogue on the Sabbaths. He even converted Crispus, president of the synagogue. His plan was always to work *only* with the Judeans.

"But after a time, many of the expat Judeans rejected and assaulted him. So he began to teach outside of the synagogue, in the house of Titus Justus. More and more non-Judeans began to listen to him and become believers. After eighteen months, the Judeans brought him before Gallio, the Roman pro-consul. They accused Paul of being a teacher of unlawful religion. Can you imagine?"

Vicky laughed. "Gallio was having none of it; he threw them all out of court. So Paul left Corinth sometime after that and went to Ephesus where he later wrote his first letter to the Corinthians."

Ruth patted Vicky on the shoulder. "You've got it all together, Vick. I wish I could take your church history classes. You really make it come alive. I feel like I'm right there on the street with Paul."

"Aww, thanks, Ruth," Vicky said. "I love talking about all this, but I get carried away sometimes. My goal has always been to shorten the distance between the pulpit and the pew."

Just before the Corinth Canal, George pulled to the side of the road. He parked near the bridge, high atop the Canal. At several small souvenir stands, Ruth saw post cards, scarves, colorful beach cover-ups, cups, key chains, and CDs of Greek folk music. She also noticed a hand-lettered sign advertising bungee jumping. From up *here*?

"I think we get out for some minutes," George said. "Not too crowdy. If you like, we come back here tomorrow. More shop time then. Now we walk out on bridge. Good view down to Canal. Come, follow me."

Beth was last in line behind the others; her face was white. "I don't know if I can do this," she whispered to Ruth. "I'm *terrified* of heights."

"Here," Ruth said soothingly. "I'll put my arm around you, and we'll walk together. Not to worry. We'll just go as far as you can; then we'll turn around, OK?" She was surprised at Beth's fear, since Beth happily rode a powerful motorcycle. Oh well, Ruth thought. There's no accounting for phobias. I've sure got a few of my own.

From the center of the bridge, they looked straight down the sheer sides of two, smooth, rock walls to the Corinth Canal below.

"Looks like somebody sliced a big loaf of bread in half and then turned the water on," Alicia joked.

"From here," George said, "is 150 feet down. Canal is four miles long. Early Roman emperors tried to dig canal 2,000 years ago. They either died or plans were stupid. This canal started in 1882; finished in 1893. Much money; several builders go bankrupt. Heavy damage by Germans during Second World War. Canal never deep or wide enough for big ships; so, today, only used by private boats or small tourist ships."

He spat down into the canal. "Good idea; but too much cost, too much corruption. Story of Greece."

"And maybe the story of America?" Vicky muttered.

"Now, George," Efie said soothingly, "don't be so grumpy. After all, we are doing the canal cruise tomorrow. From the water, it is very pretty. Now we should go. I told the hotel we would get there by noon."

They all piled back into the bus and soon arrived at the Isthmus One Apart Hotel. In front of them, they saw a square structure with three stories of small apartments. Each had its own balcony surrounded in blue glass, echoing the blue waters of the Saronic Gulf in the distance.

Efie assisted them with check-in. After they found their rooms and deposited their luggage, they met on the tree-lined pool deck for lunch. "The hotel has two restaurants and a café plus this terrace bar," Efie said. "We will eat in the restaurant tonight; but, since we were in the van most of the morning and the weather is fine, I thought you would enjoy to sit outside under the palms."

"This hotel is really nice," Beth said as she sat down. "Everything's pretty, and I love having that little fridge. Since my room is on the top floor, I can see the Canal. It's much better than standing over it. That gave me the chills."

+++++++++

After a tasty lunch of gyros and tzatziki, George drove them the five miles to Corinth. On their way, they passed the seaside village of modern Corinth; and then they approached the large archaeological site of ancient Corinth farther inland. As George parked the van, Efie said, "Please take your cameras, water, and sun hats. We will be here at the ruins for several hours."

"This place is *huge*," Alicia exclaimed after Efie bought their tickets and they entered the site. "I hope we'll have time to see it all."

"I can't believe we're really here," Vicky said excitedly. "We are actually *standing* in the same place that Paul did!"

"Yeah," Ruth said, "and I'm taking some shots to send to Jerry. Gosh, I wish Norma could have seen this. She would have loved it! Hey, you guys. Line up so that big temple is behind us. Efie, would you take a few photos of us?" Ruth handed her phone to Efie who took pictures from several different angles to include the temple of Apollo and a large, flat-topped mountain behind them.

"Since we stand here," Efie said, "I will say that these are the mountains of the Peloponnesus; and this big mountain just behind us," she gestured with her hand, "is the Acrocorinth. It is the most prominent; it is a steep, rocky slope about 1850 feet above Corinth.

In ancient times, there were many temples up there; the biggest was the temple of Aphrodite. Legend says there were 1000 slave girls as ritual prostitutes."

"Whoa!" Beth said. "Just think: For one guy, that would be a different girl every day—for *three* years! Or maybe the legend was just wishful thinking."

As they walked on, Efie told them that the seven columns of the temple of Apollo were the only ruins of ancient Corinth visible prior to early excavations begun in 1892. As she led them to the central market area called the *agora,* she said, "The American School of Classical Studies in Athens began excavating here in 1896. They have worked ever since except for three stops due to wars.

"I have made small maps for you to see where the buildings used to be. You are free to walk about as you wish. We will meet by the Temple of Apollo in one hour and then visit the Museum." Ruth took the maps from her and then passed them to the others.

Najila made a mental note: Provide maps. People like to find their own way.

Vicky headed for the theaters. At the smaller one, the Odeion, she climbed up and down several rows of seats, then out onto the stage where she took a bow. I could have been a star back then, she thought. But, hey, if I ever get my act together, maybe my book about Theodora can be televised; and then *she* can be the star. She'd like that.

Najila and Beth ventured west from the market area to the ancient health center called the Asklepieion. "This was like their hospital," Beth said as she read from a small guidebook. "Even back then, they knew to keep sick people isolated from the others. They also had a big fountain down here—the map calls it the Lerna—to bring fresh water to the hospital area. They were sure ahead of their time."

Alicia was drawn to the imposing Temple of Apollo in the center of the market area. She took photos of it from every side, then turned and took a long shot up to the Acrocorinth, the mountain towering above the ancient city. She sat down on a low wall, took a sip of her water, and enjoyed the view. She felt so happy and relaxed. It was as if her troubles at home were on another planet.

All the hustle and bustle of this big city, she thought, all the intrigues, the politics, the parties, the dinners, the births, weddings, deaths, and the lives that were lived out in this place are all gone now. Done. Game over. All that remains are these silent stones. What stories they could tell.

Thank God for Paul's letters to those people. We can see what he tried to do, his commitment, his passion, and the love he felt for them. He wanted so *badly* for them to know Jesus as he did. Paul just hung in there; he remained so committed and steadfast in spite of their crazy behavior, their pettiness, and their criticism of him. Thank goodness we've got his side of the story.

Alicia sighed. I wonder what my story is going to be.

In another section of the ruins, Ruth wandered on her own, happy to be there. After all, Corinth was the high point of their trip and the place where Paul had been so successful. She followed Efie's map through the streets until she reached the Pierene Fountain.

In her guidebook, Ruth read that the Pierene

Fountain, once enclosed within a building, had provided water, shade, and a meeting place for many citizens in ancient Corinth. Ruth had hoped to walk down closer to the fountain; but now it was fenced off, as further excavations took place. She took several photos, then sat down on a column fragment under a cypress tree. She scribbled some notes in her journal, then closed the book and leaned back against the tree.

Corinth Canal

Corinth and Acrocorinth

Odeion in Ancient Corinth

Temple of Apollo in Ancient Corinth

Pierene Fountain in Ancient Corinth

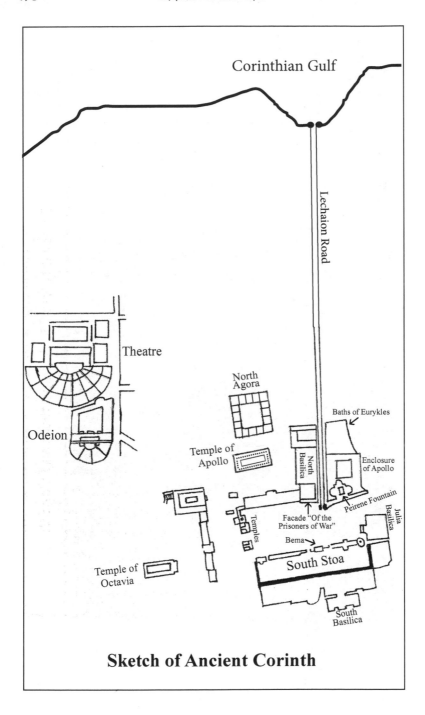

Sketch of Ancient Corinth

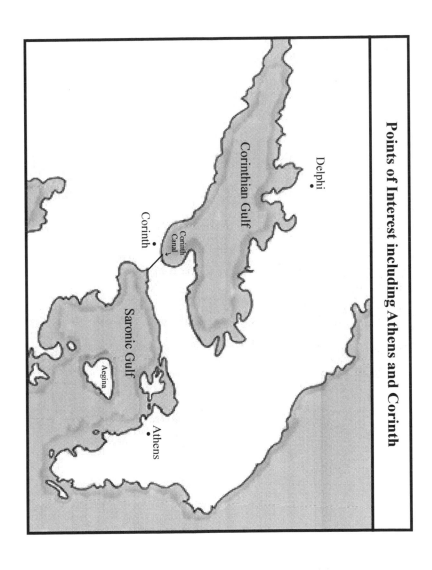

Points of Interest including Athens and Corinth

Twenty-five

July, 50 AD—Corinth, Greece

"Come, come, Timothy," Paulos said. "We must hurry. I told Priscilla we would bring her fresh water by midday; and, see, the sun is directly overhead now." They stepped into the Pierene building, filled large clay jars from the flowing fountains, then hastened out into the bright sunlight.

Paulos' face was covered in sweat as he threaded his way through the noisy crowds in the market. Standing up straight and going for a short walk was a relief for him after sitting all morning in the busy workshop. He was so grateful to his friends, Priscilla and Aquila, for inviting him to lodge with them and join them in their work as tentmakers. They had even spoken to neighbors and arranged rooms for his friends, Timothy and Sylvanus. How many others would be so generous?

A few streets away, Priscilla greeted them at the door of the workshop. "Three jars? Wonderful," she said, as she wiped her hands on the rough towel at her waist. "Now we will have cool water with our lunch. I will also be able to wash a few garments and clean the shop before our meeting with new believers tonight. Timothy, will you stay for our meal? I have prepared your favorite lentil and onion dish; and there are olives and fresh figs, as well. Paulos, Titus Justus came this morning. He asked that you stop to see him later. Ah, here is Aquila. Now let us all sit, thank God for our food, and then eat."

As Paulos sat at the table, he thanked God also for the loving hearts of his hosts. They had come to Corinth from Rome in search of work after the edict of the Emperor Claudius ordered all Judeans to leave Rome. Aquila was an excellent tentmaker with a steady stream of customers at his door. With a ready smile and a kind word, he would invite them to sit and talk while he stitched. He would listen and nod, not really saying much; but the clients left with glad faces. Best of all, they recommended Aquila to their friends: ship captains, merchants, Isthmian Games' officials, and wealthy homeowners in search of a fine tent for a garden party. Often, these same men, with faces hooded, would appear for the night meetings.

Prisca, or Priscilla as most people called her, was Aquila's wife. With her silky black hair caught up under a short veil, she was a delicate beauty. Paulos knew by her speech and mannerisms that she came from a cultured family. Yet she worked tirelessly alongside Aquila, completing the intricate finishing stitches, keeping the orders straight, collecting the payments, buying the tent-making and other household supplies, and making sure that the shop and their rooms above it were clean and tidy. Her cooking was simple but nourishing, and there was always room for a friend or a visiting missionary at her table.

On her daily trips to the market, she spoke with other women, inviting them to come and learn about Jesus several afternoons a week. It was a great sadness to her that she had no children of her own. Paulos had seen the longing on her face as she soothed a fussy baby for a young mother. Yet she never complained. She knew that bringing new believers to Jesus was offering them birth into a new life of a different sort. Her open personality was also a magnet for older, more established women with larger dwellings who could host their own house-church.

Paulos was amazed by her abilities and her energy. When once he tried to compliment her, she just smiled. "How could I not do these things? We are all family. This is what families do. This is what love is."

On days like this, Paulos could hardly contain his happiness. He had been in Corinth for only four months. Many Corinthians, even several synagogue officials, were believing and being baptized. It was so different from his experience in Athens. Perhaps the Lord had not intended for him to remain long in that city. Here in Corinth, with so many different cultures, beliefs, and peoples from many lands, they were eager to hear the message of Jesus. The time was right.

Twenty-six

Startled by voices nearby, Ruth checked her watch and then rubbed her neck, stiff from leaning at an angle against the tree. She bent down to retrieve her journal that had fallen to the ground.

I still can't believe we're actually in Corinth, she thought. All those weeks of planning and then poof! We're finally here, in this place where Paul lived and walked. I'm just sorry that Norma couldn't be with us. But then, maybe she is.

She tucked her journal into her tote bag, walked out of the fountain area, and waved to Alicia.

Alicia stood up as she saw the others coming back. "Let's go to the *bema*, or at least the sign on that wall over there," she called out. "We've got to get photos of us in front of it."

They gathered in front of the plaque stating that this was the *bema*. Efie explained that this was a speaker's platform in the middle of the market or *agora* area and was the probable place where the proconsul Gallio heard Paul's case when he was accused of teaching false religious practices.

"You know," Vicky said, "it's a good thing that Gallio threw the case out because that made Paul pack up and move to Ephesus. On the one hand, he might have felt like his work here was done; and it was time to move on. But on the other hand, if he had hung around here much longer, he might not have made it out alive."

"Yeah," Ruth said, "nothing ever happens by accident. Miracles occur every day. Trouble is, I'm usually dinking around; and I miss most of them. C'mon, ladies. I can see Efie almost at the museum."

Efie guided them through the galleries of the Corinth museum, pointing out the famous black and red pottery that had reaped vast profits for the city. They saw hundreds of marble statues, colorful and intricate mosaic floors, stone fragments with the letters *"ebrew,"* and carvings of menorahs.

But the room that interested them most displayed votive offerings from the ancient hospital, the Asklepios. Mounted on the wall were clay models of various limbs and body parts that had been healed.

"Man, all those hands and feet, and well, er, um . . . the other bits," Ruth said, blushing. "People must have been really grateful when they got well."

"Of course they were," Beth said. "If you got sick, that was usually the end of it. Life expectancy in those days was about 35. Hardly anybody would have been as old as we are."

"Some of those potters were really quite . . . um . . . creative," Vicky said as she pointed to the wall. "I'll bet trade was brisk for those guys."

Efie laughed. "I'm sure it was. Where there was money to be made, Corinthians never missed a chance. Now I think we must find George and go back to the hotel. It is still warm; you can go for a swim if you like. They opened the pool for the season just last week."

+++++++++

A gaggle of screaming little kids, splashing and jumping in the pool, made naps and a shower seem like a better option. "We will meet in the restaurant at 7:30," Efie told them. "Perhaps you can swim later."

After dinner, they gathered again by the pool. "Terrific," Ruth said. "All those little rug rats are gone. Come on, ladies; let's get our suits on. This is too nice to waste."

"I will sit here with Efie," Najila said. "We will enjoy the soft air and the fairy lights in the trees. I am not a water woman."

Soon Beth, Ruth, and Vicky were lounging on the steps in the shallow end of the pool while Alicia swam some laps.

"That felt good," she said as she toweled herself off and joined them. "I've missed my workouts."

Just then, George came out of the hotel and spoke to Efie. "Oh yes," she said in English. "What a good idea. Najila, George asked whether you would like to walk with us over to the casino in Loutraki? We do not gamble, but it's a good place to have a drink and maybe meet other tour guides. It's about fifteen minutes from here. There's a nice walkway along the beach."

Najila stood up. "That would be most nice. I will go and get my scarf. One minute, please."

"Will you be all right here, ladies?" Efie asked. "We will be back in an hour, maybe a bit longer. When guides get together, it is hard to stop talking."

"No problem," Ruth assured her. "We're doing great. This water is fabulous."

As George and Efie walked to the hotel lobby to

wait for Najila, Beth said, "I know I was supposed to talk about my chapters of First Corinthians tomorrow, but could we do it now? I mean, this is such a nice place, and we were just in Corinth today, and I . . . well . . . I kind of have a lot to say. Is that OK, Vicky?"

"Of course," Vicky said. "I'm sorry your part was long, Beth; but I gave you the biggest section because you've had so much study group experience."

"Oh, that's OK," Beth replied. "I enjoyed it. Years ago, I wasn't sure I understood Paul's letters and what he was talking about. Now they've taken on a whole new dimension. Because of what's happened in the past two years, I've changed my mind on a number of issues."

She moved down the steps into the warmer water. "The first thing I've learned is that I need to read the entire letter and not just 'cherry pick.' There are so many phrases and one-liners that people have taken out of context from Paul's letters over the centuries. Some are beautiful, but others have been used wrongly to harm others. A person needs to read the whole letter to get the whole picture."

"Yes," Vicky said. "When I did that, I got a better feel for what went on in Paul's Corinthian community."

"And here's another thing," Beth continued, "a lot of stuff must have changed during those four or five years that Paul had been gone. It sounded to me like these were not intellectuals but just ordinary folks who had been really pious at the beginning when Paul was there with them; but, after he left, they ran after the flavor of the week. You know what I mean: 'I love this minister or that preacher' or 'Well, that bossy guy Paul isn't here anymore, so we'll do whatever we please.'

Lots of people can manage the moment. It's the long haul that takes commitment and perseverance and, you know, mentoring and follow-up. Paul shouldn't have been surprised about this after five years."

Alicia scooped up a handful of water and let it run through her fingers. "Those same attitudes are alive and well in many Christian communities today. Imagine that."

"Right," Beth said. "Early on, some Corinthians probably figured that they were *saved*; so they thought: 'What the heck? Anything goes. Eat, drink, and be merry.' But now, after five years had gone by, Paul made a number of strong suggestions to the Corinthians as to how to act. He told them to tighten up and realize what a gift they'd been given: that Jesus actually had died for their sins. Could they act like they *got* this?"

She sighed. "It's interesting that he started with married people—the duties of husbands and wives—then slaves, the unmarried, and widows. I didn't want to talk about this before because . . . well . . . I didn't want to upset anybody or disrupt our trip, but now seems like a good time to tell you that . . . that . . . Perry and I were divorced last year."

"Gosh, Beth," Ruth said cautiously, "should we be happy or sad for you?"

"A bit of both, I guess." Seeing their surprised faces, Beth held up her hands. "Let me tell you what happened. We married young, grew in different directions, and eventually grew apart. We finally realized our marriage had been dead for years, so we ended it peacefully. We lived in the same house while I waited for him to retire from his job in Rome. Turns out he wasn't ready to retire, so I left. The divorce was final last year. Perry remarried; my daughter and I attended the wedding. He's still working in Rome.

"It's been a hard three years, I'll tell you. But I've survived. We've both moved on, and I think we're both happier. I sure am. I *could* tell you all about it, but I'm having fun right now and enjoying the present. My therapist said it's unhealthy to keep rehashing the past, so I'm not going to wallow in it anymore. I'm done feeling miserable. This trip with you girls means too much for me to spend any more time talking about Perry.

"So when I read the verses about the problems in Paul's congregation—questions about eating meat that had been sacrificed to idols; about some getting into idolatry, immorality, and grumbling; and about the proper behavior at worship services—and the fact that the Corinthians criticized him for not asking for support from them, I could really identify.

"Believe me, I know how it feels to be criticized by people in your church group. See, in my former church, I was a worship leader and a music leader and was very involved with a lot of people; so I know how sanctimonious people can be. They all think *their* way is the best, and they can be so harsh and judgmental when anybody differs with them.

"People I had *thought* were my friends were pretty nasty when they learned about our divorce; some were even angry that I hadn't run it by *them* first! Can you imagine? There were so many rumors and so much gossip flying around, and all this was from people I'd known for *years*." She sighed. "It was awful, and it took me a long time to get over it. I'm better now, but I sure know how Paul must have felt, being bombarded with the daily controversies among his Corinthians.

"There was all that fussing about their hair: long or short; about veils: yes or no—stuff like that. Paul's advice was always: 'Be considerate. Think of the greater good.' That's what Perry and I tried to do. It didn't always work, but . . .." She paused to wipe her eyes on her towel.

Ruth put her arm around Beth and gave her a squeeze. "It's OK. And the best thing is, *you're* OK. In fact, you're *amazing*. You've gone through hell and high water these last few years, but you've come out on top. I'm really proud of you, girl."

Beth smiled at Ruth. "Thanks. I need to hear that sometimes. Oh gosh, listen to me. I've talked too much. Does anyone want to share something?"

Ruth moved up out of the pool so that only her feet were in the water. "Well, I've always loved Paul's words in Chapter 13 about what's really important: the spiritual gifts and how love was *the* most important one. He wrote all those lines about being patient, kind, and not thinking only of yourself. We've all heard them a thousand times at weddings.

"But actually," Ruth went on, "I think Paul was really angry with those Corinthians who thought they were so high and mighty. They were so full of themselves. Like a lot of us, they had totally missed the boat. So Paul told them: 'You think *you've* got gifts? I'll show you gifts. What you've been doing is *not* love; *this* is what love is.' And then he listed it: love is patient, love is kind; and, well, you know the rest of it. There's so much to think about in that one chapter."

"I've also thought," Alicia said, "about the end

of the letter when Paul tried again to explain the resurrection to them. It sounded like many of their problems stemmed from the fact they hadn't understood, or, better yet, they hadn't accepted what the resurrection of the body really meant. But I see myself in those Corinthians. It *is* pretty hard to understand and believe. So I've asked myself: Do I really not understand, or do I just not *want* to?"

Vicky drew her towel around her shoulders. "I'd like to share something that happened recently at my book club. I realized that a service with Paul's Corinthian group might have been similar. There were people from different cultures and different countries doing cross talk in several different languages. There were people talking about food; somebody coming in late and needing a stiff drink; people talking about the discussion; people falling asleep during the discussion; some getting the point, some missing the point, and some bringing up all sorts of inane side stories. There was even a 50-year-old war going on between two members. Then there were people who couldn't hear and people who didn't want to hear.

"And here was Paul, trying to reach out and teach these people how to be a unified community. Can't you just hear him? 'People! Get over yourselves. What you eat, what you wear on your heads, your smallness in taking each other to civil courts—NONE of that is important. Jesus was talking about simple things, like being kind to your parents, forgiving your neighbors, and loving and being generous to everyone. In other words, He wanted them to act like He did. He *is* the Messiah. Contrary to what the Old Testament scriptures said—that the Messiah would be a mighty

king, a ruler, full of pomp and riches—this Jesus *is* the
real Messiah. That is His message. Try to get it.'"

Beth looked perplexed. Then she smiled and
reached for her tote bag. "Well, that's all I have to
say. Thanks for sharing, everybody. I appreciate all
your insights. Now I've got to get out of this pool. I'm
getting cold."

"Me, too," Alicia said. "Thanks, Beth. You did
a great job. I really value your honesty about your
personal life. You've been through so much. I'd love
to talk more; but, right now, I'm turning into a prune.
See you all in the morning."

"Al, wait up," Ruth called. "I'm coming, too." She
climbed out of the pool and followed Alicia towards the
hotel.

After they left, Beth moved next to Vicky. "I need to
ask you something about what you said a minute ago.
I feel like those Corinthians when Paul was telling
them to 'try to get it.' I *do* try to get it, but some of
the commentaries I've read say things so differently.
It wasn't how I was taught in my church. How can
everything I learned earlier be so wrong?"

"It wasn't wrong," Vicky answered. "It's what
everybody learned back in the day, but there's been
a lot of outstanding biblical scholarship and new
developments in the past thirty years. New documents
have come to light. The original languages have
been correctly translated and better understood,
and translations and versions have been altered
accordingly."

Vicky laid her hand on Beth's arm. "You're a
medical person, Beth. Look at it this way: Would you
want a doctor who still used eye of newt and wing of

frog? No. When you got your knees done, you wanted the best, most modern, medical technology available. And you got it. You didn't want some guy with a baggie full of leeches! All I'm saying is that medicine has moved forward and so has biblical scholarship."

"Well, OK," Beth replied slowly, "but I'll have to think about that some. Like maybe a lot." She got out of the pool, then turned around. "Thanks, Vicky."

+++++++++

Shortly after midnight, George led the way back from the Loutraki Casino. The promenade along the beach was illuminated with soft lanterns artfully concealed in the shrubbery.

"Efie, that was wonderful," Najila said, as she stifled a yawn. "I loved to meet your friends. Such a beautiful casino and so many glamorous people. When I watched at the roulette table, I noticed a man with his arm around a pretty woman. Her hair was long and black, and she wore many diamonds. I could hear she spoke American English. When he turned towards me, I saw his most blue eyes. He said to the woman that he was an ethnic . . . no, wait, an ethnobottle . . . ah, yes, an *ethnobotanist*. I have never heard of that before. George, do you know what they do?"

"Huh! That one?" George snorted. "I know what *he* does. *Tighourouni!*"

Efie laughed. "George just said the man was a pig."

The bema in Corinth

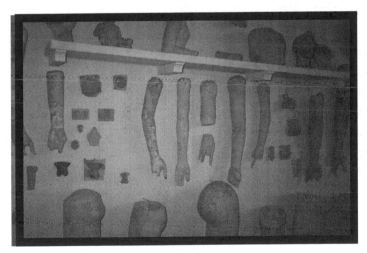

Votives in the Corinth Museum

Twenty-seven

May 10, 2014—Corinth, Greece

After a leisurely breakfast by the pool the next morning, Efie suggested that they take a drive around the area. She wanted to show them where new Corinth was. They would also pass by the port of Lechaeon on the Gulf of Corinth.

"Bring your suits and a beach towel," Efie said. "We will surely find a nice spot for some swimming and sunning."

Ruth hurried back to her room to retrieve her sun hat, and then they were ready to go. George drove slowly through several towns before reaching new Corinth, a charming village close to the sea. He pulled into a dusty parking lot near a small supermarket.

"I park van here," George said. "Market over there, pharmacy down to left, good café across street. I go now to visit friend at Coast Guard office. Meet you at café."

"Perfect, George," Efie said as she got out. "Ladies, there are also some interesting shops that sit along the sea. In one, an artist friend sells beautiful things he does with driftwood. If you like gold jewelry, look into the shop next to the pharmacy. The owner carries unusual pieces from local artists. If he's in a good mood, he might be willing to bargain . . . a little.

"Why don't we all meet back here in one hour; and then we can have a coffee at the café George mentioned, eh? They make really nice *bougatsa*. Or you can have a sandwich or other small bites—whatever you like. Now I'm going to the market. They have wonderful olives down here; I can never find them in Athens. Anyone want to come?"

"Sure," Beth replied. "I'll get some more shampoo, as long as we're here."

"Good idea," Vicky concurred. "And maybe I can find some fun little gifts for my neighbor. Never hurts to look."

Attracted by the well-kept garden, Alicia headed straight over to a small white house near the market. The owner was hard at work, weeding and trimming. She nodded and smiled broadly when Alicia asked her—using sign language—if she could take a few photos of the flowers. Seeing all the roses made Alicia think of Norma.

Alicia walked the length of the woman's fence taking close-ups of each flower then said *"Efharisto."* The woman paused a minute and then motioned for Alicia to sit down at a table under a palm tree. She hurried into her house and soon returned with a tray bearing two cups of coffee, a plate of almond cookies, and three packets of seeds. Flowers seemed to foster easy friendships.

While Alicia sat in the garden, Ruth and Najila walked towards the shops on the beach. "Just look at all those pretty cottages," Ruth said. "I'd love a two-week vacation down here. So tell me, Najila, how was the Casino at Loutraki last night? Did you win anything?"

"Oh my, no," Najila said, laughing. "I do not gamble,

although I did watch at several different tables. At one, I saw a pretty young woman with long black hair. She wore many flashing diamonds. A handsome man with such blue eyes stood close by her with his hand on her . . . uh . . . waist. He spoke to her that he was an ethnobobilist, no, wait, an *ethnobotanist*. When I asked George later, he did not explain. Do *you* know what one is?"

Ruth inhaled sharply. Her heart felt like stone. This Stavros really gets around, she thought. He's nothing but a gigolo and a bigger sleaze than I ever imagined. He probably came down to Corinth early and couldn't keep his . . . his hands to himself. He couldn't even wait until Alicia arrived. What a creep. The man's an ass!

Her brain raced as she tried to remember some of those factoids Alicia had dropped on her the other night. "Well," she stammered, "I don't know any ethnobotanists *personally*; but I think they do something with plants and flowers—you know, how things grow, what people do with them, and stuff like that."

Ruth smiled brightly as she took Najila's elbow. "Let's head over to those shops, Najila. I'd really like to see that driftwood."

And I'd like to talk about something else, Ruth thought. This has *got* to be the same guy. Now what do I do? Should I tell Alicia that he's been way too familiar with another woman? I feel like I should because I can sense that Al's about ready to jump off the deep end and do something really stupid with this moron. Most of the time she's so incredibly smart; but, these days, she doesn't act like it. She's so vulnerable.

But it's none of my business. Or is it? Yes, of *course* it is. It's *all* of our business. Here's this creepy stranger, trying to put the moves on Alicia. On the other hand, she's a big girl but possibly a little naïve . . . OK, a *lot* naïve. If I told her what Najila said, would she consider it meddling? What should I *do*? After all, I'm supposed to be in charge of our group. What would Paul have done if this were somebody in *his* Corinthian group?

Geez, I can't believe this is all happening in the exact same place where he had so many similar problems. There really is nothing new under the sun. People just keep digging the same holes for themselves, over and over. If this is the kind of thing a trip leader has to deal with, I'm not sure I'm up to the task.

She breathed a quick prayer. "Lord, show me how to help Al. Tell me what I should do. I wasn't there for my mom or for Norma; so please, Lord, let me be there for Alicia. Thank You."

In the garden, Alicia glanced at her watch and saw that the hour was almost up. She also saw George walking towards her. "*Kalimera,*" he said to the woman working in the neat rows. He expressed his admiration and knowledge of the flowers; her beaming face radiated her pleasure.

As she waved goodbye to the woman, Alicia turned and surveyed the plain sloping uphill in front of her. "Look, George, you can see the outskirts of the old city of Corinth from here. I'll bet that area was the high-rent district back in the day because their villas had a great view of the sea. There were probably some beautiful gardens up there, as well. By the way, I didn't know you were a gardener. You're a man of many talents."

George grinned and shrugged. "When I not drive

for Efie, I enjoy to work in garden. Very peaceful. Efie likes flowers in house. Smell nice."

"I do a lot with flowers, too," Alicia told him. "It's funny; but just two days ago, I met a guy up at the St. George Hotel who told me about his work with flowers, plants, crops, and things like that. He said he was an ethnobotanist. We had a nice chat." Alicia blushed. "He seemed really interested in me. I even told him a little about our trip."

"Hmm," George said with a frown. "Take cares, Miss Alicia. All peoples not what they seem. Sometimes big problems come. Blue eyes not always blue skies."

Twenty-eight

June, 51 AD—Corinth

Paulos sat in the shaded courtyard of Chloe's spacious villa on the outskirts of Corinth. In one corner, water trickled from a small fountain bordered by small palm trees and fragrant pink roses in large earthen pots. Grape vines, laden with fruit, tumbled down the courtyard walls. Despite blue skies overhead and the beauty surrounding him, Paulos' spirit was melancholy as he reflected on his earlier years when he had been a dedicated persecutor of Jesus group members. He was so different then than he was now.

He had been so self-righteous, so smug, and convinced that he was doing the right thing to purge the Jewish faith of this new cult, the people who followed the way of the crucified Jesus of Nazareth. He had hounded and hunted those early believers, often dragging them into prison. How Paulos regretted the harm that he had done. His heart ached, and he was filled with remorse when he thought of their terrified faces.

But after his vision of Jesus on the Damascus road, his whole life had changed.

Oh, it hadn't been overnight. There were those long solitary years in Arabia, Damascus, and Cilicia—seventeen years in all—while he was taught and formed before he went to Jerusalem again to meet with Peter and the other brothers. Now, in spite of his past, by God's grace, here he was, almost a year after arriving in Corinth, sitting in Chloe's garden, seeing the fruits of his labors.

Chloe was a wealthy widow with four grown children and many grandchildren. Tall and commanding, she was an imposing figure; her cool gray eyes missed nothing. After her husband's death, she carried on with his export business, maintaining many contacts in the city and beyond. She was an able administrator of her large staff; she called them "her people." She also energetically hosted a house-church in this part of Corinth. Her words of welcome to the group at the beginning of each weekly service were heartfelt and moving. Kind, generous, and possessing a deep faith, Chloe was one of Paulos' best and most trusted leaders.

Now she walked out into the courtyard. A smiling serving girl bearing a tray of fruits and chilled juice followed her. "Set it there, my love," Chloe directed. "I can see by his face that Paulos is in need of refreshment." The girl placed the tray on a small wooden table near Paulos' elbow, then bowed and departed.

"I thank you for stopping on this warm afternoon," Chloe said. "Please, try the white grapes. They are delicious this year. Now then, our group goes along well enough for the most part. Several members have moved to other cities, taking the message of Jesus with them. During our services here, there are always a few who interrupt, asking silly questions, wishing to appear important. Others worry that they must still observe all the early dietary laws. They are unsure about what they may buy at the market or eat." She sighed. "The biggest troubles continue to come from those who find it so very difficult to accept non-Judeans into our midst. I fear they do not truly believe the message of Jesus—that God's love is for all, not just Judeans. I try to soothe their feelings, but there are rumblings simmering beneath the surface."

Paulos rubbed his forehead and nodded. Now that he had established a community of believers, his next task was to ensure that things were going smoothly and that the other house meetings in Corinth were in agreement. Since their numbers had grown, believers now met in three more houses or workshops across the city. There were usually twenty or more in each group. It was not possible for him to be present at every meeting; so he tried to visit each house often, to know the group leaders, and to confirm that they all gave the same teachings.

With people coming from diverse backgrounds and different cities around the Mediterranean, holding their own ideas about how the meetings should run, problems were bound to arise. He hoped to snuff these out before they caused serious rifts. His flocks needed to focus on the teachings of Christ, not their own petty squabbles. He knew Chloe felt the same. He appreciated her gentle warning and was confident she would not hesitate to inform him if things worsened.

At 42, he was no longer a young man. Although being so busy with his work and the meetings often left Paulos feeling exhausted, he would remember the vision he received one night from the Lord. Paulos had awakened and heard God talking directly to him: "Do not be afraid. Go on speaking and do not be silent, for I am with you. No one will attack and harm you, for I have many people in this city." And Chloe, with her steadfast faith and strong leadership, was one of those people.

God's words and the love Paulos felt for these people gave him the courage to stand firm and carry on, no matter what.

Twenty-nine

After their lunch at the local café, George drove them to a beach. "Good swim place," he announced. "Quiet, clean sand, and palm trees for shade. Efie and I come back three o'clock."

"This looks great," Ruth said as she climbed out of the van. "We can spread our towels down by that little dune and take turns staying with the stuff. I'll do the first watch."

"Grease up liberally, girls," Beth cautioned. "The sun's hot today. I can already feel my nose burning."

"I can't wait to hit that water," Alicia said as she stripped down to her bathing suit and ran into the surf. "C'mon, Vick. You, too, Najila. You'll love it. It's not cold at all."

They splashed around in the clear, turquoise waters and then stretched out on their towels to dry off and rest. Soon, seeing that the others were snoozing, Alicia asked Ruth to go for a stroll. Fifty yards down the beach, from behind a clump of tall sea grass, a well-built man in ridiculously brief swim trunks came striding towards them. His eyes were very blue.

"Halloo, Alicia. What a surprise to see you here, my angel! And who is this charming lady?" he asked, nodding in Ruth's direction.

"Oh, hi, Stavros. Yes, ah, this *is* a surprise. Ruthie,

meet Stavros. Stavros, this is my friend, Ruth. So, ah, how is it that you're here in Corinth?"

Ruth stared at this Greek god as she admired his lean and muscular frame. So this is Mr. Wrong, she thought. Fair of face but black of heart. With those big blue eyes and that easy smile, he's really handsome. No wonder Alicia is attracted to him. I have the distinct feeling that I'm looking at a disaster waiting to happen.

"I had business this morning with a farmer near Corinth," Stavros said casually, "and we finished early. So I decided to take a little break at the beach. My work requires that I travel a great deal; and I don't get many chances to relax, especially not with two ladies as lovely as yourselves."

He flashed a brilliant smile. "There's a small kiosk just over that next dune. Allow me to buy you a glass of the local red. It's quite good. By the way, I'm at the little hotel near the sinking canal bridge. And where are you staying?"

"We're at the Isthmus One Apart Hotel, right on the Canal," Alicia said breathlessly. Ruth gave her a soft nudge in the side. "Ah, a glass of wine would be nice; but I'm afraid we should be getting back. Our driver is picking us up at 3:00. Maybe another time?"

"Of course, my beautiful angel. See you tonight then," Stavros said with a wink. "Delighted to meet you, Ruth. Enjoy your afternoon, ladies."

"Likewise, I'm sure," Ruth said to his retreating back. She wanted to barf.

"I'll give you enjoy," she muttered as they walked in the opposite direction. "Well, you're right about one thing, Al. He sure is good looking. But what a line.

Total crap. Listen, I'm really worried about you, setting up a meeting with this guy and all. What if he turns out to be a serial murderer or something? I mean, you've barely just met him; and you're thinking about getting together with him for a drink tonight. Are you texting him? I bet you are, or he would have never shown up here like he just did. Oh, don't make that face. I've known you too long, and I can tell what you're thinking."

Alicia waved her hand as if shooing away a fly and kept walking. "It's just a glass of wine, Ruthie."

They strolled farther, and then Ruth turned to Alicia. "Al, don't take this the wrong way, but I just thought of something you might need. 'No trial has come to you but what is human. God is faithful and will not let you be tried beyond your strength, but with the trial, he will also provide a way out, so that you may be able to bear it.' First Corinthians. I memorized it when I first read all this stuff. Just thought it might, you know, come in handy sometime, like, ah, if you should ever find yourself in a tight spot."

"Oh, Ruthie, relax, will you? Don't be such an old fuddy-duddy. I'm just fine. Everything's great. Nothing's going to happen."

Ruth rolled her eyes and tried to push down her anxiety.

++ +++++++

After they finished dinner at the hotel, the group adjourned to the lounge chairs by the pool. "In spite of my warning to you ladies, I'm the one who got burned," Beth said sheepishly. "I'm going up to put on some après-sun cream and then have an early night."

"I will also go to my bed," Najila said as she stood up. "I am not working, so I do not know why; but I am feeling some tired tonight."

"It's all this sun and sea air," Vicky said. "I'm right behind you, Najila. See you all at breakfast."

"OK," Ruth said. "I'll sit here until Al finishes her smoke; and then I'm turning in, as well."

Alicia took two more drags and then stubbed out her cigarette. "I think I'll stroll over to the Casino for a bit. Wanna come, Ruthie?"

"Nah, I'm beat. But thanks. And, uh, watch yourself, OK? I wouldn't want anything to happen to you."

"Ruthie, honestly. You're worse than my mom ever was. I *am* an adult, you know." Alicia laughed, stood up, and then strode off down the beach promenade.

Ruth fought her feelings of concern as she prayed fervently. "Please, God, protect her and keep her safe. Show her a way out."

After all, Alicia was an adult. *Wasn't* she?

+++++++++

Two hours later, concealed by the canopy of palm trees near the Apart Hotel, Alicia and Stavros were locked in a passionate embrace. Stavros ran his hands down Alicia's back and whispered, "Come with me, my angel. My hotel is very close to here. We could relax, be comfortable, and make beautiful magic together. I have wanted you since the first minute I saw you at Lycabettus. You are so incredibly gorgeous, such a woman of passion. I can feel you are attracted to me, as well."

Alicia could barely breathe. "You're right; I *am* attracted to you. Who wouldn't be? But I . . . uh . . . well . . . uh . . . I don't know. It's a bit soon, isn't it? I mean, we met only a few days ago. Besides, I'm married."

"Of course you are, my angel." He chuckled softly. "You Americans. So rigid. But where is your husband? He is not here. Ah, but *you* are, as I am. Tonight, it is just you and me. Tonight belongs only to us. We must use this perfect night . . . to make perfect love." He nuzzled her neck. "Come with me, my beauty." He stroked Alicia's hair and pulled her even closer to him.

She could feel herself falling, melting, wanting. What *would* it hurt? Who *would* know? It would be so nice really to be loved, to be appreciated . . . just for herself.

Stavros caressed her back and then her hips. With his index finger, he traced lazy spirals slowly down her arm. Chills rippled up her spine. He gently drew more circles around the gold bangles tinkling softly at her wrist. He threaded a finger inside one bracelet and paused—one beat too long.

Alicia felt a shiver of fear. She became instantly alert. What was going on here?

"Um . . . Stavros, it's getting late; and we're doing the Canal boat cruise tomorrow. I need to go."

"Not yet, my angel," he pleaded in a husky voice. "Come with me. We have only just begun, my sweet."

"Maybe, but I've got to go. Thanks for the drink."

She spun on her heel and hurried into the hotel. "Thanks, God," she prayed silently. "And thanks, Ruthie. Who would have thought a gold bangle would provide the way out?"

Four floors above, Beth stepped out onto her

balcony for a breath of air and stood in the shadows. Below her, she saw the red glow of a cigarette, followed by the small rectangle of light from a cell phone. She caught most of the man's words.

"Hallo, Tiffany? Stavros here. I know it's late, darling; but could I drop by for a minute? I would love to see you. My meeting ended earlier than I thought. What? Oh, it was OK. Not much productive. But now my arms are anxious to hold you, my angel. We must use this perfect night. What's that? Oh, you are? Ah well, another time."

Stavros stuck his phone in his pocket and walked back along the path to the Casino's parking lot. As he got into his car, he observed himself in the lighted mirror. He scrutinized the tiny lines under his eyes and frowned at the few gray hairs at his temples.

I need some repair work, a little touch up and a bit of color, he thought. This job is getting harder. Ten years ago, many women were eager for a holiday romance; they were easy pickings. Today they all seem more careful, more aware. Ah, but the young ones, they are usually ready for some fun.

He smiled at himself and then, with his fingertips, pulled the skin back from his cheekbones. He decided that a facelift wasn't in order yet. His mama always told him he was too handsome for his own good and that, one day, he would end up in jail; but, after she said that, she had always laughed, patted his head, and given him a big kiss.

Ah, Mama. You were so beautiful. Why did you leave us so soon? What did Papa do wrong? What did I do?

With a sigh, he closed the car door, turned on the

ignition, and drove off slowly into the darkness.

Thirty

An hour later, Alicia was awakened by the text tone of her cell. She sat up, grabbed the phone, and read:

Caroline has run away. Left a note saying: 'I can't take it anymore, Dad. You can find another daughter to scream at. I'm out of here. Who knows? Maybe Mom won't come back either. Then you'd finally have to deal with yourself.'

I've called her friends, but nobody's seen her. What should I do?

"Oh, my God!" Alicia whispered. Tears welled up in her eyes; one escaped and plopped onto her touch screen. She threw the phone onto the bed. Poor Carrie. Oh, my poor sweet baby. I should *never* have left. What have I done? Why did I think Carrie could handle him when I can't? She grabbed the phone and quickly typed a reply:

What were you thinking of? How could you be so rotten to Carrie? Have you called Jack, her boyfriend? Your mom? The police? I'm coming home. I'll send flight info when I know it.

Then she called Carrie. The phone rang and rang.

No answer. Oh, no. She's turned it off.

She swore softly under her breath. I can't *believe* this. This is all Jim's fault. I *have* to go home and find her. I'll have to leave this trip. I've got to go tell Ruthie.

She wiped her eyes, jerked on her robe, and flew across the hall. Tapping urgently on the door, she whispered, "Ruthie, open up. It's me, Al. Something terrible has happened!"

Startled out of a deep sleep, Ruth mumbled, "What?" She sat up, heard Alicia's voice and frantic knocking, and then hauled herself to her feet and staggered to the door. She was shocked by what she saw. Like an apparition, Alicia stood in front of her, crying uncontrollably and waving her cell phone. Her blonde hair was a stringy mess; her eyes were streaming, and she was hysterical.

"Good grief, Al! What's up? What time is it?" Ruth asked as she drew Alicia gently into the room and closed the door.

Her voice shaking, Alicia rattled off the sequence of events.

"Oh, Ruthie! I *knew* I never should have left. This is all my fault. No, actually, it's all Jim's fault. Oh, who cares? The main thing is that Carrie's gone. My baby is gone! I'm going to have to leave here and fly back now. I *have* to find her. I *have* to get there, and you've got to help me. Jim won't have a clue what to do. He never does, except when it comes to refilling his liquor cabinet."

"Geez, Al, calm *down*, will you?" Ruth pleaded. "Here, come and sit down; and then we can talk this thing over." She drew Alicia to the bed, handed her the box of Kleenex, and got her a glass of water. Then she sat down next to her.

"It's OK, you can tell me," Ruth said. "Now start from the beginning, and go slowly. My brain doesn't function all that well at 2:00 AM. By the way, what time is it in the States where Carrie is?"

Alicia blew her nose, drank some water, and talked through her tears. Slowly she told about being awakened by her cell. She recounted the details of Jim's text about Carrie's running away. She repeated the contents of Carrie's note and Jim's pitiful request for help. Then she hung her head.

"Oh, Ruthie," Alicia whimpered, "I know this is a punishment from God . . . for what I was about to do. I just *know* it. Earlier tonight, I met Stavros at the Casino. We had a few drinks, and then he walked me home. I let him kiss me under those palm trees near the pool. He was begging me to go back to his hotel with him. I'm so ashamed to admit this; but I was so close, so ready to do it, until . . . until . . ." Her voice trailed off.

"Until *what?*" Ruth said. "Good grief, Al. Don't keep me on pins and needles."

Alicia's chin came up. "Until he hooked a finger under one of my bangles and . . . and . . . waited a little too long. I felt a stab of fear and *knew* something wasn't right. I knew right then that it wasn't *me* he wanted; it was my jewelry, my money, or God knows what else."

For a fleeting moment, Ruth wondered if she should tell Alicia about Najila seeing Stavros with another woman the night before. Nah, what's the point? Would it make any difference? It will just make her feel worse. She already knows he's a creep.

"It was one of those moments of insight," Alicia continued, "when you just know what's *really* going on. It was like . . . no, it was not *like* . . . it *was* a gift from God." Though her lips trembled, she managed a weak smile. "But now, you've got to help me. I've got to get out of here, get to Athens, and get a flight home. I've *got* to find Carrie. Every minute counts!"

"Oh, Al," Ruth said sympathetically, "I feel really bad for you about Carrie. I know how I felt when one of my cats ran away. I can't *imagine* how it would be to have a daughter run away; but, somehow, I don't think she's gone far. I don't know what makes me say this, but I think she may have been on her last nerve. Have you tried to text her? See if she'll respond to you?"

Ruth peered at the bedside clock. "Al, it's almost three o'clock. There's no way we can do anything now. It would take several hours to drive up to Athens, and there are no flights to the U.S. before 7:00 AM anyway. I could call my agent, Carol; and she could book your flights. I'm sure Efie has her own airline person who could do it even faster, though. We'll just have to wait a few hours. Meanwhile, why don't we say a little prayer and then try to rest a bit?"

She took Alicia's hands in her own, bowed her head, and said, "Lord, protect Carrie, keep her safe, and return her to her family. Give Alicia the peace she needs. Show me how I can help her, and help us to get a little sleep. Amen."

Alicia leaned forward and gave Ruth a tight squeeze. "Oh, Ruthie, what a good friend you are. You're *always* there for me." She blew her nose once more and then yawned. "You know, I think I *will* lie down. I'm sure I won't sleep, but I'll try to rest my eyes. I've cried a year's worth in the last hour. Oh, and would you mind opening the window? It's really hot in here. There's not a breath of air. Thanks."

Ruth opened the window and then helped Alicia get settled. She covered her friend with a sheet and then curled up in the recliner close to the bed. "I finally did it right," she whispered. "I was there. Thanks, God,"

When the sun's first warm rays streamed through the window, both women were sleeping peacefully.

Thirty-one

August, 51 AD—Corinth, Greece

Although it was still early, the summer heat was stifling. Paulos propped open the door of the workshop with a stone, so that he might catch a breath of air. He was occupied with preaching much of the time these days but still made it a point to work with Aquila several times a week. He was insistent upon earning his keep by supporting himself and not taking help from the Jesus group members. Now, Aquila had gone out for supplies; and Paulos worked alone.

As he plied his needle through the stiff tent leather, he reflected on recent events. Things had run smoothly for many months as the number of believers increased; but, then, as had often happened in other cities, whisperings among non-believing Judeans increased. A few weeks ago, a hearing was held at the bema in front of Gallio, proconsul of Achaia. Paulos and several others were accused of teaching a false religion, worshiping God contrary to the law. Gallio had no interest; he dismissed the case, saying that no crime was committed, that it was only a religious quarrel, and the accusers should see to things themselves. In their anger, the Judeans then beat Sosthenes, who was a new believer and head of the synagogue. Gallio merely shrugged and walked back to his home, saying it was not his concern.

Paulos realized that these were the things Chloe had warned him of, all those months ago. In spite of his weekly preaching, some new believers were not living according to Jesus' message. They were impatient and unkind to each other, seeking their own interests. They were quick to judge, even taking one another to civil courts instead of settling matters amicably among themselves. A few even engaged in illicit relationships. They all boasted that they possessed many spiritual gifts but often acted like children.

What was it that Priscilla had told him? She said that "We are family, and this is what love is." Why was it so hard for many new believers to grasp this concept: the importance of love and to live it every day?

In his prayers, Paulos asked for guidance. He felt pain for Sosthenes but fortunate that he, himself, had avoided a beating or worse. Paulos knew that he must strengthen the leaders in each house-church group here because God was calling him to move on—to spread Jesus' message to other cities. He knew he must prepare to leave. He had been reasonably successful in Corinth, a bustling city in Achaia. Now he would set his sights on Ephesus, third largest city in the Roman Empire. It would be a huge challenge, but he had faced harder things in his life.

Pulling the last stitch tight, Paulos determined

that he would contact his friend, Phoebe, at Cenchreae, the eastern port of Corinth. She would help him.

Thirty-two

May 11, 2014—Corinth, Greece

At 6:00 AM Alicia's cell chimed again. She threw off the sheet, groped for her phone, and gasped as she read:

Caroline is back. She was at Kathie's house. We need to talk when you get home. Maybe we can turn over a new leaf. Jim.

In her chair, Ruth yawned, stretched, and rubbed her eyes. "What's up, Al?"

Alicia shook her head as she handed the phone to Ruth. "A lot. You won't believe this. It doesn't even sound like the Jim I know. He must have had the living daylights scared out of him. But, hey, talk is cheap; and we've been down this road before. I'll believe it when I see it. It's too early to get my hopes up. I'm just happy that Carrie's back. I'm so proud of her for having the courage to stand up to her dad. That's good enough for me today."

Ruth scanned the message, gave the phone back, and then enveloped her friend in a hug. "Wow. All I can say is: 'Thank You, Jesus, *big time.*' Al, you've just been given two fabulous miracles; yet you're *still* waiting for the airplane with a banner out the back. Well, maybe now you'll be able to enjoy the rest of this trip."

She looked at her watch. "Now you've got to get out of here, so I can shower and dress. We're all supposed to meet for breakfast at 7:30. After last night, it's gonna take me longer than usual to make myself gorgeous. Bye."

"I'll beat you there," Alicia called over her shoulder as she hurried out the door, "because you're older than I am."

True to her word, Alicia slid into a chair in the sunlit breakfast room at 7:25. She was fresh in tan Capris, a beige shirt, and gold hoop earrings. The dark circles under her eyes had been carefully concealed, and her damp hair had been pulled into a French twist at the back. The bangles on her wrists were gone. She laid a finger along her lips when Ruth took the seat next to hers.

The rest of the group soon appeared. They enjoyed their breakfast, had seconds of the strong coffee, and were waiting at nine when George pulled up in front of the hotel. He drove the few miles to the boat landing at the mouth of the Corinth Canal on the Saronic Gulf where they boarded a small cruise boat. Since it was still early in the season, there were few other passengers. Lively, Greek folk music played on the loudspeakers; the blue and white striped Greek flag fluttered from the back deck.

"Perhaps you would like to sit on the top?" Efie said. "You can see much more that way. There is a small bar for coffee or other drinks on the lower deck inside; the rest rooms are there as well. I will sit under the sunroof; but, please, sit wherever you like."

The captain made lazy circles in a holding pattern

at the mouth of the canal. "Canal one-way street," George informed them. "See, when two yachts come from other end, then we go."

Ruth, Najila, and Alicia found places on benches at a rectangular table on the top deck; while Beth and Vicky stood opposite them at the white metal railing taking photos. Ruth took several selfies and then said, "Vick, take a picture of us three, OK? Then I'll get one of you two. We'll send them to Jerry; he'll love it."

"The water is so blue and calm," Najila observed. "Norma would have enjoyed its beauty." Ruth and Alicia nodded in agreement.

Soon the larger boats emerged from the canal, and the captain began his approach. Once they were underway, the folk music stopped; and recorded commentary, alternating between Greek and English, began. It elaborated on the history of the Canal's construction: Several attempts during ancient times had failed, and the present Canal was finally completed in 1893 at an enormous cost. It had taken eleven years to build.

They were told that during World War II the Germans had gone to great lengths to sabotage the waterway by dumping huge chunks of concrete, machinery, and other impediments into the Canal. Today's gargantuan ocean liners are much too large for the Canal, which is now used only by pleasure craft and small cruise boats such as theirs.

At first, the sides of the Canal were low and rocky, dotted with small trees and bushes. As they progressed further, the walls grew gradually higher and straighter.

Vicky leaned back from the railing, tilted her head, and gazed upwards. "Look, ladies. There's the bridge we walked out on two days ago. Just *think* of the engineering and the labor, not to mention the *time*, it took to build this thing. Somebody really followed his passion. It must have been incredibly tough, but they stayed with it."

"Kind of like Paul," Beth added as she joined the others at the table. "In a way, this canal is a metaphor for what he did, isn't it? No matter how difficult his missionary work became, he never gave up."

The women were quiet, relishing the slow pace, the soft purr of the diesel engine, the cloudless blue skies, and the warm sunshine. The water lapped gently against the sides of the boat as they glided along, occasionally passing tiny clusters of wild flowers and green plants clinging bravely to crevices in the rock.

Finally, Ruth spoke. "Wouldn't Norma have absolutely *loved* this? I'm so glad we're here, doing this in her honor. You all know how much I didn't want to do this, I mean, lead this trip; but I'm *so* glad I did. Sometimes our worst fears just don't materialize. Things often turn out differently than we thought they would. Yeah, I know—not terribly profound but true."

She sighed. "After all the worrying I did as a kid, you'd think I'd know that by now. I guess God has to keep whacking me on the head, giving me that lesson over and over."

Alicia had taken off her sandals and was drowsing in the gentle heat of the morning. Now she opened her eyes and turned to the other women. "Well, friends, maybe it's time for me to share a few lessons that I've learned the past few days. I wasn't sure I would tell you all this—some of it's pretty embarrassing—but now I want to. I'm tired of keeping dark secrets. It concerns a couple of potentially disastrous situations and a whole lot of fear on my part. Some things turned out OK—in fact, *way* better than OK."

And so, for the next half hour, Alicia sketched the years of her stormy relationship with Jim: his constant verbal abuse accompanied by his increasing dependence on alcohol. She went on to explain about Stavros and his smooth tactics, her interest and vulnerability during their meetings, and her lifelong struggle with low self-esteem. She related last night's drama: her near capitulation to Stavros' advances, Carrie's running away, and then the double miracles this morning of Carrie's returning and the possibility of a real change in Jim's attitude. She remained surprisingly objective, laid no blame, and stated only the facts.

While Alicia was talking, Ruth slipped down to the bar and bought lemonades for them all. She carried the glasses and a stack of napkins up to their table on a small tray.

"Thanks, Ruthie," Alicia said. "I know you guys think I'm smart; but sometimes—no, a *lot* of times—I don't act like it. I act like a total idiot—a *naïve* idiot to boot. I guess what happened to me as a kid, you know, the abuse thing with my dad, affected me more than I realized. It's sure influenced my relationships with men . . . and myself. I thought I had all that behind me; but it's obviously still there, lurking in the background. Otherwise, I wouldn't have given a sleaze-ball like Stavros the time of day. I'm pretty disappointed with myself." Hot tears stung her eyes.

Beth reached into her pocket, found a packet of tissues, and offered one to Alicia. "Bless your heart, Alicia. I understand that totally. Who was more upset and disappointed about getting a divorce than righteous church leader me? But, hey, don't be so hard on yourself. We all have our weak spots, and you know something? I just realized how being around water makes us open up. Last night, I told about my divorce while we were sitting in the pool. Now you're telling us all this while we're on a boat in this canal . . . oh, gosh, forget it. Maybe that's just stupid."

"Or," Ruth said slowly, "maybe that's why we're all here."

"What do you suppose," Vicky asked, "the disciples talked about when *they* were in the boat with Jesus?"

"Are you kidding?" Ruth said, laughing. "I'll tell you how it *really* was. Here's the short version of what probably happened. Peter was standing in the bow, griping about his mother-in-law; Jamie and Johnny were in the center, arguing about who was top dog; Judas was in the back, counting out the shekels; and, beyond a shadow of a doubt, Thomas wasn't even there. He'd missed the boat completely!"

Alicia chuckled. "The Gospel according to Ruth. I love it!"

Beth then leaned over and put her arm around Alicia. "You know," she whispered, "late last night, I . . . I . . . I had a feeling . . . I just had this feeling that . . . that something was going on with you; so I started praying for you. I asked God to put a fence around you and protect you. Guess it must have worked."

"Thanks, Beth. That means a lot to me." Alicia nodded to Ruth. "Miracle number three."

They had reached a small bridge almost at the end of the Canal. Their little boat stopped, and they waited while the bridge slowly submerged to let them pass. Several rustic cafes crowded the shore by the bridge. Further inland, behind a stand of trees, they saw a small hotel.

Ruth winked at Alicia. "Hey, maybe that's Stavros' hotel. Want to get off and run up for a little visit?"

Alicia made a face. "Want to get a frontal lobotomy? I think I'll pass."

The captain steered their boat out to the end of the Canal, made a wide circle in the Bay of Corinth in the Ionian Sea, and then turned around, heading back in the direction from which they'd come.

As they began the return trip, Alicia heard her cell tone; it was a text from Carrie.

Hi Mom,

Sorry I scared you; but I was so mad at Dad, I just didn't know what else to do. It was pretty terrible around here for the last week or so; but since I've come back, Dad's really different. Fingers crossed that it lasts.

School is OK. I took my AP government and AP calculus exams today; I think I did fine.

Hope your trip is fun. The dog misses you. Me too. xoxoxo Carrie.

Alicia passed the phone to Ruth who skimmed the message, and then gave Alicia a high five.

"Listen, ladies," Ruth said as she finished her lemonade, "why don't we meet on the hotel pool deck around four or so? It will be shady there by then, so I'll do my stuff on Second Corinthians. Al, do you want to do yours after dinner?"

"Yes, but no," Alicia replied. "I'd rather wait and do mine tomorrow in Delphi, if that's OK. After last night, I'm pretty beat. I need some time to get my head together."

"Fine," Ruth said. "Meanwhile, I'm going down to the back deck to get some pictures from that angle. Now then, where's my sun hat?"

Thirty-three

At the end of the cruise, George drove them back to the Isthmus One Hotel. They helped themselves to the informal noon buffet and then retired to their rooms for a siesta.

Shortly before four, Ruth sat at a white, metal table under a palm tree on the pool deck; she was shuffling and re-shuffling a set of papers. Najila was the first to appear.

"I am glad we are alone, Ruth," Najila said. "I wish to say such good work you did for Alicia last night. Once a lady got the heart attack on one of my tours. It was very frighted, but I quickly learned it is most important to keep rest of group calm. The leader must show calm."

"Gosh, thanks, Najila," Ruth said, blushing, "but I didn't really do all that much. Oh, I mean, I *did* have Al stay in my room so she wouldn't have to be by herself. But by early this morning, when she'd gotten another message from Jim, the crisis had passed. From there on out, everything was fine."

Ruth's heart felt very full. She appreciated Najila's compliment.

As the other women gathered around the table, Ruth re-arranged the papers and opened her folder. Her hands were shaking. Leading a study was definitely *not* her thing. Maybe she'd just say a little bit and then see if the others had anything to share. She knew they all loved to talk.

"Well," Ruth said haltingly, "at first, I thought these chapters were hard to understand, you know, with Paul being so complicated and all. Then a few things popped out at me. According to the Murphy-O'Connor book, Paul probably wrote Second Corinthians from Macedonia. It might have been compiled from several letters, or maybe it was just one. Sometimes he sounds normal, like he did in First Corinthians; while in other parts he gets so emotional, like he's really upset.

"Here's something I noticed. In Chapter 1, Paul mentions 'encourage' or 'encouragement' at least ten times. He said that God encouraged him, so he can encourage others. It seemed like somebody was trying to undermine or run down Paul's work and reputation because he spends an awful lot of time justifying what he does or has done. They were so critical of him, and it really cut him to the core. I get that, big time."

She removed her sun hat and laid it on the table. "See, I worked for the College Challengers for five years as a legal secretary. During one of my bad depressions, some CCers suggested that I was *possessed;* while others spread it around that I was spiritually inadequate. Nice, huh? And there I was, working so hard, trying to do my best, being so holy about everything, thinking I had been *called,* thinking that I had a *mission* to do this work. They obviously didn't think so, and that really hurt.

"But who knows? Maybe some of those Corinthians were just like that and didn't *want* to change. They loved their old ways and wanted to hang onto them with a death grip. Paul talks a lot about Moses and the old covenant, as well. Maybe Paul thought that they didn't really believe that Jesus was the new covenant."

Ruth felt herself getting into deep waters. Time to hear from the others. "So what do you ladies think? Anybody have anything to add? Reflections you'd like to share?"

"Well," Beth said, "I think that those Corinthians didn't understand what Paul meant, that belief in Jesus—using His life, suffering, and death as a model for *their* lives—was what they were *supposed* to be doing. They might have *said* they were believers, but they sure didn't act like it. It's kind of like at my old church. Paul probably taught them a lot of things while he was in Corinth. They'd nod their heads, look really wise, and say, 'Yes, sure, no problem.' So, naturally, Paul *thought* they understood. Later, when he heard the news about the troubles there, he realized that they didn't get it at all. You know, my kids used to do the same thing to me."

All the women laughed.

"Mine too," Vicky said. "But when you think of the wide variety of people who were in Paul's community, it's no big surprise that problems arose. There were slaves, common laborers, soldiers, sailors, tradesmen, merchants, and only a few wealthy, educated types. Some might have been Judeans; but many were from other religious backgrounds, as well. They all thought theirs was the best way."

Alicia swatted away a mosquito. "And don't you *know* that some of them must have heard about Paul's earlier track record, of how he had persecuted Christians and all? They probably thought, 'Right. This dude says he's been changed and that he wants to tell us about this Jesus. Who does he think he is?' It's hard for people to believe that somebody has changed—I mean, *really* changed. Old images hang around for a long time."

"But," Najila said tentatively, "there were some in Corinth who *did* understand and who *did* believe because someone saved those letters. Perhaps they thought Paul's letters were the treasure and stored them in earthen vessels, like . . . like . . . a water jar."

"You're incredible, Najila," Vicky said admiringly. "You *always* get it."

Ruth fiddled with her hat rim and then looked up at the others. "Thanks, ladies. You all had great ideas to share. I knew you would. You all saw deeper things than I did. And, hey, that's good. We're all at different stages of our walk. After I read these chapters at home, I knew I couldn't do every last thing that Paul recommended; so I decided to try just one thing at a time. I can handle one new action a day. Maybe that's not much, but it is a step forward for me.

"So here's what I did. In my journal, I wrote a little plan for a week: my objective and then how it worked out. It was an eye-opener, I'll tell you. I started out easy; so the first day was for encouragement: trying to encourage somebody, even myself, one whole day. The next day, I worked on not being so judgmental and critical. Pretty tough.

"The third day was for patience. Now *that* was hard! I couldn't *believe* how many times I caught myself being impatient: when the water in the faucet took three forevers to get hot; or sitting at a stoplight; or waiting behind some older person in the check-out line; and, especially, trying not to scream while Pete told a story I've already heard nine times.

"Kindness was on the fourth day. That wasn't too hard. Day five was thinking of myself as a temple of God and remembering that if God lives in me, He also lives in everybody else. Now that we've seen all these beautiful, ancient temples, I have a better idea of what that means. I might go back and do that one again, like, in what ways am I a temple of God—me personally *and* my house? Is my temple clean, in good shape, with doors open, with the welcome mat out, and with a light in the window? Is it the friendliest place in town?

"Day six was to be an ambassador for Christ. Do I act like a believer? Am I a good advertisement for Christianity? Would anybody want to become a Christian, based on how I act?

"And that led right into day seven when I tried to be joyful all day long. That happened to be a tough day for me; but I decided that, even when I'm depressed, I can still be joyful and have a smile on my face. So many good Christians I know go around looking so down and grumpy. I mean, really! Who would want to join a group like that? Could they just *smile*? My first Bible study teacher used to say, 'If you've accepted Jesus as your personal Savior, would you please inform your *face*?'"

The group erupted in laughter.

Ruth heaved a sigh and then flashed a big smile. "OK, that's it. I'm done. Anything else, ladies?"

Beth spoke first. "Ruth, that was terrific. Bless your heart; that was one of the best explanations of a scripture passage I've ever heard. You sure made things clearer than lots of sermons I've heard in church, plus you gave me some great examples of how to live."

"Amen to that," Alicia said. "Super job, Ruthie. Listen, I'd like to ask you a few questions about this stuff later. Maybe we can sit together at dinner?"

"Sure," Ruth replied. "I'd love that."

As the group dispersed, Ruth stood next to Vicky. "Was that OK? Gosh, I was so nervous. Look at me— my hands are still sweating. I've been in a million Bible studies, but this is the first time I've ever *given* one. I mean, Al is such a brainiac, Beth has led studies forever, and you're the church history lady—but me . . ."

Vicky put her arms around Ruth and gave her a big hug. "You were fantastic, Ruth. You *are* fantastic— every day, all the time. You're so smart, down-to-earth, and have so much common sense and so many good insights. When will you start *believing* that?"

+++++++++

Seeing that they were finished, Efie came out to the pool deck to collect them. George then drove them to the village of Cenchreae, where they took photos and waded among the ruins of the early port. Efie explained that this was where Paul's friend, Phoebe, had lived and that Paul probably embarked for Ephesus from here. She also told them that, in Chapter 16 of Romans, Paul praised and commended Phoebe, saying that she was a minister or deacon of the church in Cenchreae and was a benefactor for Paul and many others. It was possible that Phoebe had delivered Paul's letter to the Romans.

Modern houses now stood further inland. Due to earthquakes over the centuries, only fragments of ancient buildings and the pier remained, now partially submerged and surrounded by sea grasses frosted with white foam from the gentle waves. Sitting on a low stone wall, Ruth smiled as she dried her feet with her neck scarf and visualized Phoebe doing the same thing as she waited for Paul.

Thirty-four

September, 51 AD—Cenchreae, Greece

Paulos gave the driver a few coins, climbed down carefully from the dusty wagon, and waved a farewell. He had been fortunate to find a merchant going to Cenchreae, Corinth's eastern port on the Saronic Gulf. While the walk would have taken only a half day, riding with the merchant gave Paulos more time to visit at the home of his friend, Phoebe.

Carrying his tent-making tools and meager belongings in a rough leather bag crafted for him by Aquila, Paulos started up the small hill near the beach at Cenchreae just as Phoebe stepped away from her white-walled house.

She turned and shaded her eyes. "Yes, I think the new rooms will be perfect on this side, Zachos," she said. "I am pleased that there is enough space back here. It will be away from the road, thus allowing visitors a place of peace and quiet; but they will still hear the sea. When can you have them finished? Perhaps a bit of silver will hasten your men?" Tilting her head back, she smiled up at the burly carpenter in front of her. Zachos had been her man of all work for twenty years. They understood each other perfectly.

Her face lit up as she saw Paulos approaching.

"Ah, Paulos, my friend, how wonderful to see you again. But you are a day earlier than your letter said, are you not? Or is my memory failing more than usual?"

"No, dear sister, your memory is as sharp as always. I completed my preparations and decided to come down early. If you have no room, I can sleep under your fig tree there. Priscilla and Aquila had much to do to close down their shop, so they arrive tomorrow. I was finished and came ahead."

"Room?" Phoebe said with a laugh. "Of course I have room. For you, Paulos, there is always room. Come, let us move inside where it is cooler. Carry on, please, Zachos. It will be wonderful when the new rooms are ready. As you can see, they are needed."

Paulos smiled as he followed his friend into her house. Tiny, bird-like, with wispy gray curls around her face, Phoebe was an unassuming yet powerful force in Cenchreae. Phoebe's mother had died birthing her; so, as the daughter of a ship owner, Phoebe grew up freely, near and on the water. As a small girl, she had often accompanied her father on his voyages, laughing as they flew through the waves on the Aegean Sea. As his only child, she inherited the shipping company her father had left her. Now she guided it with a firm hand.

These days, she was usually at home; but, even though she had hired an overseer, a few times a year she would sail with a ship to ensure that the cargo and the mail arrived intact and on time. In her eyes, good business was the result of good management. God help any man who tried to short-change her. She could administer a tongue-lashing not soon forgotten. The captains respected her; crews adored her.

Never married, she had raised her neighbor's three daughters after their parents were killed in a carriage accident. Now the girls all had families of their own, but Phoebe remained everybody's mother. She knew everything and everyone in Cenchreae. No fuss or fanfare, she was always the first to appear with food or medicine when a child was sick. Small purses of silver often passed quietly when a father was out of work. As a deacon of the church in her house, she thought of all the members as family.

Paulos loved to visit in this seaside community. Although only a short distance from Corinth, it was another world, providing an oasis of peace and rejuvenation. And Phoebe was always full of stories. She made him laugh with her adventurous tales.

That evening, as they watched the sunset from her terrace, Phoebe asked, "So what are your plans, Paulos? Where do you travel next?"

Paulos' eyes shone. "There are now many believers in Corinth; and, although there are problems, my work there is done. After Priscilla and Aquila rest here a few days, we will set sail for Ephesus. I feel God is calling us to spread His message there. I am so grateful for you, my sister. You do a great service for the Lord, caring for your own community and providing hospitality for travelers like us. We will surely remain in contact. Perhaps someday, God willing, I will return here."

Phoebe patted his arm. "Your room will always be ready, Paulos. There is always room for family."

Thirty-five

May 12, 2014—Delphi, Greece

After they checked out of the Isthmus One Hotel the next morning, George loaded their things into the van. Just before he climbed into the driver's seat, his cell phone rang. He spoke rapidly in Greek.

"Yah. We're in Corinth; we are leaving now for Delphi. What? Not him again? I'll keep my eyes open. Call me later, OK? *Efharisto.*"

Efie looked puzzled. "George, who was that? Nothing serious, I hope?"

"Nah. It was only Niko, asking me to keep a look out for some guy. Now we go."

They were on the road shortly after 9:00. As they left the shoreline, the road began to rise gently upwards onto the coastal plains.

"From Corinth to Delphi," Efie spoke into the microphone, "is a distance of about 240 kilometers."

"One hundred forty-four miles," Alicia told the group softly.

"Traffic is usually light on this road," Efie continued, so we should arrive by 12:30, or so—in time for lunch. Before we get there, I will tell you a few things about Delphi, eh? This afternoon, we will have a guide who will explain more about the oracle and all the ruins of Delphi. Meanwhile, sit back, relax, and enjoy the scenery."

Beth took pictures of the changing landscape as George sped along. Graceful palms gave way to scrubby bushes and neglected stands of gray-green, wild olive trees. Tall pines appeared as George drove up into more mountainous terrain. Although the skies were overcast, the air was warm.

In the back, Alicia and Ruth sat side by side. "So, tell me again, Ruthie," Alicia said, "why *exactly* are we going to this place—this Delphi? Paul didn't even come here."

"Look who's done her reading," Ruth joked. "Here's the deal. We're going to Delphi in order to learn about some of the other religions Paul had to compete with and because the travel books made it sound like a very nice place. And since I was designing the trip, I got to pick, didn't I? Nyahhh.

"Seriously, since modern Delphi has only 1,500 people, I figured it would be a change from the hustle of Athens and the big ruins in Corinth. When I planned the trip, I figured we'd need something low key by this time. As it's turning out," she nudged Alicia's arm, "it will be a good spot to rest. *Somebody* kept me up pretty late the other night."

They paused for coffee at the Thiva exit while George filled the van's gas tank. Soon they were back onto E75, driving towards Livadia.

Efie turned on her microphone. "I think you will find that Delphi will be one of the most beautiful and impressive places of your whole trip. For almost ten centuries, it was the cultural and religious center of the Hellenic world. The first temples were built here in the 9th century BC, and they attracted the faithful until the 2nd century after Christ.

"The town lies at the foot of Mt. Parnassos, in a valley between two big rocks named the Fedriades. The Plistos River flows through that valley and waters the olive groves planted there. Many nice hiking trails are in the area; you can walk all the way down to the port of Kirrha, the route ancient pilgrims used when they came to seek an answer from the oracle whom they believed spoke for Apollo."

Ten minutes later, after George drove through the small towns of Livadia and Arachova, they arrived in Delphi. "Here we are, ladies," Efie announced. "This is Delphi, once a busy city with hundreds of visitors and many rich buildings; but, today, it is only a village with two streets and a few small hotels. It is one of my favorite places in all of Greece."

George turned down a narrow street called Filellinon, drove two minutes more, and parked in front of a two-story, wooden structure. The sign said 'Acropolo Delphi Hotel.'

"Let's go in," Efie said. "I'll get your room assignments, then you can come back and collect your luggage. George will set your suitcases on the sidewalk here."

Within fifteen minutes, Ruth was in her room. She loved everything: from the rustic wooden furniture, to the wicker rocker with bright yellow pillows, to the rugs woven in shades of the sea. A small, earthenware jug of wildflowers stood on the dresser. What a fun place, she thought. This reminds me of a state park lodge back in the 1950s. There's even the smell of wood smoke, probably from that stone fireplace in the lobby. I'll bet it's really cozy there in the evenings.

The bathroom was a pleasant surprise. It was newly renovated with white, ceramic fixtures embellished by gleaming, chrome faucets and handles. Hand-painted tiles in delicate blues and yellows formed the splash around the sink and tub. Thick, blue towels hung from chrome towel racks. She picked up the liquid soap container and sniffed. Rosemary. Nice.

Ruth walked over to the window, pulled back the lace curtains, and opened the window. The clouds had dissipated, and the sun was shining through the trees.

She drew in a deep breath. "Thanks, God," she prayed. "We're on Day Eight; we've passed the halfway point, and things are going super. In spite of a few glitches, we're all doing OK; nobody's sick, and everything's working out. Even Alicia made it through her near calamity with Mr. Serial Seducer. I still can't believe what a jerk that Stavros is. Anyway, this whole trip is beyond my wildest dreams. I love what we're seeing and learning, I love that we're all still friends, and I love the smell of these pine trees. This is gonna be a great day."

She closed the window, set out her small cosmetic bags, and went down to join the others. After a quick lunch in the hotel's restaurant, they met Helene, a local guide.

"Helene is an old friend," Efie told them. "She and I were in school together. Since you were sitting in the bus all morning, I think you will enjoy to stretch your legs and walk around the ruins some. Helene will tell us a bit of the history of Delphi here and also as we go from place to place. Tomorrow, we will visit the museum; and you will have free time to walk through the site again."

Helene Manos was a slight, fifty-something woman with masses of curly, black hair tied back with a ribbon from her beautiful, classic Greek face. She wore blue jeans and a white blouse; a pale green sweater was draped over her shoulders. Her feet were shod in dusty hiking boots. Her only jewelry was a thin, silver chain with a dolphin-shaped pendant.

"I am most pleased to meet you ladies," Helene said in heavily accented English. "I live in Delphi since twenty years; one can live here a hundred years and not know all. I will tell only most important things. We start in here where you can sit comfortable. Please forgive that my English not always good."

"Oh, Helene," Ruth said, "your English is wonderful. It's a lot better than my Greek. You're doing just fine."

Helene smiled as she stood in front of their table. "Delphi's first religion rituals came from more than 4,000 years ago in cave on Mt. Parnassos. Cult of Apollo start and then sanctuary and oracle begin around 8th century BC. By end of 7th century BC, early stone temples to Apollo and Athena were built. In former times, other gods worshiped here, too. Maybe you hear of Artemis, Poseidon, Dionysus, Hermes, and Zeus, yes?

"Like today, early peoples like to organize, want to run things, make money. That was the Amphictyonic League—strong association of twelve tribes from north and south-central Greece. League controlled operations and finances of sanctuary here. Sanctuary grow much bigger, have great influence on politics and religion in large area of Greece. Later, same group make much money from Pythian Games, second only to Olympics."

"Sounds like a labor union and the United States Senate—all rolled into one," Alicia said.

"Greece always same—yesterday, today, and tomorrow," George grumbled. Efie patted his hand.

"Between 6th and 4th century BC," Helene continued, "was peak time for oracle of Delphi. Everyone—city officials, rulers of countries, generals, even ordinary people—come here from whole world, pray to Apollo, ask questions of oracle. Answers given by Pythia, priestess who sit on three-legged stool near smoking rock—small opening in ground where fumes come up from underworld. Her speech then interpreted by priests of Apollo.

"People very grateful for answers and guidance, so give much money and donations, build beautiful buildings. These were called treasuries and stored that money or artwork. Treasuries were built by individuals, organizations, and city-states.

"As sanctuary grow, especially one to Athena, other things added: a gymnasium—place for sports and learning—a theater, and even stadium."

She glanced at her watch. "OK. Is enough for now. We go out to look. Please, come follow me."

Efie stood up. "Ladies, we will be out for about two hours. Bring your sun hats and maybe your water bottles, eh? We will meet you in front of the hotel in ten minutes."

When they re-assembled, Helene handed each woman an admission ticket to the archaeological site. "I buy these ahead, save much time. Good for two days. Please do not lose. You need tomorrow. Now we go."

George drove them to the main entrance of the site. They all got out quickly, and then he parked the bus down the hill. After they went through the main gate, Helene turned to them.

"Delphi built on this hillside, start first with temple to Apollo, then grow bigger, up this hill on terraces built from many stones. Much hard work. Whole site," she spread her arms in a wide arc, "was sacred to Mother Earth, was guarded by terrible serpent, Python. Long time later, Python killed by Apollo."

"Hmm," Alicia whispered to Vicky, "do you suppose there are echoes of the serpent from the Adam and Eve story, you know, like in the Garden of Eden, here?"

"Maybe," Vicky replied tentatively. "It's incredible how those ancient myths got around."

"After Apollo kill Python," Helene continued, "sanctuary built here by Cretans who walk up from port at Kirrha. Apollo come with them in shape of dolphin. That why you see dolphin in much Greek art." She fingered her necklace. "Dolphin very important symbol to early peoples. Later, many stories and plays celebrate and remember these things. Legends and myths very powerful here, last long time.

"By 3rd century BC, changes in beliefs made sanctuary less important; but rituals continue until 2nd century AD. Even Roman Emperor Hadrian come for consult oracle. Also Pausanias, traveler who write descriptions of many buildings and 300 statues. Make later reconstruction possible."

"Hey, Efie," Ruth asked, "is that the same Pausanias who wrote about Corinth?"

Efie nodded. "Yes. You have a good memory, Ruth."

"He really got around," Ruth said. "My kind of guy."

As they walked along the Sacred Way, Helene pointed out the ruins of many small buildings that housed votives, or gifts, from grateful cities or individuals for favors received or answered prayer.

"Like people donating a stained-glass window or new hymnbooks today?" Ruth said to Vicky.

"Yeah, kind of," Vicky replied. "Or throwing a half a mil into the building fund bucket."

Helene then took them to the Temple of Apollo and showed them where the Pythia would have sat to deliver oracles. Ruth took several pictures of the site with her phone.

"I think," Najila said, "it is interesting that the ancients asked for advice and direction from the god, Apollo, who spoke through the oracle. Imagine how much money flew to pay for their trip to Delphi, the temple fee for oracle, and then in saying *shukran*, oh . . . I mean, thank you."

"Absolutely," Vicky said. "In fact, in later years, people thought it was *only* about the oracle. They thought it was just some lady who got high by breathing sulfurous fumes, saying whatever came into her head—or whatever she'd been *coached* to say—and that the more money one paid, the better the advice would be. Imagine that."

"Yeah, but," Alicia said as she took a swig from her water bottle, "I have to ask myself how often do I pay big bucks to the 'seers' of our times—doctors, lawyers, beauticians, even horoscopes—when, instead, I should be asking God?"

Beth moved next to Vicky, grasped her elbow, and pulled her away from the group. "I need to tell you something," she whispered angrily. "All this talk about Apollo and these other gods is making me really upset. I mean, I thought we were all Christians here, that we believe in God, and that Jesus is His son. So I feel it's wrong to talk about other gods. It's like I'm being disloyal or even breaking the second commandment—you know, about not having false gods. Didn't those early Greeks *know* that?"

Vicky took a deep breath as she considered her answer. Then she put her arm around Beth. "I know exactly how you feel, Beth. I asked those same questions when I first enrolled in my church history courses. Fortunately, I had a really nice professor explain to me how things developed. He told me that Christianity grew out of Judaism, which grew out of Canaanism, which grew out of earlier religions. Monotheism, the belief in one God, was rather late in coming. The early Greeks did not know Jesus, but they *did* know that they needed help from a Being greater than themselves.

"Then my professor said that the basis of every religion is, or at least *should* be, about love . . . how we love our neighbor and how we love ourselves. That's what Jesus is all about, and that's what Paul was trying so hard to teach the Corinthians, many of whom came from pagan backgrounds and had worshiped different gods in places just like this. So learning about different religions isn't going to harm us. It doesn't mean we believe in them. Anyway, look at Najila. She's a Samaritan, and you certainly don't object to her."

Beth laughed nervously. "Well, that's different. She's . . . she's . . . so nice. I mean, she's . . . she's . . . just like . . . like one of *us*."

"Yes," Vicky said quietly. "She is."

Delphi, Greece

Thirty-six

After Helene finished her tour, the women spent the rest of the afternoon hiking up and down the various terraces of the site, taking photos, or just sitting and contemplating the view. Shortly before five, they left the site and wandered through two souvenir shops in Delphi. Najila noted several ideas about merchandise, like olive oil soap and scarves printed with scenes from the area, that she could offer in her own shop in Nablus.

Later, at the casual, family-style dinner in the hotel dining room, they shared long, wooden tables and visited with fellow guests from Italy, the United States, Germany, and Japan. When Efie finished her coffee, she folded her napkin and said, "Breakfast will be in this room beginning at 7:00. Sunrises are spectacular here; so you might want to wake up a bit early and take some pictures, eh? We will meet at 9:00 tomorrow."

Najila said her goodnights and started towards her room; but when she saw Alicia head out to the terrace behind the hotel, she changed her mind.

As Najila stood in the doorway leading out to the terrace, she pulled her gray, woolen shawl around her shoulders; evenings were cool at this elevation. She waited while her eyes adjusted to the darkness, and then walked towards the glow of Alicia's cigarette.

"Do you mind I sit with you some minutes?" Najila asked. "How are you feeling now? Are you some little relaxed after such terrible events of last few days?"

"Sure, no problem," Alicia answered. "Come and sit." She put out her cigarette, slid over on the white, wicker sofa, and patted the place beside her.

"Yes, I am better, Najila. Thanks for asking. The quiet up here on this mountainside is very calming. I love the idea that this place has always been sacred to Mother Earth. It sort of makes me feel, oh, I don't know, like, connected. I've just been sitting here asking God what I should do about . . . about . . . about everything."

Najila sat very still, as if she were listening for something. Finally, she spoke. "Alicia, you know I would never interfere or critical you; but this man, Stavros . . . he was not best solution for you. In my country, there are many men just like him: handsome, persuading, and secure of themselves. Their mamas raise them to think they walk in water.

"But what is reality? He is already fifty and is not married. So that means he will not marry . . . whatever the reason. Flirting is a game for such men. In Arabic, it is called *almoghazalah*. You do not need an arrangement with a man who only runs after foreign women. You are attracted to him, yes? You think he is attracted to you? Hah. He is attracted only to your money. He would only bring you much troubles. You are too fine for such a man, Alicia."

She paused and then continued. "A doctor I am not, but I know that before you can do anything else, you must work to heal yourself. I learned this after my

Kanaan died; and I was so destroyed, no, wait . . . uh
. . . *devastated*. Your past will always be with you. You
cannot forget it, but you can choose to not let it keep
wounding you.

"You have accepted that your father did abuse you.
Was Jim abusing you with his words? Perhaps when
you are home, you will be able to speak with him and
talk things over. You cannot change the past, but you
can choose your future."

Najila sighed as she pulled her shawl tighter. "I
cannot change what happened in my country, but I
am still very lucky. I can choose to live how I want,
where I want, and do the work I want. In my early
years, when I could not choose, many bad and sad
things happened. Now that I can choose, I want things
that make me happy and that I love to do: like my
souvenirs, my tours, and even the dancing. Being with
you wonderful ladies on this trip has helped me to see
that more clear. Life is too short to be unhappy most
of the time."

"Thanks, Najila," Alicia said softly. "We must be on
the same wavelength because I've come to almost the
exact same conclusions. I realize that I've allowed a lot
of baggage from my past to color my thinking and my
reactions, and I'm ready for a change. I know it won't
be easy, but I want to try."

"Perhaps," Najila said, "words of prophet Isaiah
might fit here: 'Peoples who walked in darkness have
seen the great light.'"

She reached out and grasped Alicia's hands. "Good
night, my friend. God bless you, and keep you, and
give you peace."

Thirty-seven

May 13, 2014—Delphi, Greece

Ruth's alarm jangled at 6:00 AM. She tapped the snooze button and pulled the covers over her head. Then she remembered: sunrise photos. She jumped out of bed, splashed cold water on her face, and dressed hurriedly. She started out the door, went back for her jacket, and then tiptoed quietly down the stairs.

She needn't have bothered. Alicia, Beth, Vicky, and Najila were already standing in the lobby. "Well, if it isn't Sleeping Beauty herself," Alicia said softly. "We were going to give you another two minutes, and then you'd have been on your own. Let's go. We're wasting time."

They started their photo tour on the terrace and moved on through the deserted streets of Delphi. "This sunrise," Beth said, "is beyond wonderful. It's gorgeous! Look at all those pink and purple stripes. I wouldn't have missed this for anything." The women stood mesmerized, as the soft glow from the dawn light crept over the ancient ruins in the distance.

"For sure," Alicia said. "It's a good thing we're doing this early. We could get some showers later on today. You know that old saying, 'Red skies at night: sailors delight. Red skies in the morning: sailors take warning.'"

"What?" Ruth scoffed. "Who knows *that*? Oh, I know. *You* know it, Al, because *you're* so old."

"Ha, ha, very funny," Alicia commented dryly. "Listen, you ladies can stay out here longer if you want, but I'm heading back. My *old* body needs coffee now."

George and Efie met them at 9:00, and they drove to the Delphi Museum. Efie led them through rooms packed with finds from the surrounding hillsides: beautiful statues, pottery, glassware, and jewelry inlaid with precious stones.

"This museum," Efie said, "is a tribute to the creativity of the inhabitants of Delphi down through the ages and a rich legacy to be enjoyed by all who enter each room."

The high point for most of them was the marble charioteer, a graceful young man who had, at one time, been driving a chariot. Now horse and chariot were gone; but the man was still perfect: his curly hair, the graceful folds of his robe, and even his toes.

"Just look at him. *Look* at that artistry," Alicia said reverently as she pointed to his feet. "It just shows that we've got to do our work carefully, get all the details right, even down to the toenails, because you never know what will be left behind."

When they took a coffee break in the museum's café, Ruth urged Vicky to give brief explanations of several other major religions and cults prevalent during Paul's time. Besides the cult of Apollo, she said that belief in Mythras, a strong bull, had been very popular with the many rough soldiers and sailors who would have visited Corinth and other parts of Greece.

"Gosh," Beth said thoughtfully, "Paul really did have a lot of competition, didn't he? I had no idea. Well, look at our part of the world. There are lots of different 'brands' of religions and cults out there, too. The more things change, the more they stay the same."

Efie passed out large maps of the Delphi archaeological site. "Now you will have two hours to visit here on your own. Allow some time to just sit and think about this shrine and what it meant to early Greeks. It is a most special place. Please meet at the main entrance at 12:20. George will pick us up, and we will take our lunch at a nice *taverna* nearby, eh? Enjoy yourselves."

With the maps in hand, they strolled, alone or in pairs, through the archaeological site's different terraces. The theater perched above Apollo's temple, while the stadium was tucked into a terrace higher up the mountain, some distance away.

Vicky hiked up to the stadium by herself. Hot and out of breath when she reached the top, she spied a bench under a stand of pine trees. As she sat down, she mopped her face with a tissue, took a long drink from her water bottle, and then gazed at the landscape in front of her.

Down the hill to the left were the sites of the Temple of Athena and the gymnasium where athletes would have studied and trained for the Pythian games. At the bottom of the mountain lay a vast sea of olive trees. Although she couldn't see it, she knew that the bay of Corinth was in the far distance.

As she relaxed, Vicky imagined the long line of people who would have trudged the several miles up the steep, winding path from the port at Kirrha to visit this sacred shrine. They had come for over eight hundred years, all seeking answers to problems they faced or wanting guidance about major decisions: where to build, where to colonize, who should rule, who to marry, or whether to go to war.

All of them, she reflected, just wanted to know if they were doing the right thing. They wanted security and happiness.

Her mind drifted to her own family—to that long, long line of people behind her—all those generations of marriages, divorces, re-marriages, having kids, leaving kids, dumping kids, and creating scars that wouldn't heal. Were they like the pilgrims who came to this shrine? Were they also searching for security and happiness?

Vicky's chest tightened as she thought of her mother and all those years of different husbands, lovers, and children in her life. Was her mother just reacting to her own past and pursuing happiness however she could? Had she ever found it? Why not? And if I call myself a Christian, why am I still hanging on with a *death grip* to all the bitterness, the anger, and yes, even the hatred I've felt towards her? It hasn't changed her, but it sure has changed me . . . and not for the better.

A light breeze fluttered through the pine trees. Vicky sighed deeply and then came to a decision. Maybe it's time I laid this burden down, she thought. It's been weighing on my heart, hurting me, crippling me, freezing me, like some gigantic iceberg, for so many years. I've dragged it around for too long, and I'm tired of it.

Tears welled up as she whispered, "Mom, this is really hard but . . . I . . . I . . . I forgive you. I forgive all the times you left my brothers and me alone when we were little. I see that, with all your jobs and working eighteen hours a day, you were just trying to provide for us. With those different husbands, you were trying to provide for us. Even when you left us at Grandma's, who was drunk so often, you were trying to provide for us. It was awful; and I was so, so afraid. We survived, though, because God provided help for us, too. I realize now that you were just trying to do the right thing and be happy. I . . . I hope you'll find happiness someday, somehow."

Vicky fished in her pocket, found another tissue, wiped her eyes, and blew her nose. She took several deep breaths. She felt exhausted but somehow relieved. Slowly she also felt a comforting presence, like she was being cared for and everything would be OK. She knew it was Norma.

As she stood up and started down the path, she realized she was changed. She was also positive that this mountaintop experience would remain with her forever.

Two levels below, Ruth and Alicia took pictures of Apollo's temple and the remains of the many treasuries. Alicia pointed to her map. "Look, Ruthie. The more important the city or organization was, the closer to the big temple their treasury was. Location, location, location!"

"Yeah, I see that," Ruth said. "You know, Al, a flyer I read said that this place was up and running for *eight* centuries—all supposedly to honor the god, Apollo. Do you think that, back in the day, people lived and behaved like they really *believed* in Apollo? He was called the god of light and supposedly taught people about prudence, modesty, and peace. Those twelve tribes in that Amphictyonic League were all about friendship, brotherhood, and peaceful co-existence of peoples—you know, sort of like a Delphic ideal."

"What do *you* think, Ruthie?" Alicia asked.

Ruth shrugged. "My money says it was probably about like it is today. There were some true believers and then maybe some who thought that all the treasuries and statues were just to show off—you know, to try and impress others who came to visit the oracle, as in 'anything you can do, we can do better.' But, hey, what did all those fancy and luxurious treasuries say about prudence and modesty?"

She kicked a pebble from the path. "You know, Al, this place reminds me of the Vatican Museum. All those art treasures were collected through *fifteen* centuries. Yet what do they *really* have to do with Jesus Christ?"

"Sometimes, not a lot," Alicia admitted. "However, some of those masterpieces were created by artists who really believed they were giving their best to honor God. Other pieces were commissioned by wealthy supporters who were keen to flaunt their wealth and loved looking pious. Of course, there were some affluent people who were also very spiritual and wanted to leave a legacy that expressed their devotion. I guess we shouldn't lump people all into one basket. There are as many different motives and agendas as there are people."

She glanced at her watch. "We'd better head back to the main entrance. It's time to meet the others."

+++++++++

Late that afternoon, Ruth found Vicky and Beth relaxing on the hotel terrace.

"C'mon, ladies," Ruth said briskly, "go for a little walk with me. It's too nice out just to sit there in the shade and waste all this beautiful scenery."

"Actually," Vicky said as she stretched lazily, "I was thinking more along the lines of ordering a cup of tea. My feet hurt from climbing up to the stadium."

"Oh, for heaven's sake," Ruth scolded. "Will you two just get up and come *on*? The exercise will do you good. Let's go." She slung her orange tote bag over her shoulder and marched down the steps of the terrace.

Vicky and Beth slowly got up and reluctantly followed her along a path that wound down the hill towards the sea. As they rounded a gentle curve, they saw a small grotto formed by clusters of tall, leafy oleander bushes adorned with fragrant pink flowers. Inside the grotto, Alicia and Najila sat on an ornate, white bench. A second bench formed a right angle.

"Hey, how cool is this?" Alicia said. "I was wondering when I could talk about my part of Second Corinthians, and then you ladies turn up. Perfect timing."

"What a view," Vicky said as she settled herself on the second bench. "I've got goose bumps just thinking that we're on the same ground that those ancient pilgrims were."

Beth chose a spot next to Vicky. "Here, Ruth, sit by me. Look out there. Isn't it gorgeous? Those sure look like storm clouds on the horizon. Alicia, your earlier prediction of rain could be right."

"That's why we're sitting in this grotto," Alicia said with a grin. "Anyway, I really don't have a whole lot to say. I thought that, in the last half of Second Corinthians, Paul's mood was pretty much the same as in the first half. You can feel the contrast and conflict in these chapters. One minute he's happy and encouraged; the next minute, he's down in the dumps and upset and angry with the Corinthians, who have obviously blown off a lot of his early teachings. He was on an emotional roller coaster. What do you all think? Did anything strike you? Any thoughts to share?"

The group was quiet for several minutes while they considered their answers.

Ruth spoke first. "Well, when I read this back home, I remember thinking that Paul seemed happy in Chapter 7 because Titus had returned from Corinth with good news. Then Paul sounds all sad, worrying that he had been too harsh in an earlier letter. I never realized before how much Paul depended on men like Titus, Silas, and others on his team to go back and forth, deliver messages, and check on things in the various towns where they'd worked—you know, to prop up what he started. They were like his personal mailmen, keeping him updated on what was happening in these groups. I used to think that Paul did everything himself, but even really smart guys like him needed help. That's comforting to me."

"Having been in the business world," Vicky said, "I really admired his tactics in Chapters 8 and 9, where he moves to financial matters. In order to stimulate the Corinthians, he brags about the generosity of their Macedonian neighbors for their contributions to help the poor brethren back in Jerusalem who needed money and food. I think that every alum director, foundation chairman, or grant seeker should memorize these two chapters: How to Make Your Members Run to Open Their Wallets. It was a brilliant move on Paul's part: to create a little competition between the communities—

as in 'Those Macedonians, who had so little, were clamoring to donate; so I know that you Corinthians ("with all your money" implied) surely won't do any less.' Then he closes on a really gentle note when he tells them that supplying the needs of others is a way of thanking God for His gifts. That's such a beautiful idea. I want to remember that."

"In Chapters 10 to 12," Beth observed, "I noticed three things. First, Paul goes after people who puffed themselves up by making insulting remarks about his size and his speech. Second, he defends his practice of not taking payment for his work from the local group in Corinth but, rather, from communities where he'd already been. That way, he avoided charges of favoritism and influence peddling. Very politically savvy, I'd say. And, third, he had to deal with those super apostles: false and dishonest guys who masqueraded as apostles of Christ and thought they were such hot stuff. It looks like Paul had to deal with a lot of the same issues we do today."

"Absolutely," Alicia said. "He lays it on them when he boasts about all the persecutions he endured during his missions. He saves the best for last when he describes his visions and revelations from God. It's like he's saying, 'Here's what I've done. So what have YOU done today?' Then he reels off a list of bad stuff he's heard that the Corinthians had been up to. He warns them to pull up their socks and clean up their act before he arrives a third time. The last verses of Chapter 13 are nice, though, aren't they? He says they need to get over themselves and kiss and make up. Then he leaves them with a really sweet blessing."

Najila nodded. "I am inspired when I think how

much Paul was injured by all the hurting criticism against him from these people he knew; and, yet, he kept going. He even took cares for the collection for suffering believers in Jerusalem. I will take a lesson from this and not let criticism, even from my family, push me from my goals. I must also keep going in my work."

At the first rumblings of thunder, Najila stood up. "Thank you, Alicia. You show us how those Corinthians made Paul crazy, yet he still loved them. He never gave them up."

"You're welcome, Najila," Alicia said. "Now let's go, everybody." She hurried out of the grotto and started up the path. "We've gotta hustle, or we'll get drenched."

"Be careful going up those steps," Beth called after them. "They'll be slippery."

"Yeah," Ruth said, "and I already know how to fall up steps and trash my leg in the rain."

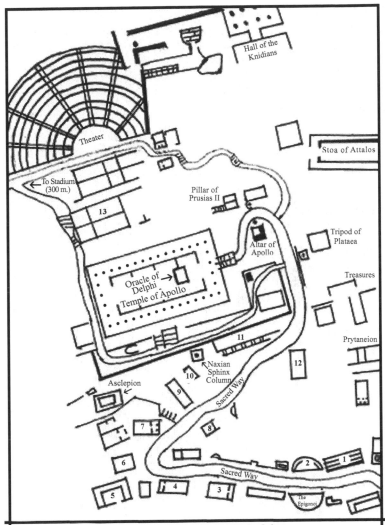

Map of Ancient Delphi

Some Points of Interest (This plan is not all inclusive.)

1. Hellenistic Monument
2. Offering of the Kings of Argos
3. Treasury of the Sicyonians
4. Treasury of the Siphnians
5. Treasury of the Thebans
6. Treasury of the Boetians
7. Treasury of the Athenians
8. Treasury of Knidos
9. Bouleuterion (Council House)
10. Rock of the Sibyl
11. Stoa of the Athenians
12. Treasury of the Corinthians
13. Offering of Crateros

Thirty-eight

Halfway through dinner at the hotel that evening, two local musicians arrived: a bearded, older man with a bouzouki—a four-stringed instrument similar to a mandolin—and a young man with an accordion. They stood in the doorway between the lobby and the dining room and performed for the guests, while waiters pushed the wooden chairs and sofas next to the walls, clearing the area for dancing. Bustling around, the manager rolled up the small throw rugs, lit the fireplace, and then came into the dining room.

He clapped his hands for attention. "Special music we arrange for you tonight," he announced proudly. "We very happy to have guests from so many countries here, and we want you should enjoy nice Greek music. Please, come and sit. Later, maybe you like dance, too. George, you lead?"

George nodded.

After the plates with baklava crumbs and the coffee cups were cleared away, the guests moved into the lobby and found seats. When they were all settled, the kitchen door opened; and Helene came in carrying a guitar. Her long, white dress rippled gracefully as she walked slowly to a spot near the musicians. A silver shawl was draped around her shoulders; its fringe shimmered in the firelight. The ribbon gone, her black hair flowed loosely down her back.

"Wow!" Ruth whispered to Alicia. "What a transition: from archaeological guide to goddess. Did she just step down from Apollo's temple? She looks fantastic."

After she tuned her guitar a bit, Helene enchanted them with several, soulful, Greek love songs. Her throaty alto voice caressed the sinuous melodies. When the final haunting strains of the last song died away, the room was still. Then the guests applauded long and loud.

Efie wiped her eyes. "I know Helene since we were girls, and her voice always brings me to tears. She could sing on any stage in Greece, but she loves it here in Delphi." She turned her head and smiled. "George, now we must dance!"

George stood up and gave a signal to the musicians who began to play a lively folk tune. He motioned for the guests to stand and then organized them all— Germans, Americans, Japanese, and Italians—into two lines. The instrumentalists played three folk dances with Helene joining them on the last one. Amidst the laughter and clapping, it was easy to see the guests enjoyed themselves immensely.

When the music changed, George danced a short solo and then beckoned Najila to join him. Embarrassed, she shook her head; but Efie shooed her forward. "Yes, yes, you must. You dance so much better than I do, and you do him a favor. He loves this."

"Go on, Najila," Ruth urged. "You are so good at this. Please?"

Najila smiled and then stood up. As she reached for

George's outstretched hand, his cell phone rang.

"Ah, sorry, Miss Najila. One minute, I come back." He stepped away from the group and spoke urgently into the phone. "Yah. Here at Acropolo. What? You got him? How much taken? OK. I'll be there in 15 minutes."

He went to Efie, spoke quickly in her ear, kissed her on both cheeks, and then waved to the manager. "Business." He bowed over Najila's hand. "Most sorry, Miss Najila. I go help friends. We dance another time." He hastily pulled on his jacket and then hurried out into the night.

The manager stepped to the center of the room. "Mr. Pappas called away. Too bad. Now, I lead dancing. Boys, a new tune, please."

Efie leaned towards the women who were all seated near her. "George still does a little undercover police work, and sometimes they call him. It makes him happy." Ruth could see from Efie's eyes that it didn't make *her* happy. Nevertheless, she carried on. She was a true professional.

"I know you have the itinerary," Efie told them, "but I wish to remind you that tomorrow we should leave around 8:00, as we will drive from Delphi to the harbor at Piraeus, south of Athens. The distance is 190 kilometers."

"114 miles," Alicia whispered.

Efie smiled and went on. "Normally, it takes three hours, but that depends on the traffic. Your reservations are at 1:00 on the hydrofoil for Mykonos. You should have time to get some lunch near the boat dock. All OK? Then I see you in the morning. Now I retire to my bed."

Ruth looked at Alicia and shook her head. "How do

you *do* that?"

"Do what?" Alicia questioned.

"Convert kilometers to miles in two seconds flat."

Alicia pointed to her head. "Nothing to it."

After Efie left them, they enjoyed the music awhile longer and then wandered out to the hotel's terrace. They saw the moon peeking out from behind the clouds, burnishing the Temple of Apollo with a soft glow.

"The books were right," Vicky said softly. "This place really does have such a mystical atmosphere."

As the women turned to leave, Najila said, "Here we are: I, a Samaritan, and you four Christian ladies, all near the ancient shrine of the god, Apollo. We have seen so many different ways of worship through the centuries, and we all worship differently today. Yet, our differences do not matter. We are bound together by our love and concern for each other. In the end, *that* is what matters."

Trust Najila to get to the heart of the message, Ruth thought. She's lived through war after war after war in her country—really bad, faith-killing stuff—yet she has the strongest belief of us all.

"You're right, Najila," Ruth said, "and *you* are the oracle for us tonight. You've given us a message straight from God."

Thirty-nine

May 14, 2014—Mykonos, Greece

In spite of looking tired the next morning, George was cheerful, as he stowed their luggage into the Volkswagen bus shortly after eight. Ruth was dying to ask him where he'd gone last night but thought better of it.

On the road, traffic was light; and he made good time driving down from Delphi to the port of Piraeus. Efie started to turn on her microphone, but George put his hand on her arm. "I see in the mirror. They're all sleeping again. Take a break, sweetheart." He left the freeway just before the turnoff to Athens, took a short cut, and reached the harbor by 11:30. He parked next to the hydrofoil dock.

The sleepy women all stretched and yawned, gathered up their belongings, and slowly climbed out of the bus.

"Just down there, by that green and white striped umbrella," Efie said when they were on the pavement, "is a very nice café. The food is good, and the owner is our friend. Tell him George sent you and that you wish a table next to the sea." She and George then hugged them all goodbye and promised to meet them at this same spot in three days.

Ruth spun around. "Wow, guys. Look at all these big boats! We've gone from a rustic mountain sanctuary to this luxurious yacht scene—all in one morning. We're livin' the dream." She checked her watch. "We should probably grab a bite of lunch. We're supposed to board the hydrofoil fifteen minutes before departure, so we've got an hour and a half. That should be enough."

Following an exceptionally tasty lunch of seafood salads, crusty baguettes, sparkling white wine, and profuse greetings from the owner to George, they ambled slowly back to the dock area. They obtained their tickets from a friendly, uniformed steward standing next to the Sea Jet I, a large, white hydrofoil that had pulled in minutes before and was now idling at the pier.

After the arriving passengers disembarked, the women joined the line of passengers boarding. As they found their seats, Alicia read the small brochure she'd been handed at the gangway. "Ladies, it says here that this trip will take three and a half hours and that we can get up and walk around, but we're advised to keep our seat belts on in case of a big wave. There's even a little map that shows where the bar and the rest rooms are. We're all set. We should be in Mykonos by 4:30."

Beth pointed to her tote bag. "I've got some motion sickness meds if anybody needs them."

"Thanks, Beth," Ruth said. "Smart thinking; but with this bright sunshine and no wind, I don't see much rough water happening. Still, you never know."

Vicky stowed her carryon in the luggage area, returned to her airplane-style seat, and fastened her seatbelt. "Ah, this is really the life, isn't it? I could get into this. What a far cry from the little fishing boats Paul traveled on. I'm really glad we're doing this trip today and not 2,000 years ago."

Najila's face was white, and her eyes were glassy with fear. "This is first time I am on such a boat. Will we go terribly fast?"

"Probably not," Ruth said, "I think the boat kinda raises up and skims over the surface of the water. I'm not really sure, but I know I'm gonna love it." She patted Najila's hand. "You'll be fine. We're right here beside you. But just in case, take this motion sickness bag. If it gets too wavy, look at the horizon, OK? Focus on the horizon."

And so, for the next three hours, the women chatted, napped, and (mostly) enjoyed the smooth ride on the clear waters of the Aegean Sea. Najila finally got up her nerve and carefully made her way to the front of the boat to look out the big windows.

The water is very blue and quite calm, she thought. Over there I see another island. This is not so bad, after all. Why was I so afraid?

She managed a smile and then went to the bar area. A cup of tea would be nice. Ruth and Beth were already there, seated at a small table, finishing their coffee and pastries.

"Come and join us, Najila," Beth said. "You're just the person we want to talk to. We're still complaining, no, make that *whining*, about the difficulty of getting jobs. In America, once a woman hits 55, it's game over. How is it in Palestine?"

"Just *being* a woman," Najila said as she sat down, "makes it hard to get the job in my country, no matter what her age. There are still many old traditions that have very strong hold on many people. Things are changing, but it is slow. Over the years, I have done many things not normal for women. Oh yes, some do teach school and study law or medicine; but I know no other woman who runs a travel company or a souvenir stand. Mama and Auntie Rania think I am strange, but I *wanted* to do my jobs. So I did. I find a way." She smiled at them. "When I try alone, nothing works. But when I ask God, a way comes."

"Bless your heart, Najila," Beth said as she finished her coffee. "In your quiet, courageous way, you live your faith every day. You're such an inspiration to me."

Embarrassed, Najila shook her head. "Thank you, but it is nothing. You and Ruth can do the same. Now I go to my seat. My legs feel a little . . . wavy."

Back in her seat, she observed Vicky, who was now snoozing behind her gold-rimmed dark glasses. How are things with her, Najila wondered. She is always so perfectly dressed, knows such good scripture, but cannot write her book. I think she starts, then runs away, abandons herself, just like her mother abandoned her. In spite of all the wars in my country, Mama was always there, was always with me. And I knew she loved me. Perhaps Vicky fights a war with herself. Her mama left her alone so often and even ran away completely when Vicky was a small girl. Now Vicky does that to herself. It is what she knows. I wonder if she can ever change that?

+++++++++

The sun was still high and hot when they arrived in the small harbor of Mykonos at 4:30. After they collected their luggage, they followed the other passengers slowly down the gangplank and onto the busy dock area.

"Since we have our suitcases and don't know where we're going," Ruth said, "let's just take a taxi to the hotel, OK? We can figure out how to walk around here, once we check in and dump our stuff. We'll have kitchens in our apartments, so I thought it would be fun to cook dinner there tonight—you know, since we've been eating out so much. We can find a little grocery store, I'm sure. Look, there's a big taxi right across the street. C'mon, girls. Let's grab him."

Soon they were in the taxi, driving slowly up a winding road away from the harbor. Beth took pictures of the rocky landscape dotted with white houses and tiny chapels. In five minutes, the driver pulled into a parking lot enclosed by green shrubs. "Here is Agnandi Homes and Suites," he announced as he turned off the ignition. "Reception just over there. Ten euros, please."

After Ruth paid the driver, they walked into the reception area and were greeted by Ionna Sciafanos, the owner. "Welcome to Agnandi," she said graciously. "I am happy you all made it here. I hope your trip over was calm? Now if you will just sign the register, I will give you your keys and then show you to your apartments. And which one of you is Ruth Hanford?" Ruth stepped forward, extended her hand, and then introduced the other women, who quickly signed the hotel register.

Fresh in an embroidered, white cotton dress and turquoise hoop earrings, Ionna was the picture of cool, summery elegance, as she led them from her office to their building. They walked along a stone path, bordered by fluffy pampas grass; broad yucca and agave plants stood guard nearby. Pink, crimson, and white bougainvillea flowed over the white adobe walls of their terrace.

Ionna leaned down to scoop up some fallen blossoms and then unlocked the main door. "We have eighteen separate buildings here on our property," she explained. "This one has three small apartments; two of them have two bedrooms and the third only one bedroom. You'll all have your own space but won't have to go far if you wish to come together for drinks or a meal. You will be close to the pool but still a bit away, so you will have peace and quiet. Please step in."

She showed them around one apartment, explaining how the stove and various kitchen appliances worked. "The current in Greece is 220 volts, but you probably know that by now. We do have an adaptor under that counter, if you need one. There are hair dryers in the bathrooms, so you should be fine."

"Look," Beth called as she opened a narrow door next to the fridge. "There's even a washing machine, ironing board, and iron in here. You've thought of everything, Mrs. Sciafanos."

"Oh, please call me Ionna. Everyone does. Yes, when we remodeled these buildings two years ago, I told Demetrious that today's guests want clean clothes when they travel. I know I certainly do. It was just too hard for guests to use the laundromat down in the village; many tourists, like you, have no cars here. Now, do you have any questions?"

"Yes," Ruth answered. "We want to fix our own dinner here tonight in this beautiful kitchen. Where's the nearest grocery store? Also, I hope you won't think I'm nosy; but do you get your hair cut here or in Athens? It looks terrific."

Ionna looked very pleased. "Thank you, Ruth.

How kind of you to notice. Yes, I get it cut here on the island. Stefanos has a salon in town, just off the main street. He's the best. Now, if you'll excuse me, I must get back to the office. I'm expecting more guests shortly. I hope you'll enjoy your apartments. Call me if you need anything. Someone is always at the desk. Please think of this as 'your home away from home' here on Mykonos."

She started to walk out the door but then turned around. "And to answer your first question, there is a fine, small market just at the bottom of the road. Go left out of our driveway, walk down the hill about a mile, and you'll come to it. It's called Manos' Market. They have a delicatessen with organic meats and cheeses, plus local fruits and vegetables. If you want, you can come back on the public bus; it runs up the hill every half hour. The stop is just across from the market."

After Ionna left, the women explored their apartments. Ruth said, "Al, how about if you and I share this one; Beth, you and Vicky can have the one to the left of the terrace, and, Najila, we've gotten you the single. That must be your door in the middle out there. I think all three apartments share the big terrace; but," she peered out the kitchen window, "it looks like each place also has another smaller terrace off the living rooms. This one does anyway."

Vicky began opening the kitchen cupboards and drawers. "Look at these beautiful blue and green dishes and glassware, and there are matching placemats and silverware. And here, under the counter, are all sorts of pots and pans. There's even a big fish steamer. They've thought of everything."

While they were salivating over the kitchen and its equipment, Alicia had slipped out the door and run up the shaded path to the pool. Now she was back. "You won't *believe* that pool and the deck area. It's like something out of a magazine. I can't wait to take a swim."

Seeing Alicia's excited face, Beth made a quick decision. "Vicky, how about if you, Najila, and I walk down to town and pick up some groceries— just something simple for dinner? We'll fix it in our apartment tonight; and, then, Alicia, you and Ruth can take care of dinner tomorrow night. Najila, you can supervise . . . or pour the wine. That way, Alicia can have her swim, we three will get in a walk, and Ruthie can have a little time off or even a nap. How does that sound?"

"Sounds like a plan to me," Ruth said happily, as she opened the cupboard above the stove. "Look, there's salt, pepper, oil, vinegar, sugar, even a bit of coffee in here. Other guests have obviously left it. Nice."

She tore a piece of paper from the pad next to the phone. "Here, let's make a list of stuff we'll need for breakfast: eggs, bread, jam, fruit, more coffee, and some of that Greek yogurt, for sure. I bet the terrace will be beautiful in the morning. First person up starts the coffee."

She did a little dance in the middle of the kitchen. "Girls, I am *so* glad that I found this place online. You never know; people can put up any kind of photos. This is the real deal, though. It's beyond my wildest dreams."

After they stashed their suitcases in their bedrooms and freshened up a bit, Beth's plan got underway.

Armed with their tote bags, Beth, Vicky, and Najila made their way out of the hotel's grounds and down the hill to Manos' Market. They found all the items on Ruth's list and then added a tempting selection of cold cuts and cheese, breads, salad makings, olives, fresh fruits, and, of course, some Greek pastries.

"Wait, wait," Vicky said as they stood at the cash register. "Wine. We need wine. We can't forget that." She dashed back to the wine section to rectify this grievous error. A sturdy lady standing in the aisle pointed to a display of white wine and smiled broadly. "This very good. Come from local grapes. My brother make."

"Then it must be terrific," Vicky said. "*Efharisto.*"

As Vicky picked up two bottles, the woman added, "You know, even Jesus turn water into wine. He make wine, too. His wine the best." Vicky laughed and walked back up the aisle.

After they paid, they stopped for iced coffee frappes at a café next to the market. Minutes before the next bus arrived, Vicky noticed a stand with free brochures advertising the neighboring island of Delos. She took one, paged through it, and then stuck it in her tote.

While the three women were shopping, Alicia changed into her swimsuit and hurried to the pool area. She was on her tenth lap by the time Ruth joined her. "You're right, Al. This is gorgeous. Straight out of *House and Garden.*"

She spread her towel on a brown, wicker lounge chair topped with a long, white cushion, sat down, and rubbed on sunscreen. "Ahh. This is what it don't get no better than. I *might* get in the water later; but right now," she said with a yawn, "I feel a nap coming on.

That is, if you can keep the noise down." She stretched out, covered her face with her sun hat, and then closed her eyes.

"No problem, Ruthie," Alicia called from the water. "I'll try to swim softly."

They were both asleep on adjacent lounges when Najila appeared an hour later. In her hand, she cradled a small bell that she now rang gently. "Ladies, I am to tell you that dinner is served. Please to come."

The late afternoon sun filtered through the pine trees behind the pool as Alicia and Ruth slowly sat up, slipped on their sandals and T-shirts, and followed Najila back down the path.

"Thanks for coming up to get us, Najila," Ruth said as she covered a yawn. "That little salad back in Piraeus didn't fill me up. Here I am, starving again."

Her problem was soon remedied as they all helped themselves to the lavish buffet Beth and Vicky set out on the main terrace. Najila had pushed two tables together, covered them in a green and blue checked cloth she'd found in her kitchen, and had arranged five chairs around the tables. There was even a blue candle in a tall glass chimney for later. With a stunning view of the harbor, it was the perfect setting for their *al fresco* dining.

Tea towel draped over one arm, Najila passed among them, pouring wine and bringing out more platters from Beth's kitchen.

"Do you work here?" Ruth said, laughing. "C'mere and sit down, Najila. You don't have to wait on us. Al here *could* stir herself . . . if she weren't so busy eating."

They decided that, before the pastries and coffee, they needed a break; so, after rinsing the dishes, they put on their walking shoes and went for a stroll up the road behind the hotel. The landscape was strewn with gray-green rocks alternating with tufts of wild flowers. Houses were small and scattered far apart.

"Look," Ruth said. "All those houses are stark white with the doors and windows trimmed only in bright blue or turquoise. The Paint Police are tough here." She laughed. "You know, I can't *believe* this. It's just like my dream: the one I had when I first started planning all this. All I need is to meet some old guy in scruffy clothes called Petros. I'd fall down dead if that happened.

"Now, is it time for dessert? Did you buy the low-cal baklava? Oh well, I'll diet when I get home."

The hydrofoil to Mykonos

Forty

May 15, 2014—Mykonos, Greece

The next morning, Vicky was the first one up. She savored her coffee alone on the terrace in her robe. Soon the others came straggling out, attracted by the aroma of the fresh brew.

"Girls," Vicky said as she helped herself to some yogurt and fruit, "yesterday, I picked up a flyer about the nearby little island of Delos. The archaeological sites cover almost the whole island, and there's a small museum. It was supposedly the birthplace of Apollo and his twin sister, Artemis, and is one of the most important sites in all of Greece. In ancient times, it was second in importance only to Delphi."

"Really?" Beth asked. "Tell us more."

"Well, at one time," Vicky continued, "Roman traders made it the center of the slave trade. In the late Hellenistic and Roman times, it became a busy port and then grew into the financial and trading center of the entire Mediterranean. By 100 BC, there were 30,000 people living there. Now it's pretty much deserted except for the site guards. It's only two miles away, ferries run every hour, and it takes twenty minutes. Anybody interested in going?"

Ruth, Beth, and Najila agreed; but Alicia shook her head. "Amazing. You must have a photographic memory, Vick. You did such a super job on the background that I don't *need* to go. No, just kidding. Actually, I'm pretty much OD'ed on ruins. Tell you what: You guys float over to Delos and check it all out. I'll go for a quick swim and then walk down to the market, get some groceries, and bring the stuff back here on the bus. I'll meet you in town for lunch when you get off the boat. Then we can poke around in the shops and cafés in the afternoon. I'll be in charge of dinner, OK? Ruthie, if I buy the veggies, can you do a salad?"

"Sure," Ruth answered, "and I just want to add that we're here to relax; so there's no pressure and no stress. We all get to do exactly what we want. After all the touring and sightseeing we've already done, this is playtime. Fun in the sun, OK?'"

Everyone was happy with that idea; they planned to meet at 12:30. By the time the four women were on their way to catch the ferry, Alicia was back in the pool.

She loved swimming and had done it a lot as a kid, but she had gotten out of the habit the past few years. She wanted to change that. Churning through the water not only worked her body but also allowed her brain to drift into a meditative state.

I can't believe how nice this place is and how relaxed I feel, she thought, as she counted off another lap. This trip is helping me to get some perspective on myself, on Jim, and on our marriage. I've learned a lot about Paul and Greece but more about myself. Money well spent, I'd say.

Now if I can just keep this focus, this feeling that things might be OK once I get home. I don't want to get my hopes up; but I'm happier than I've been in a long,

long time. I know that I want to keep moving forward. Only time will tell whether or not Jim will be on that journey with me.

She completed fifty laps and then, pleased with herself, returned to her apartment. After a quick shower, she put on her tan Capris and the sparkly, cream top she'd bought in Athens that first day; she was in the mood for something glamorous. She surveyed the spices in the kitchen cupboard and then took off down the hill.

Her first stop was the fish market, three doors from Manos' shop. She listened to the owner's advice, memorized his recipe for *Fish Plaki*, and then purchased two large fillets of fresh halibut. Just as she stepped outside, she caught a glimpse of Stavros, coming straight toward her, with his arm around a beautiful young woman with long, black hair.

For an instant, Alicia considered ducking back inside the shop; but, then, the 'new Alicia' thought, "Ah, the heck with it. Let's see what he'll do."

"Oh, hi, Stavros. Imagine meeting you here," she said sweetly. "Are you in Mykonos on business? Checking out the lentil fields here, are you?"

"Ah, well, ah, yes, in a way," he stammered. "Ah, Alicia, here is my friend, Tiffany. I met her recently at, ah, the Loutraki Casino near Corinth."

"Yes, I remember that casino," Alicia said, as she looked straight into his eyes. She tilted her head and smiled. "It's especially nice at night, isn't it?"

Stavros' eyes shifted rapidly from left to right as bright red patches appeared on his cheeks. She loved watching him squirm.

"Ah, Tiffany, this is Alicia . . . an, ah, an old

acquaintance."

"Pleased to meetcha, I'm sure," Tiffany said in a shrill New York accent. "It's always nice to see *old* friends, right, Stavi?"

Her glance brushed over Alicia's face and figure in a nanosecond. Alicia knew she'd been instantly relegated to the geriatric department.

Tiffany hooked her arm possessively through Stavros' and started to move away. "Sorry, uh, Alison, is it," she said, "but we've got to run. We're meeting friends for lunch, aren't we, Stavi?"

Then she pointed to the jewelry store window behind Alicia. "Oh, *look*, Stavi. Look at those fabulous *diamonds*! Let's go in, OK? *Please*, Stavi?" She tugged at his hand. "See ya, Alice."

Alicia managed a wave as they turned and entered the store. She also managed not to laugh. He's got his hands full with that gold-digging piece of arm candy, she thought. Tough. Serves him right.

I wonder if I should have told her what a jerk he is. Nah, she'll find out soon enough; and then she'll scratch his eyes out. It's too bad I won't be around to see it.

Still grinning, Alicia made a fast trip through Manos' shop, selecting salad greens, tomatoes, rice, cherries, and wine. She paid for everything, tucked it all into her large tote, and caught the next bus back up to the hotel. After she concocted a marinade for the fish and washed the vegetables and cherries, she placed everything in the fridge.

The clock above the stove told her it was just eleven. She walked out to the terrace, gazed at the harbor, and then sat down in a padded, wicker chair.

I love all this, she mused. It reminds me of the year I studied art in Italy. That was one of the best years of my life. Could I ever feel that free and calm again? The good news is that my hands aren't shaking all the time these days, and I'm not craving a cigarette. Maybe I could actually kick that habit.

She closed her eyes and let the soft breeze drift over her. She felt every fiber in her body slowly relax as she melted into the thick cushions. There really is life beyond yelling, screaming, and fighting she thought. And I aim to find it.

But now, I'd better get myself moving and down into town. Ruth will be wanting lunch.

Alicia was standing at the dock as the other four stepped off the ferry at 12:30. At a picturesque seaside café, they chattered about Delos and showed her their photos while they ate. "I'm glad you guys enjoyed yourselves," Alicia said. "I had an interesting morning, as well." She made a mental note to share her encounter by the jewelry store with Ruthie later.

When they finished their cappuccinos, Ruth led them on a leisurely walk along the harbor and beach area and then into crooked side streets lined with attractive boutiques and shops.

"While we were waiting for the ferry," Ruth told them, "I found a map of the town. On the back, it says that these funny streets and alleys were designed like this on purpose in the 16th century to confuse pirates. Hold it—this one looks interesting. Let's go up this way."

They turned and were winding their way up the narrow street when Ruth stopped and pointed. "This sign says 'Salon Stefanos.' This must be where Ionna gets her hair cut."

All five women peered through the plate glass window. "Must be a slow day," Beth said. "I don't see any customers in there."

Suddenly, the door opened; and a slim, fifty-something man beckoned to them. "Come in, come in, ladies, and get out of this dreadful heat." He wore a long black apron over his white polo shirt and pale blue shorts. "My name's Stefanos. Welcome to my salon."

"Oh, sorry," Ruth said as her face reddened. "We were just passing by. We didn't mean to gawk. I guess we *could* come in but only for a minute. OK, ladies?" She looked around and the other four nodded their assent.

"Perfect," Stefanos said. "Please take a seat. Oh, yes, this is my assistant, Sean. Next to me, he's the best hairdresser in all the islands. He's brilliant. He's also Irish, but we won't hold that against him." Stefanos laughed heartily. "Can I get you something to drink?"

The group perched on two flowered sofas in the waiting area. "Oh, no thanks," Alicia said. "We just finished lunch; but if you don't mind my asking, how do you come to have such a splendid British accent here on Mykonos?"

Stefanos leaned back against his workstation. "My father is Greek and my mother English. I grew up in London and went to university for a while but found it boring. I started cutting hair for friends and then got lucky and learned my trade properly at some top salons in Knightsbridge. I vacationed in Mykonos once with my parents when I was young. Then I just kept coming back. I ended up moving here eight years ago."

He looked out the window. "This place is as close to

paradise as I'll probably get in my lifetime. The only way I'll leave is by being floated off on a raft, covered by a wreath of jasmine . . . you know, that sort of thing."

He laughed again. "I'm joking about the raft, of course, but not about the paradise bit. This place is wonderful."

Beth had been biting her lip as he spoke. Finally, she said, "I'd like to ask you something, Stefanos. Oh, gosh, this is embarrassing. I'm a nurse, and I *hate* it when people ask me for medical advice at a party. Anyway, I'll pay you for your time. You're a professional, and Mrs. Sciafanos recommended you highly. I know you'll know: What should I do about this white hair?"

She held up a few strands of her hair. "I'm only 62, and I'd like to get a job. When people see my white hair, though, they start offering me wheelchairs! I'm at my wits' end about this hair thing."

Stefanos came over to Beth, fingered her hair gently, then tilted her head from side to side. While he did this, Ruth whispered to Alicia. "Come on, Al. Now's your chance to lose all that long hair. You got a new face at *Attica*, so the hair's next. You can at least *ask* him."

Alicia shrugged. "OK, *OK.*" Then she turned and said, "Excuse me, Stefanos. I know you probably have other clients this afternoon, but I'm wondering if you'd have time to cut my hair. I'm ready for a new look." She turned to Vicky. "How about you?"

Vicky laughed. "You guys are something else. Sure, I'd *love* a haircut. I hate it when mine hangs over my collar, which it's been doing for two weeks; but these men are probably booked solid."

"We might as well go for all the gusto we can," Ruth

added. "I'm so over my salt and pepper color, but I'm not sure what would be best. But, hey, we *could* come back in the morning, if you're busy now."

Stefanos looked at his partner. "Why not?" Sean said in his lilting Irish accent. "I can't think of anything more grand to do this afternoon than to look after you lovely ladies."

"I couldn't have said it better myself," Stefanos said. He then walked to the window, pulled down the blinds, and turned the sign on the door around. Closed.

"Let the games begin," he said, as he retied his apron. "Ladies, this is going to be a great adventure. We'll have you all sorted out in no time. Sean, let's get the colors mixed; and they can be processing while we do the other cuts, right? Now then, who wants to go first?

Soon, all but Najila were in the four chairs getting shampooed or having their new colors applied. She declined, shaking her head vehemently, saying she wanted to go for a little walk. The truth was that she didn't have much cash left, and she didn't know these men. American women are certainly different than women in my culture, she told herself.

She left the shop and walked a long way down the promenade until her feet started aching. She stopped for a coffee in a small seaside café, happy just to sit. She was fascinated with all the boats in the harbor.

When she looked at her watch, she realized that ninety minutes had passed. "Aiyee. I must get back. They will be done and waiting for me." She hurried back to the salon; but when she knocked softly and walked in, her eyes widened.

Beth's hair was cut much shorter; the white had

been updated with chic blonde and gold highlights. Ruth's former salt and pepper was gone, now replaced by reddish-brown tones. Vicky's hair was blunt cut; it gleamed with subtle auburn shades.

Alicia's was spectacular. Her long, blonde hair had been drastically cut and thinned; it now reached to just below her chin. When she moved her head, the hair flowed like rippling wheat. She couldn't stop smiling. "My head feels so . . . so . . . so much lighter; and, to be honest, it matches my whole mood these days."

She looked into the mirror and ran her fingers through the new cut, watching as each hair fell back into place. Then she turned. "My hair hasn't been this short since grade school. I love this, Stefanos." Impulsively, she stepped forward and gave him a big hug.

"And you, Madame?" Stefanos asked Najila. "Just a trim, perhaps? A little off the sides with some shaping in the back? Get those wispy bits under control? It will be fantastic, I promise."

Najila put a hand to her thick unruly hair. "Oh, no. I could not. What would Mama say? Or Sami? And, and . . . it will be too expensive."

"Come on, Najila," Alicia said encouragingly. "Do it. You'll love it. Never mind about your mama or Sami. You're a big girl. It's your hair. Stefanos did a great job on mine. If he can cut my horse's mane, yours will be a piece of cake. Besides, he's just going to cut your hair, not shave your head. If you don't like it, you can always let it grow back. Not to worry about the price. It will be my treat, my pleasure."

After more cajoling from the others, Najila finally gave in. "I have a small station in the back," Stefanos said to her, "that's a bit quieter. Besides, the light's better there." He had heard Najila's Middle Eastern accent and knew she would appreciate the privacy.

"Don't go away," he said to the others as he ushered Najila down a short hallway. "We'll be back in a tick. Sean, perhaps you could offer these ladies some refreshment?"

While Najila and Stefanos were gone, the women occupied themselves by taking selfies or reading Greek movie magazines. "These things are the same the world over," Vicky said. "Just page after page of glitzy glamour and steamy personal drama."

Sean brought them a selection of cold fruit juices combined with sparkling wine.

"I can't *believe* we're in a hair salon," Ruth said as she sipped her drink. "It feels like a resort. Whatever— I'm loving every minute."

Forty-five minutes later, Najila walked out, with Stefanos right behind her, tooting a fanfare on an imaginary trumpet.

The other four were speechless. Then they all started clapping.

Najila's naturally curly hair had been cut very short, thinned, and cropped close to her small, delicate face. Her hair looked fantastic, but her eyes looked uncertain.

Beth ran over and gave her a squeeze. "Oh, Najila! Your hair is wonderful. You look ten, no wait, *twenty* years younger. You look like a little pixie. Your mama will love it, and Sami won't even know you." She winked at Najila. "Maybe that's the idea, right?"

"Oh, but, I mean, you are *sure* this style is right for me?" Najila stammered as she stared in the mirror and saw how Stefanos had completely changed her look.

"You're going to be the prettiest tour guide in all of Palestine," Beth said, "maybe even all of Israel. Wait 'til Efie sees you. She'll be so proud of you."

Ruth pulled out her phone. "Stefanos, would you take a few pictures of us? I want to send them to the husband of our good friend, Norma. She . . . ah . . . she . . . couldn't make this trip." Ruth's voice caught, and she wiped her eyes.

After taking several pictures of the group for Ruth, Stefanos took some with his own phone. "Would you mind if I hang these in the salon? I want to show off your beauty and our work," he said. "You ladies all look incredible! You'll be a great advertisement for us."

"Sure" Ruth said. "I can see the sign now: *Holiday Hair and Highlights*. Nah, that's corny; but you'll come up with something."

As the women paid their bills, they all thanked Sean and Stefanos profusely. They exchanged contact information and promised to stay in touch. Then they caught the next bus and were soon back on their terrace—tired but happy.

"What a day, huh, girls?" Alicia said. "Totally serendipitous. We all did what we wanted to, ended up at Stefanos', and now look better than we have in years. We all certainly look *younger* than we did two hours ago. It's amazing what a new cut and some color can do. Listen, I've got dinner under control. We'll eat in about an hour, OK? Ruthie, everything's washed, so you can do the salad whenever. Najila and Beth, you can just kick back. Vick, you can be the waitress tonight. I think there's enough cheese and olives left to make up a plate of munchies."

Ruth grabbed Alicia's arm on the way to their kitchen. "Al, I don't know about you; but that was one of the neatest things that's happened on this whole trip. You know, it was the exact opposite of what happened to Samson. When he got his hair whacked off, he *lost* all his strength; but getting your hair cut . . . well, you look like you've *gained* strength. It's almost like you're a new woman. I'd even go so far as to say *fabulous,* but I don't want your head to blow up."

Tears glistened on Alicia's long lashes as she gave Ruth a hug. "Thanks, Ruthie. Let's hope you're right. Now I've got to get dinner started."

Beth and Najila reclined on the terrace with a glass of wine, while the other three took over. Soon the smells from the kitchen were tantalizing. Within an hour, Vicky had set the tables; and Alicia was carrying out a huge platter laden with the halibut covered with a sauce of tomatoes, onions, garlic, and aromatic spices. Ruth brought out tossed salad in a green ceramic bowl and then went back for the rice and a basket of garlic bread.

As Ruth sat down, Beth held up her hand. "I know we all use different prayers before meals; but I'd just like to say thanks to God for all the gifts He's given us, for this food and the hands that prepared it, and special thanks to you, Ruthie, for organizing this trip to this beautiful place. I don't know when I've had so much fun in such a short time. Stefanos is right; Mykonos *is* a corner of paradise."

She raised her glass. "To life, to love, and to Norma. She's the reason for this trip. Amen."

"Thanks, Beth," Ruth said, as she wiped her eyes with the corner of her napkin. "That was perfect." They all looked at her for more, but she just smiled and said, "Dig in."

They took their time but managed to polish off every bite. Ruth used her garlic bread to mop up the last traces of the tangy tomato sauce. "Al, this was terrific. You know, we're *all* great cooks. We could open a restaurant and call it Five Girls."

"And get sued for copyright infringement," Vicky said dryly as she cleared off the tables. "Sometimes, I think you guys are nuts."

As they relaxed after dinner and watched the lights twinkling in the harbor, Ruth said, "Maybe now would be a good time to read Norma's letter. I'll go get it."

"This isn't quite our last night together," she said as she returned carrying an envelope, "but almost. It's so pretty up here with all the flowers and everything; I think Norma would have loved it." She opened the envelope, drew out a folded piece of paper, and saw that the writing was very spidery and uneven.

Ruth's voice trembled slightly. "Norma probably wrote this when she was near the end. It says: 'This is a little memory of our trip to Samaria. You gave me so many gifts. Now here's one for you.'"

Inside the folded paper was a laminated card. Ruth held it up. "Look, ladies: nine rose petals are in a circle. Oh, I'll bet anything they're from that rose she showed me on the plane when we left Tel Aviv. She meant the nine petals to symbolize the nine of us on that trip; and, underneath, she printed the words . . . oh . . ."

Tears trailed down Ruth's face. "I can't," she said haltingly. "Beth, will you read it?" She passed the card to Beth.

"Sure," Beth said. "It says, 'The greatest of these

is love.' Oh, Norma . . . of course you *would* say that. Those are the last words of I Corinthians, Chapter 13. Paul wrote that when he was telling the Corinthians about their gifts and that none mattered as much as the gift of love."

"How beautiful," Vicky murmured. "That gives me goose bumps. Do you remember, back in Cincinnati, when we were on the riverboat discussing this trip, I said I thought Norma was helping us because it felt like something phenomenal was going on? Well, she did; and it is."

Najila laid her hand on Ruth's arm. "Norma was right. It *is* great love that binds us together."

"To Norma! To Norma!" they all said as they clinked their glasses.

They grew teary, as they realized how much they missed their dear friend.

Forty-one

May 16, 2014—Athens, Greece

The next morning, they all slept late, tired out by the events of the previous day. After breakfast on the terrace, they folded their clean laundry, happy to have the machines right in their kitchens. Then they completed their packing and straightened their apartments.

Alicia smiled when she saw Ruth lay 30 euros on the bed for the maid. "Yeah, I know: 'Always remember the little guy.' You're such a good kid, Ruthie. You never forget that, do you?"

When they were finished, they trooped down to the office and expressed their gratitude to Ionna, who then called a taxi for them.

"I know you could take the bus into town," she said, "but you'd still have a good walk to the pier. This way, you'll be more comfortable and won't get so warm. I am so glad you all enjoyed your stay. You ladies were wonderful guests. Please tell your friends about us, and come back to the island soon. Have a pleasant journey home."

The taxi driver let them out near the dock. "I'll get the tickets," Ruth said. "Look, this boat is even bigger than the last one. Man, I could ride one of these things every day. I wonder if they ever need any extra crew members?"

The hydrofoil left promptly at noon. Ruth hurried to the back of the boat to take pictures, as the island of Mykonos grew smaller behind them. Several of them bought sandwiches at the bar on board, but Najila declined. "My stomach is . . . a bit . . . uneven," she said. "I will wait."

As Efie promised, she and George met them at Piraeus as they docked at 3:30. She was effusive with praise for their new "dos." Everyone looked tan, rested, and relaxed.

Traffic was heavy, so the ride back to Athens took longer than their previous trip. It was almost five when they arrived at the *Amelika* Hotel.

"Shall we pick you up later and find a *taverna* for dinner?" Efie asked.

After a quick discussion among themselves, the women decided they'd prefer to eat at the *Amelika's* rooftop restaurant and then have an early night.

"Thanks for the offer," Ruth said, "but I need a little time to savor our island experience—you know, take it easy tonight and not just blast right back into the noisy city life here in Athens. It was so quiet and wonderful on Mykonos. I loved it. I think we all did."

"Me, too," Alicia agreed. "It was just what I needed."

"Fine," Efie said. "We'll do a few things around town in the morning and then have our last night at a special *taverna*, right, George?"

George nodded. As he handed Najila her suitcase, he bowed and said, "We make one last dance, Miss Najila?"

After they agreed to meet at nine the next morning, the women waved goodbye to Efie and George. Ruth glanced at the clock behind the desk as they walked into the lobby. "Ladies, it's 5:30. How 'bout if I make a reservation for 8:00? Then Alicia will have time for a nap. She does need her beauty sleep."

"Girl, I might have to kill you one of these days," Alicia shot back. "You know I'll be there before you and will have gone for an hour's walk besides. Get over yourself, OK?"

At dinner, they each ordered a different entrée; so they could sample a variety of dishes. "I want to learn to cook some of these Greek things, once I get home," Beth said. "They're all so delicious, and they're good for you—very heart friendly."

Vicky nodded. "While we're out tomorrow, I'll keep my eyes open for a cookbook. That will make a nice souvenir for us."

As they stood up to leave the table, Najila moved beside Vicky. "Do you have some minutes, Vicky? I have a few questions."

"Sure," Vicky said. "Let's go sit outside on the terrace. I see an empty table over in the corner."

After they said goodnight to the others, they walked to a table next to the railing. They could see the lights of the Acropolis shimmering in the warm night air.

When the waiter arrived, they both ordered sparkling water. "I must remember myself to take much water," Najila said. "Auntie Rania says water makes young skin. Young is important for her."

Najila came right to the point. "I need your help, Vicky. We do not have much more time together; so I want to ask you how to write and publish the story of Sapha, the woman of Samaria. You remember I have the notebook from my grandmother, the copy of the old documents from my family? I think other people might wish to meet Sapha, but I do not know what to do."

"Oh, Najila, how wonderful!" Vicky said. "I'm happy to share what I know. Probably the first thing you'll need to do is to type up everything from your grandmother's notebook. Include her notes at the beginning as well; those were fascinating and made it personal. Your readers will be able to identify.

"When you've got that finished, send it to me as a pdf; and I'll read it. I'll make comments when things aren't clear, so we'll be writing back and forth quite a bit. That's just what writers have to do. Writing the material is only a small part; the real work is in the re-writing and the editing. Don't feel bad if I make a comment or ask a question. I just want to help you make it clear for your readers, OK?"

Najila nodded, her eyes sparkling.

"Since it's so hard these days," Vicky went on, "to get picked up by a big publishing house, I'd suggest going with one of the online self-publishing companies. I'll help you select the right one when you're ready for that step."

"That sounds very wonderful," Najila said. "I would like to offer these books in my souvenir stand and maybe to the tour groups I take to the Samaritan woman sites. Her life was difficult but very inspiring, yes? Visitors might like to know more about her. Can I put pictures in the book?"

Impressed, Vicky smiled at Najila. "Wow. You've really given this a lot of thought, Najila. You're already planning marketing strategies. Yes, photos are possible and would be a great asset. Also, it would be good if you could include a few pictures of those early papyrus scrolls. I think you told us that an uncle of yours still had them?"

"Yes, Uncle Ramzi keeps the scrolls. He is most protective of those ancient documents. Perhaps if I take my brother, Hani, along, we can convince Ramzi to let us make some pictures. He can be difficult sometimes, but I will bring him some *baba ghanoush*. He likes my recipe."

Vicky gave Najila a business card. "Here's my contact information. Please email me, and send me your work as soon as we're all home. I'm excited about this and so happy for you. I know your book will be great." She rubbed her eyes and then stifled a yawn. "Oh, sorry. Excuse me. I don't mean to be rude, but I'm really tired. Maybe we should call it a night." They hugged, and Najila walked inside.

As Vicky returned her card case to her purse, her fingers touched something round and smooth. It was the green glass mirror. I should get back to my own writing, as well, she thought. Theodora had an incredibly challenging life; but, in spite of her world and the whole Roman Empire falling apart around her, she came out a winner. She was one tough lady.

That's a story worth telling.

Forty-two

May 17, 2014—Athens, Greece

At 9:00 the next morning, Efie met them at the hotel and then walked them down Apollonos and Adrianou Streets to the ancient Greek marketplace called the *agora*. As they entered the site, Efie explained that, from the 6th century BC to the 2nd century AD, the *agora* had been the heart of Athenian government and law, a place of public debate and worship, and the central marketplace for almost a thousand years.

"Amazing," Beth exclaimed. "That's a really long time. Why was that?"

"Three reasons," Efie answered. "The ground was flat, it was accessible to early Athenian farms, and the farmers and merchants could easily reach the port of Piraeus."

She moved under some trees. "Come, let's sit here in the shade." They sat on a stone wall, while Efie showed them a map with a layout of the extensive early buildings: courthouse, law courts, artisan workshops, many temples, and even a theater.

Ruth pointed to the map. "Look at all those buildings. I'll bet the *agora* was *the* place to see, and be seen, back in the day. This is the same place where Paul walked. It has to be. Now look around us: there's almost nothing left."

"What happened?" Vicky asked. "Why are most of the buildings gone now?"

"Sadly," Efie replied, "there was much destruction from outsiders over many centuries. In 267 AD, the Heruls invaded; then, in 396, the Visigoths; and, later, in the 6th century, the Slavs raided the city. This area was then deserted for 300 years and lay buried under thick mud."

"That sounds very familiar," Najila said. "It has been like that in my country as well."

"As if all that weren't enough," Efie said with a sigh, "in the early 1820s, more destruction happened during the Greek revolution. One happy result of that struggle was that excavations and restoration began in 1831 under King Otto; and, so, here we are today, seeing what Otto paid for."

Ruth stood up, stretched, and then dusted off her slacks. "Thanks, Efie. That was super. You know so much about all this history and stuff. You're the best. Listen, I know we just had breakfast an hour ago; but I'd really love a coffee. Anyone else?"

"Thank you, Ruth," Efie said, as she rose from the stone wall. "You are very kind to say that. Yes, of course we'll get coffee. I need one as well. We'll go to that small café just over there. By the way, there is a glass floor in the WC. You look down onto the ancient ruins."

Alicia sidled over next to Ruth. "Let's hope there's not some ancient guy down there, looking *up!*" she whispered.

Ruth smiled and shook her head. "You are really *disgusting* sometimes. You know that?"

"Girls, just think of it," Beth said as they found a

table. "Paul must have walked on these same streets while he was here in Athens. I'm so grateful that I got to come on this trip to see all these things."

Alicia was pensive as she sipped her coffee. "After his vision of Jesus on the Damascus road, he was so changed. For years he'd been *persecuting* Christians; now he began *recruiting* them. Oh, sure, he had his ups and downs; but he was so convinced that he was doing the right thing. I wonder what he'd think about the ripple effect of his letters: how inspiring and helpful they are and how they're often quoted by all kinds of people. There's also the flip side, though, with his words being *misquoted* and misinterpreted—even used to dominate others. It all depends on who's doing the talking."

"I am so impressed," Vicky said, "that even though most of the buildings from Paul's time are gone—no churches, cathedrals, or even congregations left here or in Corinth—because Paul took the time and wrote to people in places like Corinth, Philippi, and Rome, etc., we still *have* his writings. They're among his greatest. Buildings come and go, but writings remain."

After she ordered a *bougatsa*, her favorite cream pastry, Ruth said, "Do you suppose those ancient people understood and actually did what he wrote about? Now that I know a little more about him, I like him because he encourages people to be more like Christ. I wonder if they got that?"

Vicky laughed. "It's hard to say, but I'll tell you one thing: This trip has convinced me that I need to get back to my own writing and show people what kind of a person the last Empress of the Eastern Roman Empire was. If I don't, who will?" She took the green glass mirror from her purse and held it up for them to see.

"Good for you," Beth said, "and don't forget what Chopin's father told him: 'They *won't* remember what you played, but they *will* remember what you wrote.'"

"That is very good, Beth," Najila said. "I must remember that. Writing about the Samaritan woman will be hard, but I feel I must do it. I must also tell you how I have loved being with you ladies and how I have learned so much from you, Efie, about being a good tour guide—perhaps even a better-looking one. *Shukran.* I thank you. This journey has brought us all together. I thank Paul and Norma and all of you for that."

Ruth finished her *bougatsa* and wiped the powdered sugar off her mouth. "I've loved *everything* about this trip: the preparations, reading Paul's letters, all the new sights, the people we've met, and, of course, the foods . . . as you can see. I thought it was going to be so hard, but it was all so much fun. You all know how reluctant I was even to *think* about organizing a trip like this; and, yet, things have gone so well—beyond my wildest dreams even. I'm just sorry that Norma isn't here to enjoy it with us; but, somehow, I think she knows."

Efie looked at her watch. "Well, if you ladies aren't too tired, we have time for a little shopping in *Monastiraki*, if you like."

"I'm on it," Ruth said.

Visiting a number of elegant shops, they all selected souvenirs and gifts to take back. Vicky even found small Greek cookbooks. "Send me a report of what you've cooked, once you're home," she said as she handed each woman a copy.

An hour later, they stopped at *Savvas* for a stand-up lunch. "Our last *souvlakis*," Ruth said mournfully.

"For *this* trip," Alicia said. "My money says you'll be back some day."

Efie said she and George would pick them up at 8:00 and then left. Alicia and Vicky took the Metro to the Byzantine Museum, so Vicky could soak up the atmosphere one last time. Beth, Najila, and Ruth walked back to *Attica* to show Liana their hair.

After an excellent dinner that night at *Psaras* in the *Plaka* district, George once again led all the guests in a festive line dance. When the music changed, a few people started to dance but then sat down when George began a slow solo. Halfway through, he clapped his hands; and the musicians picked up the tempo. He stood in front of Najila, offered his hand, and led her to the floor. This time, they did an even longer, more complicated dance together as the music accelerated; and they whirled to an electrifying close.

The applause was tumultuous. Even the bearded bouzouki player clapped for them.

"*Shukran*, ah no, thank you, ah no, ah *efharisto*, George," Najila said breathlessly. "*Mumtaz*, oh sorry, I mean, excellent. That was wonderful."

As he led her back to her chair, George reached into his jacket pocket, drew out a CD of Greek music, and presented it to her.

He smiled shyly. "So you not forget to dance."

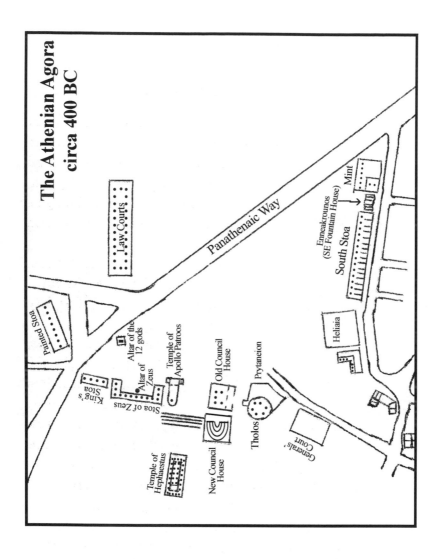

Forty-three

May 18, 2014—Athens, Greece

Their last day was a flurry of activity. They packed, had a quick lunch, and then checked out of the *Amelika*. George and Efie picked them up at 1:00 and drove them to the airport at Spata. When she got out, Ruth patted the side of George's blue and white Volkswagen bus. "Well done, good and faithful servant."

As the others were unloading their suitcases, George and Efie beckoned to Alicia. "Ah, Miss Alicia, I want . . ." George said haltingly. "Ah, you say, Efie. My English not so good."

Efie then spoke quickly and softly. "Last night, George told me about Stavros. He thought you should know that Stavros is not an ethnobotanist at all. His real name is Spiros Minos. He used to be an actor: doing bit parts in commercials, openings for trade shows, even teaching drama for a short while at the American College. He was dismissed when he became too friendly with the Dean's under-age daughter."

"Good grief," Alicia said. "How disgusting."

Efie nodded her agreement, then continued. "Stavros then began preying on foreign women tourists, ones who looked wealthy and were alone. After the encounters, the women often reported jewelry gone missing. In such a large city as Athens, it is very difficult to catch someone who is like a shadow. But, finally, George and several of his colleagues did. They were aided by Stavros' last lady, a bold young woman from New York. As he tried to remove her diamond necklace, she knocked him down, called him many bad names, tied him with her metal belt, and then sat on him while she rang the police on her cell phone. When the officers arrived, she told them she was a black belt in karate. Stavros is finished."

Alicia's face had been a sea of emotions while Efie spoke. Now she broke into a huge smile. "Wow! Good for her. You know, I saw them together in Mykonos. She was beautiful. Nobody would ever think she was that strong. Thank you so much for telling me all of this, both of you. I was feeling so vulnerable when I first met him; I am ashamed to admit I *was* attracted to him. However, there were a few things that didn't seem quite right about him. At the beginning, he seemed to know a lot about botany; but when I asked him some specific things, he changed the subject. Then, when he put his hand on my gold bracelet, I *knew* something was wrong. After hearing all of this, I'm really glad that I trusted my intuition."

She looked at her watch. "Gosh, I'd better get going and join the others. I don't want to miss my flight. Thank you both again. George, you were my guardian angel. *Efharisto.*" Alicia stepped forward and gave him a big hug.

They joined the other women and, with more hugs all around, said goodbye. As they stood at the curb, Ruth dug into her tote bag. "Efie and George, *efharisto* and a thousand thanks. This was an absolutely fantastic trip, we all loved it, and we love you. To show our sincere appreciation, we've gotten you a little gift. This is just something to remember us crazy women by."

She leaned over and whispered to Najila. "Tell your mom that we got the best price, OK?" Najila nodded while she smothered a laugh.

Efie looked very surprised. Her eyes said she was deeply touched. When she unwrapped the package, she saw a wonderful photo in a silver frame. The five of them were standing by the waterfront in Mykonos. They were all sporting new hair-dos and laughing.

"You ladies are so kind," Efie said as she wiped her eyes. "This picture is beautiful. No one ever gives me gifts at the end of their tours. I have loved every minute I have spent with all of you, eh? *Efharisto*. Thank you."

After more goodbyes, tears, and pictures, they entered the Athens airport terminal. As soon as they cleared security, they walked with Najila to her gate. More hugs and promises to keep in touch ensued. Ruth said, "OK, Najila. You have to plan a trip to the States. Wouldn't that be fun?"

As Najila got in line for her flight to Tel Aviv, the other women waved goodbye, blew kisses, and wished her a safe flight. "Be sure to email us tomorrow to let us know you made it home safely, OK?" Beth called out.

The other four flew to Frankfurt and on to Atlanta. During the flight, as they sipped a glass of wine, Alicia recounted to Ruth all that she'd learned from Efie and George at the airport.

Ruth reached over and gave her a hug. "You are one smart lady. I'm so proud of you. You saw through that jerk in time. I'm glad everything worked out for the best. Who knows? Maybe Stavros can set up a drama group while he's in prison. There'll be no more silk shirts, but won't he look super in a striped jump suit?"

They both laughed and then resumed sharing their many photos of the trip.

After they'd cleared customs in Atlanta, they all hugged one last time before they went to their separate gates. "Stay in touch, OK?" Ruth said. "Text me when you get home; and, later, send more news—you know, of how you're doing. Bye, ladies. Love you all."

Four hours later, Ruth walked in her front door. "Pete, I'm home. I caught an earlier flight and took a taxi from the airport."

Pete came out of his study with arms extended. "What? You weren't supposed to be back until tonight. But who cares? C'mere once."

He enveloped her in a huge bear hug and kissed her soundly. "Man, am I glad to see you!"

"Me, too. I've missed you, honey. It's good to be home."

+++++++++

Late that night, Ruth began to unpack. She opened all her small cosmetic bags and set the empty containers on her bathroom counter. That was so much fun, she thought. I'm thrilled that things worked out so well. Everything was beyond my wildest dreams.

Then she laughed and turned out the light.

Epilogue

Two months later—July 18, 2014—Louisville, Kentucky

The summer night was warm, but Ruth was too lazy to get up and turn on the overhead fan. She was propped up on her sofa, holding her laptop, re-reading recent emails in her Inbox.

The first was from Najila.

My Dear Friends,

Greetings from Nablus. I hope you are all well and happy.

Many things happen since I am home. A few weeks after my return, I invited Sami for tea one afternoon and told him that I was flattered by his interest but very happy in my single life, in all the projects I want to do, and that I have no desire to marry again.

His face looked upset, but I went on. I told him I understood that he needs a wife who can assist him in his work, but that would not be me.

Last week, I saw him at a birthday party. He was with the new lady friend. Fine.

The fighting in Palestine has again stopped, so tour business is better for now.

I have talked with Mama and Gran Najet and asked them

to say me what they know for the story of Sapha. Vicky, I will send my writings soon.

Thank you for invite me, Ruth. I am missing you all.

I am most happy. I do what I want to do. I wish the same for you.

My love to you,
Najila

PS Mama likes my hair. Sami said nothing.

****

Ruth closed Najila's email and opened the next one; it was from Vicky.

Hi there, ladies,

A big hello from Dallas where it's hot as Hades. Oh, how I miss those cool Mykonos breezes.

The big news is that, a few days after I arrived home, I set up a room just for myself. I moved a writing desk, my laptop, some lamps and plants, and a comfy chair in there. It's simple and quiet. Best of all, it's mine.

For a start, I've given myself a schedule of writing: three hours each morning. I still have time for the house, exercise, and social stuff. It's nothing really out of the ordinary; I just stopped putting everyone else's needs first. Now the writing takes priority. I'm halfway done with a first draft. It's rough, but it's coming.

After all, look at what Paul did with the slim resources he had. I've got it so easy.

I'm loving getting back into the research about Theodora, the Byzantine times, etc. There was so much color, action, violence, and intrigue—about like today. Ha, ha. Anyway, I'm really excited.

Thanks again, Ruth. Super job on the trip.

Much love,
Vicky

PS. I've found a guy to cut my hair like Stefanos did. He's not quite as good, but it will have to do until my next trip to Mykonos.

* * * * * * * * *

Ruth clicked on Beth's next.

Ladies,

It's taken me some time to get rested up after the trip, and I fell off a stool while I was cleaning windows in my kitchen. I put my knee out of whack a bit, but it's better now.

I have some exciting things to share. Two weeks ago, at a neighborhood coffee, I made a new friend; her name is Sally. You'll never guess what we talked about. I told her a little about myself; and, then, bless her heart, she said she's in a dead marriage and doesn't know what to do. Just like that. I couldn't believe what was happening. I knew right away I was supposed to help her.

Anyway, Sally and I have gotten together several times. She invited me to attend her church with her, and I went. Since it was Methodist, it was a bit different than what I'm used to but still very nice. Everyone was so warm and welcoming. The sermon was on First Corinthians 13. Of course I cried, remembering Norma's rose petals.

In the past month, I've had three calls about nursing jobs; and I've bought a new Ducati. The guy at the dealership looked surprised when I said it was for me. He also looked very cute! Life is good.

I miss you a lot. Thanks again for organizing the trip, Ruth.

Be well and God bless you all.

Love,
Beth

****

Ruth opened Alicia's last.

Hi, Gang,

I've got some incredible news. After our daughter, Carrie, returned home, she told Jim that she was disgusted with his behavior and that he needed to get help. He realized what he might lose, so he joined AA that day. Later, he told me that he didn't want to; and it was really hard. When he went, though, he was surprised to see so many people just like him. He's heard lots of awful stories but also some really positive things about recovery and how it works.

We've found a Christian counselor we both like. She's a really sharp woman: no holds barred and takes no prisoners. Sometimes we see her alone and sometimes together. We've got a long way to go, but it's a start.

The dynamics are changing around here now that Jim's stopped drinking, and I've stopped being the victim and the enabler. It's all new territory for us, so we're going slowly. The main thing is: we're going forward.

I've started reading Pope Francis' new book, "The Joy of the Gospel." It's amazing how often he quotes Paul's Corinthian letters. I love it that I know them now.

I've also joined a health club and swim four times a week. A month ago, I started volunteering three days a week at the Harry Leu Gardens, here in Orlando. At first, I just cleaned the paths and the perennials; but, after the manager talked with me one day, I'm now helping in the office and redoing the visitors' guides. Last week, I even made a short video presentation. It's so much fun.

Once a week, I deliver plants from the Gardens to a nearby nursing home. It's my favorite thing. Norma would get a laugh out of that.

You guys be good. Miss you.

Love to you all,
Alicia

PS. Jim liked my hair. It's the first time he's even noticed it in 20 years!

****

Ruth laughed and set her laptop on the coffee table in front of her. Suddenly, her cell phone rang. She groped among the sofa pillows and finally dug it out on the fifth ring.

"Hi, Ruthie, it's me, Carol. How was Greece? Super? Glad to hear it. Oh, Ruthie, one of my assistants called yesterday. She was supposed to run a trip for a group from Louisville. They've booked Austria in September. Now she tells me she's having foot surgery on September 15 and can't do it. Of all things! I tell you, I was pretty annoyed . . . but what are you gonna do?

"I was up all night, racking my brain, going crazy trying to think of someone I could get. At 4:30 this morning, your name came to me. Of course. Ruth would be perfect. Remember how we used to fly in and out of Vienna, and we loved it and thought it was so pretty there?

"So, would you be up for this, Ruthie? Please? *PLEASE?* I know it's short notice, but you're so organized. All the Greece plans you made were spectacular. It would really help me out. You'd get the trip, of course, and the money would be good. I'll see to that. What do you say?"

Ruth was flabbergasted. She was also thrilled. What? Somebody wants me to lead a trip . . . *professionally?*

"Geez, Carol, this is incredible. I mean, I've only been home for two months; and now you're asking me to do a trip? It sounds really fun, but I don't know. I mean . . . to plan and run a trip all on my own with a bunch of *strangers?* I don't know. I'll have to think about it and talk it over with Pete, of course. Give me a day or two, OK? I'll get back to you. Bye. Oh, and thanks."

Ruth hugged herself with excitement. I can't believe this, she thought. Carol is asking, no, she's *begging* me to do this whole trip on my own. She thinks I can do it.

But this would be so much harder. No. No way. I could *never* do this.

On the other hand, during the Greece trip, we all discovered, like Paul, that we have our own particular

Corinth: something that's *really* tough to do. I was so scared and unsure in the beginning, but look how things turned out? We got on the bus and just rolled along.

"What do You think, God? Should I do this? *Can* I do this?"

She got up, paced around the living room, and then sat down again. She wanted to pray longer, but it was late. Also, her beloved brown sofa was doing its thing again, calling her to curl up. She was really excited, but she was also tired. It had been such a busy day.

I'll lie down, she thought. Just for a minute.

As her eyelids fluttered, there it was, that same, funny little laugh: Norma's laugh.

"Go for it, Ruthie."

Historical Notes

Women were a vital and important part of Paul's work and ministry. Paul lists at least ten women in Romans 16: Phoebe, Priscilla (Prisca), Mary, Junia, Tryphaena, Tryphosa, Persis, Julia, Rufus' mother, and Nereus' sister. He mentions either the churches in their homes or the work they performed for the Roman community.

Priscilla, wife of Aquila, appears six times in the New Testament, portrayed by three different authors: Paul twice, First Corinthians 16:19 and Romans 16:3; Luke three times, Acts 18:1-3, 18-19, and 26-27; and by the author of Second Timothy 4:19.

Paul writes of Chloe only in First Corinthians 1:11 when he states: "For it has been reported to me about you, my brothers, by Chloe's people, that there are rivalries among you." Paul had left Corinth and gone to Ephesus at least four years earlier, before he received this report. The contents of the report were Paul's reason for writing First Corinthians. Therefore, Chloe would surely have been a close associate of Paul's in Corinth, possibly a leader in a house-church. Chloe had obviously maintained contact with Paul during those years after he left Corinth.

Phoebe is described in glowing terms in Romans 16:1-2 when Paul commends her to the Romans as his sister, ". . . who is also a minister of the church at Cenchreae, so that you may receive her in a manner worthy of the holy ones and help her in whatever she may need from you, for she has been a benefactor to many and to me as well."

Many scholars feel that it was Phoebe who carried this important letter of Paul's to the Judean members of the Jesus group in Rome. It is quite possible that she hosted a house-church in her home in Cenchreae. She was well known, respected, and trusted by Paul because for him to call her "sister," "a minister of the church at Cenchreae," and a "benefactor to many and to me as well" was very high praise indeed.

Paul's usual method was to arrive in a town, begin preaching at the synagogue, establish a Jesus group of believers, appoint outstanding members for leadership in the community, and then depart for his next city.

But what happened when he left? Who was in charge? Who arranged for the weekly meetings and services? Who often presided at these services? Who saw to it that a house was prepared, swept, necessary items ready for the Lord's Supper, and, often, provided food for poorer members who had come directly from their workplaces? Who looked after the widows, the orphans, the sick, and the elderly? Who spoke to the women and the children? Who managed meals and lodging for visiting missionaries? Who kept things going and continued to spread the word about Jesus to these communities and others as they traveled?

By and large, it was women like those in Romans and like Priscilla, Chloe, Phoebe, and the many others who are nameless but no less important. Without the dedication, work, love, and courage of these women, especially during times of persecution, Christianity would most likely not have survived.

May we always remember these women and honor them. These early Christian women provided a model for Christian women today, who still serve in churches the world over to feed, care for, and nurture the congregations.

Cast of Characters for
The Well Women: Crossing the Boundaries

Kay Hunter—Kay is the color-coded, on-time, super organizer of the trip to Samaria; she even packs her whiskbroom. Being a single mother and losing her son to heart disease have taken their toll, but Kay chooses to focus on the bright side.

Ruth Hanford—A comedian with Kleenex and empathy, Ruth lost her mother when she was nine. Life got very hard when her new stepmother's shrieking and her father's drinking catapulted their home into a nightmare. Ruth compensated by being perfect in every way, while struggling with cystic acne and depression. Now retired, she misses her job as a flight attendant and finds humor in every situation.

Alicia Corrigan—Trying to sublimate memories of childhood abuse by her alcoholic father, Alicia self-medicated by rocketing through high school, college, and grad school in only seven years, followed by art studies in Europe and then becoming super mom. Four months' hospital bed rest proved a turning point when she begged for God's help—and got it.

Julia Wagner—Constant prodding by female family members in her storybook hometown afflicted Julia with a painful complex about her weight. Her intelligence and wit reacted by creating a caustic complaint for every occasion, but the negative self-talk continued.

Inez Varez—Finding a Higher Power through a 12-Step program allowed Inez to move past her addictions to food and other self-destructive behaviors generated by her troubled home life. The civil war in Inez's country was a metaphor for the war in her house and her head.

Corinne Zartley—A St. Louis girl, Corinne was privileged to witness a miracle: the appearance of a perfect cross in the moon. The experience strengthened her faith and changed her life forever.

Norma Schaffer—At home in the Middle East, Norma had the perfect marriage. Then, one day, her husband declared that he wanted a divorce and shipped her back to Washington, DC. Alone in a new city, with no husband, no friends, and no job, Norma began her conversations with Jesus. Her life blossomed when she made new prayer group friends, found a new job, and, soon, found a new husband. In spite of her advanced lung cancer, Norma's laughter and kindness inspired everyone on the trip.

Beth Cassel—Beth became a nurse, wife, and mother before moving with her husband, Perry, to Rome. There they embraced the international party scene until her affair almost shattered their marriage. Christian friends supported them as they rebuilt their lives. Knee surgery prevented Beth from making the trip to Palestine, so she sent her story in the form of a letter.

Vicky Bright—Vicky's family was strewn with the wreckage of multiple marriages and divorces. Frequently abandoned by their mother, Vicky and her baby brother were home alone again and again. During a college trip to Mexico, she had an incredible encounter with evil. Married, with two grown children, Vicky is a fashionable former business executive who keeps trying to finish a novel.

Najila Danfi—Najila is a thoroughly-modern Palestinian woman who flouted local traditions most of her life. As a young widow, she taught school, lived alone, set up a souvenir stand at the Samaritan well, and then founded her own tour business. As guide for the trip, Najila shared writings from ancient parchments, possibly set down by her ancestor, Sapha, the real Samaritan woman.

Minor Characters:

Huda Danfi—Najila's mother, Rania's sister

Rania Danfi—Najila's gad-about aunt

Acknowledgements

Many hands and minds worked to put the *Bus to Corinth* on the road. Huge thanks go to Monica Chappell—chief mechanic, book designer, and publisher—and Vevonna Kennedy—creator of the cover and the mini-bus art.

I am grateful for comments and encouragement from Barbara Abendschein, Sharon Armbrust, Reverend Donald Cornell, Susan Duncan, Jeanette Evans, Margie Gibson, Vevonna Kennedy, Irene Lewandowski, Dr. John Pilch, Laurie Orth, Fr. Donald Senior, CP., Verlon Stone, Carol Tilley, and Barbara Veres.

Particular thanks go to Margie Gibson, who taught me the intricacies of em and en dashes and hyphens; to Barbara Veres, who cheerfully corrected endless stray commas and semi-colons; and to my daughter, Laurie Housholder Orth, who gifted me with story concepts and her sharp red pencil. As ever, my husband, Frank Housholder, provided great meals and his insights into what Jesus and Paul were really about.

The Greek recipes were contributed by fantastic cook Tanya Papadopoulos and enhanced by professional food editor Margie Gibson.

In an effort to bring Paul the Apostle and the important women in his ministry to life, the five vignettes portraying them were created from scriptural sources and my imagination. Any errors are solely my responsibility.

Ladine Housholder
July 2016

For Further Reading

Blair, Edward P. *The Illustrated Bible Handbook.* Nashville: Abingdon Press. 1975, 1987.

Bowe, Barbara Ellen, RSCJ. *A Church in Crisis— Ecclesiology and Paraenesis in Clement of Rome.* Minneapolis: Fortress Press. 1988.

Bristow, John Temple. *What Paul Really Said About Women.* San Francisco: Harper & Row. 1988.

Brown, Raymond E., Fitzmeyer, Joseph A., & Murphy, Roland, E. *The New Jerome Biblical Commentary: Student Edition.* Englewood Cliffs, New Jersey: Prentice Hall. 1968, 1990.

Caldwell, Taylor. *Great Lion of God.* Glasgow: William Collins & Sons, Co. Ltd. 1970.

Corley, Kathleen E. *Private Women, Public Meals— Social Conflict in the Synoptic Tradition.* Peabody, Massachusetts: Hendrickson Publishers. 1993.

Furnish, Victor Paul. *The Moral Teaching of Paul— Selected Issues, 3rd Edition.* Nashville, Tennessee: Abingdon Press. 2005.

Getty, Mary Ann, RSM. *First and Second Corinthians— Collegeville Bible Commentary.* Collegeville, Minnesota: The Liturgical Press. 1983.

Gillman, Florence M. *Women Who Knew Paul.* Collegeville, Minnesota: The Liturgical Press. 1992.

Johnson, Luke T. *The Writings of the New Testament: An Interpretation*. London: SCM Press. 1986.

Keller, Marie Noël, RSM. *Priscilla and Aquila: Paul's Coworkers in Christ Jesus*. Collegeville, Minnesota: Liturgical Press. 2010.

Malina, Bruce J. and Pilch, John J. *Social-Science Commentary on the Letters of Paul*. Minneapolis: Fortress Press. 2006.

Mavromataki, Maria. *Paul The Apostle of the Gentiles: Journeys in Greece*. Athens, Greece: Editions Haitalis. 2003.

Meeks, Wayne A. *The First Urban Christians: The Social World of the Apostle Paul*. New Haven and London: Yale University Press. 1983.

Meinardus, Otto F. A. *St. Paul in Greece*. Athens, Greece: Lycabettus Press. 1972.

Morton, H. V. *In the Steps of St. Paul*. Cambridge, Massachusetts: Da Capo Press. 1964.

Murphy-O'Connor, Jerome. *Paul: His Story*. Oxford, England: Oxford University Press. 2004.

Newsom, Carol A. and Ringe, Sharon H., Ed. *Women's Bible Commentary, Expanded Edition*. Louisville, Kentucky: Westminster John Knox Press. 1992, 1998.

Puskas, Charles B., Jr. *The Letters of Paul: An Introduction*. Collegeville, Minnesota: The Liturgical Press. 1993.

Themelis, Petros G. *Ancient Corinth—The Site and the Museum*. Athens, Greece: Editions Hannibal. 1998.

Thurston, Bonnie. *Women in the New Testament: Questions and Commentary*. New York: The Crossroad Publishing Company. 1998.

Wilson, A. N. *Paul—The Mind of the Apostle*. New York & London: W. W. Norton & Company. 1997.

Further Useful Information

Agnandi Hotel
P.O. Box 417, Mykonos 846 00, Greece
+30 2289 023242
www.agnandi.gr/index.php/agnandi-location

Benaki Museum
Koumpari 1, Athens, Greece
+30 21 0367 1000
www.benaki.gr/index.asp?lang=en

Byzantine Museum
Sofias Ave., 106 75 Athens
www.byzantinemuseum.gr/en/

National Archeological Museum, Athens
28is Oktovriou 44, Athens 106 82, Greece
+30 21 3214 4890
www.namuseum.gr/wellcome-en

Aliki Pelteki
Greek tour guide
alikipelteki981@hotmail.com

Bus to Corinth Study Guide

Lesson One—Introduction and Background

1. **Read the Acts of the Apostles 6:1-9:31 and 11:25-19:41.** Who are some of the leading personalities in this section? What action is taking place? What picture do you get of Paul?

2. **Skim First Corinthians 1-16.** Jot down your general impressions, and make a short synopsis. Make a note of any passage or any concept that really jumps out at you. What was Paul trying to say? What does Paul tell us about himself? Has your picture of Paul from Acts changed?

3. Who were the people in his Corinthian community? From what backgrounds did they come?

4. From Paul's words, what are some of the issues he raised with the Corinthians? What is relevant for us today?

5. **Read *Bus to Corinth*: Prologue to Chapter 6.** Have you ever shared an exciting adventure or a dangerous situation with someone and promised to stay in touch afterwards but never did? Or did you perhaps mean to write and say thanks for something special but never quite got around to it? What were the consequences?

6. After she received the news of Norma's passing, Ruth experienced another long-buried feeling. What was this all about? How are the two events connected?

7. In Chapters Two and Three, what clues suggest that Ruth is working outside of her comfort zone? How

does she do?

8. In what ways were Norma's funeral and the luncheon afterwards a celebration of Norma's life? Who were some of the people she had influenced during her life?

9. Describe the group of women who sat with Ruth at the funeral luncheon and at dinner that night. Who were they? How had they known Norma?

10. Given the circumstances, do you think that discussing tentative plans for a trip to Greece in Norma's honor was appropriate? Why is Ruth so adamant about not leading such a trip?

11. What were some of Alicia's problems?

12. In what ways does Ruth help Alicia later that evening? What steps did Alicia take to help herself?

Lesson Two—Making Plans

1. **Skim Second Corinthians 1-13.** As in Lesson One, jot down your general impressions; and make a brief synopsis. Does any passage or any concept speak to you? What was Paul saying? What more does Paul tell us about himself? How has your earlier picture of him changed?

2. Were there any new issues?

3. Some scholars have thought that this letter is a composite of fragments of several of Paul's letters, written at different times. Others have felt that Paul wrote just one letter, but the abrupt changes in tone

and subjects are due to his fluctuating emotional state. Why would this second choice be possible? What had happened to the Corinthian community, and why was Paul so upset?

4. **Read *Bus to Corinth*: Chapters 7-12.** After her talk with Alicia, Ruth also had difficulty getting to sleep. What was she worried about? Who "appears" to her? How did Ruth seek help?

5. What roles will Vicky and Beth play during the trip to Greece?

6. During a riverboat excursion the next day, Alicia gives Ruth several gifts. What are they, and what is their significance—especially for Alicia?

7. Chapter Nine opens with Ruth sending tentative ideas for the Greece trip to Alicia, Beth, Najila, and Vicky. Were you impressed with Ruth's plans for the trip? What has inspired her? Does she take her job seriously?

8. What is the meaning of the laminated card Ruth finds in her Bible as she begins to read the Corinthian letters?

9. Who is Najila Danfi? Why does she wish to join the other four women on the Greece trip? What problems does she have? Have you ever been faced with similar choices? How did it work out?

10. Why does Ruth read First and Second Corinthians at this point? What are her thoughts? What does she mean by "a new calling?"

11. What is *your* calling? Has your calling changed

throughout your life?

12. What do you learn about Alicia, Vicky, and Beth from their emails in Chapter Twelve?

Lesson Three—Arrival in Athens

1. **Read *Bus to Corinth*: Chapters 13-17.** When the women meet the first time in the Atlanta airport, what gift does Vicky give them? Was this helpful?

2. Why was the loss of Alicia's suitcase particularly upsetting for her? Have you ever had a similar occurrence? What was your reaction?

3. In what ways do Ruth's own travel experiences prove helpful at this time?

4. As the group is boarding the airport bus into Athens, Ruth promises Alicia that "This is gonna turn out to be a fine day." Describe the ways that this prophecy comes true. Has anything unexpected like this ever happened to you?

5. When Najila arrives from Tel Aviv, she fills them in on her life. What has been going on with her during the past two years? What are some of her concerns today?

6. What accounts for Ruth's mood at the close of their first day?

7. Why is Ruth so surprised when she first meets Efie Pappas, their Greek guide? Will Efie be a good model for Najila?

8. **Read Acts 17 again.** What was so special about the Areopagus? What was the focus of Paul's speech to the Athenians there? Why did this become a starting point for Paul's journey to Corinth?

9. Have you, like Ruth, ever wondered if you've turned people off by the ways you've shared your faith?

10. Why was Najila's list-making about the pros and cons of marrying Dr. Sami a good idea? What was she able to discern? Were her answers conclusive?

11. What was the main topic of conversation at dinner that night? Can you share similar instances about the difficulties for women over 50 getting a job?

12. Why was Ruth so excited at the end of Chapter 17?

Lesson Four—Big Changes

1. Read *Bus to Corinth*: **Chapters 18-23.** What were your impressions in this scene with Paulos, Timothy, and Sylvanus?

2. What insights do you get from Alicia's conversation with God at the end of Chapter 19?

3. How is Alicia influenced by her visit to the National Archaeological Museum?

4. What is especially moving for Alicia in the Benaki Museum? Why? Have you ever been greatly affected by a work of art or a piece of music?

5. Why is Vicky so excited about her visit to the Byzantine Museum? What does this mean for her?

6. How does the purchase of a small book on flowers evolve into something much more for Alicia? What does she share with Ruth at dinner that night? What is Ruth's reaction?

7. What do we learn about George and Najila after dinner?

8. What does Alicia's reply to Jim's text about the defective appliances signify for her?

9. At the laundromat, when Najila asks Beth's opinion about whether she should marry Sami, how does Beth respond? Besides the emotional upheaval after Beth's divorce, what was even more hurtful to her? What steps is she now taking?

10. Describe some of the ways that Efie chose to update herself in order to be a successful tour guide.

11. **Read First Corinthians 1-6 again.** After Vicky's informal study on these chapters, how would you answer these questions:

    A. What does the "Power of God" mean to me?

    B. Do I live as though my body is a temple of the Holy Spirit?

    C. What am I being called to do?

12. Later in the afternoon, when the group is at Sounion, watching the sunset, they contemplate their own particular calling. Summarize each woman's thoughts.

13. Has your direction or calling in life changed in the past ten years? Are there things that you need to get

rid of to lighten your load and help you through the storms in your life? What two things will you do *today* to start this process?

Lesson Five—Bus to Corinth

1. Read *Bus to Corinth*: **Chapters 24-29.** During the drive from Athens to Corinth, Efie relates background information about the Corinth of Paul's day. What items were new or impressive to you?

2. What did you learn about Paul from Vicky's introduction?

3. After Efie's tour at the archaeological site of ancient Corinth, which areas attracted the women?

4. In Chapter 25, what was your impression of Priscilla? What was her role in Paul's ministry?

5. Why did Paul have to leave Corinth?

6. **Read First Corinthians 7-16 again.** During an after-dinner swim at the Apart One Hotel pool, Beth gave her reflections on the second part of First Corinthians. What does she reveal? How does she tie her situation to that of Paul's?

7. Have you ever been critical of church leadership? What was the outcome?

8. When is it time to move on from a toxic or a dead relationship? How long must one stay?

9. Are you accepting of people from different cultures and backgrounds, people who look and think

differently than you do?

10. Are you open to new discoveries and new teachings, especially about religious matters?

11. Who was Chloe, what was Paul's mood when he first arrived at Chloe's home, and what service did she provide for the Jesus group members in Corinth?

12. Summarize the recent developments between Stavros and Alicia. Why do you think Alicia is so interested in Stavros? What has Najila learned?

13. What causes Ruth great concern? In a similar situation, what would *your* reaction be? When does helping become meddling?

Lesson Six—Being a Temple

1. Read *Bus to Corinth*: **Chapters 30-34.** Why is the news about her daughter's running away doubly devastating for Alicia? Who does she blame? What do you learn from her initial response? What do you learn about her husband, Jim?

2. In what ways does Ruth help her? Have you ever tried to help a friend mired in an abusive situation? What was the result?

3. As Paul sat in Aquila's workshop, what troubles was he facing in Corinth? What decisions did he come to?

4. The next morning, what lies behind Alicia's guarded reaction to the happy news in the second text from Jim?

5. Why is the cruise on the Corinth Canal boat a perfect excursion for the group at this point? How does each woman reflect about what she's learned?

6. Why did Alicia explain to her friends what had happened in her relationship with Jim and her recent experience with Stavros?

7. **Read Second Corinthians 1-6 again.** Later that day, Ruth leads the group in a study of these chapters. Describe her insights and applications.

8. How do you encourage the people around you?

9. Do you make Jesus' life a pattern for your life?

10. In what ways are you a temple of God—you personally and your house? Is your temple clean, in good shape, with doors open, welcome mat out, and a light in the window? Is it the friendliest place in town, a place where people feel wanted?

11. Using these guidelines, can you say that your church is a "Temple of the Living God"?

12. Who was Phoebe, and what part did she play in Cenchreae and in Paul's ministry? How had her earlier life prepared her for this work? Do you know anyone like Phoebe?

Lesson Seven—Decisions in Delphi

1. Read *Bus to Corinth*: **Chapters 35–38.** List the reasons that Ruth chose to have the group visit Delphi. What accounts for her happiness as she was getting settled in her hotel room?

2.   What was the original purpose of the shrine of Delphi? What were most people searching for?

3.   Why is Beth so upset about being there? How did Vicky handle Beth's fears?

4.   What was the topic of the conversation between Najila and Alicia after dinner on the hotel terrace the first night in Delphi? What effect did it have on Alicia?

5.   In the Delphi Museum, what was so special about the statue of the Charioteer? What is its message?

6.   What did Vicky experience as she sat in the stadium above Delphi? Why is forgiveness often so difficult?

7.   Do you agree with Ruth's comparison of people in the time of worship of Apollo and those of today? What is often the focus of people's worship—at any time?

8.   **Read Second Corinthians 7-13 again.** In a leafy grotto near the hotel, Alicia led the discussion on these chapters. What were some of the reflections of the group?

9.   Are you like those early Corinthians in any way?

10. What does your checkbook or credit card statement say about how generous you are to those in need?

11. Is it easy to be steadfast in following your faith?

12. Later that evening, how did Najila summarize the real meaning of their time together in Delphi?

Lesson Eight—Mykonos Magic

1.   Read *Bus to Corinth*: **Chapters 39-40.** What was the main reason the group traveled to Mykonos? Was this important? Do you think that Paul ever needed breaks from his work?

2.   During the boat ride to Mykonos, Beth and Ruth question Najila about the difficulties of women seeking employment in Palestine. What is Najila's recipe for success?

3.   How were the living arrangements and dining plans made for the first evening? How did each woman take part?

4.   On their after-dinner walk, what was relevant concerning Ruth's initial dream about Mykonos?

5.   The next morning, Vicky suggests a tour to the nearby island of Delos. Why was this small island so important in ancient times?

6.   Why does Alicia beg off the Delos trip? What does she choose to do instead? What decisions does she come to during the morning by herself?

7.   On Alicia's shopping trip, how does she get more than she bargained for?

8.   In what ways did the discovery of Stephanos' Salon develop into such an uplifting experience? What happened to each woman?

9.   Why was Najila so reluctant at first?

10. That night, after dinner on their apartment terrace, Ruth opened the envelope that Jerry had sent

her. What did it contain? Why was this last gift from Norma so poignant?

11.   Have you ever received a similar gift or letter?

Lesson Nine—The Last Dance

1.   Read *Bus to Corinth*: **Chapters 41-42**. As Ruth is packing and preparing to leave her apartment at the Hotel Agnandi, what kindness does she do? What is her rationale?

2.   What made the group decline Efie's invitation for dinner at a taverna when they returned to Athens from Mykonos? What would you have chosen?

3.   Later that evening, Najila sought out Vicky for advice. How did Vicky help her? What did Vicky receive in return?

4.   The last full day in Athens proved to be very busy for the group. Their first stop was at the ancient Greek marketplace, the *agora*. What was this place, and why had it been so important? What did they actually see?

5.   During their stop for coffee at a nearby café, what reflections do the women share?

6.   How have they been inspired?

7.   What does each plan to do when she returns home?

8.   How does each woman spend the last afternoon?

9.   At the close of the evening, why is George's gift

to Najila so meaningful?

10.   In what ways might this provide encouragement to her?

Lesson Ten—Conclusion

1.   Read *Bus to Corinth:* **Chapter 43 to the Epilogue.** What did Alicia learn from Efie and George as they were saying goodbye at the airport?

2.   What is special about the group's gift to Efie?

3.   What are Ruth's feelings about being home again? Does she have any future travel plans?

4.   In the Epilogue, what reports do Najila and Vicky give? List several important things about their decisions.

5.   What has happened in Beth's life since she's returned home? Were there any surprises?

6.   What changes are occurring in Alicia's life? What things impressed you about her email?

7.   Why was the call from Carol such a shock for Ruth? What did Carol need, and what was Ruth's response? Who was there to help her?

8.   During his day, Paul used his method of communication: a stylus on parchment. Today, we use emails and other media. We type on tiny keyboards and send things electronically through the ether. Which will have the most effect? Which will last longer?

9.   Because of Norma's funeral, the women in *Bus to Corinth* got together again after a two-year

separation. Why is a funeral often a wake-up call for those remaining?

10. Many changes had taken place in the women's lives during those two years. What have *you* been doing the last two years of your life: personally, professionally, in your community, and in your church?

11. What would you *most* like to do in your life?

12. What steps are you taking to achieve this goal?

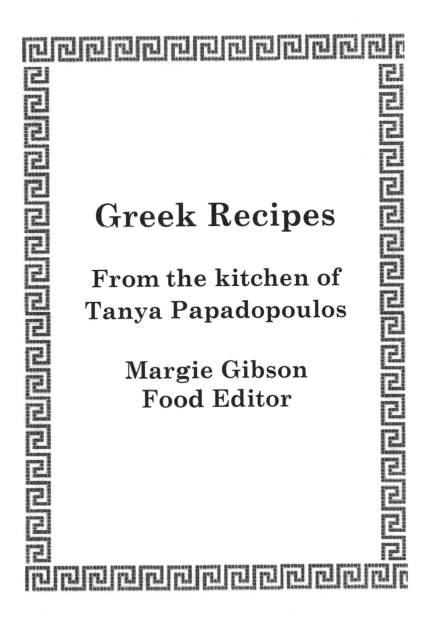

Greek Recipes

From the kitchen of
Tanya Papadopoulos

Margie Gibson
Food Editor

MEZE

Greek cuisine offers a wide range of *meze*, Greece's version of the "small dishes" that have become as popular as Spain's tapas. It is not difficult to make a meal out of *meze*, but they can also be served as a precursor to a full dinner—with glasses of Greek wine, of course.

TZATZIKI
(Yogurt Cucumber Dip)

The combination of cucumber and yogurt makes a refreshing sauce for summer meals. Don't be afraid to make a large amount; this sauce is even better the second day.

1 Tbsp. minced garlic
1 tsp. olive oil
2 c. Greek yogurt (about 20 oz.)
1 tsp. dry mint (optional)
2 medium cucumbers (peeled, grated, and drained)
Salt and pepper to taste
1 Tbsp. white vinegar

Mash garlic with olive oil. Combine with yogurt. Add remaining ingredients, and combine gently. Chill before serving with crackers or vegetables. This can also accompany roasted lamb or ground meats.

SAGANAKI CHEESE

Saganaki is a diminutive form of the Greek word for a frying pan, *sagani*. Thus, dishes that are labeled *saganaki* refer to the type of cooking pan, not the food itself.

Serves 6-8

1 lb. cheese, such as kasseri, feta, or kefalotiri
6-8 Tbsp. butter
3 Tbsp. lemon juice
2 Tbsp. brandy (optional)

Slice cheese into 1-inch-thick slices. Melt butter, and fry cheese in a small frying pan over medium heat for 2-3 minutes on each side or until melted and lightly brown. Sprinkle with lemon juice. The brandy may be poured over the cheese and ignited, if desired. Serve immediately with crusty bread.

KEFTEDAKIA
(Cocktail Meatballs)
Although this recipe calls for ground beef, ground lamb or a combination of beef and pork can be used.

Serves 6-8

1 lb. ground round
½ c. grated onion
1 Tbsp. minced garlic
salt and pepper to taste
½-1 tsp. dried oregano
¼ tsp. dried mint
½ c. plain bread crumbs
½ c. white wine or water
1 egg (beaten)

Mix meat, onion, garlic, salt, pepper, oregano, and mint. Moisten bread crumbs with the wine or water. Add to meat mixture along with the egg. Mix well. If mixture is too dry, slowly add more water or wine. Refrigerate for at least an hour.

Preheat oven to 350 degrees F.

Shape the meat mixture into 1-inch balls.

Place on a greased, shallow baking pan; and bake. Check the meatballs after 15 minutes, and turn them over. Continue baking until the meatballs are browned: about 15 additional minutes.

AVGOLEMONO SOUP
(Chicken Soup with Egg-Lemon Sauce)

Even if you've never eaten this Greek classic, the tart, silky combination of chicken broth, eggs, and lemon juice screams "comfort food." In the depth of winter, this soup soothes sniffles and worse. In summer, a chilled version perks up taste buds and, as a sauce, adds flavor and a welcome acidic note to grilled meats.

Serves 6-8

Chicken Soup:
one 3-3½ lb. roasting chicken
3 qts. water
1 small carrot
1 stalk celery
1   onion
salt and pepper to taste
1 c. raw rice or orzo

Avgolemono Sauce:
2-3 eggs
2-4 Tbsp. fresh lemon juice

Prepare the Broth:
Clean chicken, rinse well, and place in a heavy soup pot with water. Add carrot, celery, and onion. Bring to a boil, cover, and simmer about 2 hours or until chicken is tender. Add salt during the last hour of cooking.

Remove chicken and vegetables, strain broth, and remove as much fat as possible. (Or chill until the fat turns solid, and remove the fat before reheating.)

Add the eggs and lemon. Bring the chicken broth back to a simmer, and add the rice or orzo.

Simmer, covered, until rice or orzo is tender, about 10-20 minutes. Then reduce heat to maintain the broth just below a simmer.

In a large bowl, beat eggs until frothy. Gradually beat in lemon juice. Beating constantly, slowly add two cups of the hot, strained broth to the egg sauce. Do not add the hot broth too quickly because this will curdle the eggs. Slowly pour this mixture back into the pot of remaining broth. Heat, *but do not boil*, stirring vigorously until thickened. To serve, ladle soup into bowls; and add slices of cooked chicken.

Note: A 46-oz. can of chicken broth can be used. Bring to a boil, and add rice or orzo. Simmer about 10-20 minutes, and follow above directions for *avgolemono* sauce.

BOUGATSA
(Custard Phyllo Pastry)

Bougatsa is a filled phyllo pastry that can be filled with a sweet custard or savory cheese. This recipe for a custard *bougatsa* is served as a breakfast pastry or at midmorning (or mid-afternoon) with a cup of strong coffee.

Phyllo dough can be found in a large grocery store (in the freezer section) or in shops that specialize in Turkish, Middle Eastern, North African, or Greek foods.

When working with phyllo, don't open the package until you are ready to begin layering the sheets. Unroll the phyllo dough, and place the stack on the counter. Cover the phyllo with a sheet of wax paper and damp dish towel, and remove one sheet at a time to your baking pan. Cover the stack with the paper and towel before you brush the melted butter onto the sheet you have laid in the pan. If you break the sheet as you lay it into the pan, simply fit it together and continue the layering.

Serves 12-16 (in 3 x 4-inch pieces)

Custard Filling:
2 c. milk
¾ c. sugar
¾ c. farina
12 eggs, beaten

Pastry:
1 lb. phyllo
½ - ¾ lb. unsalted butter, melted
Confectioners' sugar

Prepare Custard:
Preheat oven to 350 degrees F.

In a heavy, 4-quart saucepan, combine milk and sugar; and bring it almost to a boil. While stirring constantly, slowly sprinkle the farina over the hot milk and sugar. Cook over moderate heat, stirring until thickened. Remove from heat. Set aside for five minutes, while whisking occasionally, before adding eggs.

Very slowly add a small portion of the eggs as you whisk or beat the milk mixture vigorously until smooth. Continue until all the eggs have been added.

Layer the Phyllo and Custard:
Brush the bottom and sides of a 12 x 16-inch pan with butter.

Lay a sheet of phyllo into the pan, and use a pastry brush to coat it lightly with melted butter. Continue until you have used half of the sheets. Pour the custard over the phyllo, and smooth the custard out with a spatula.

Continue layering the remaining phyllo sheets over the custard, brushing each sheet with butter and tucking the phyllo ends in for a neat finish. Score the top few phyllo sheets into serving-sized pieces.

Bake for about 40 minutes or until crisp and golden. Remove from oven and cool at least 30 minutes before cutting. Can be served warm or cold. Just before serving, sift confectioners' sugar on top.

Note: When preparing phyllo, the bottom leaves are usually layered to overhang the pan. After filling is added, the overhanging sheets are then folded in; and the top sheets are added.

SPANAKOPITA
(Spinach-Cheese Pie)

Spanakopita may be the quintessential Greek food. In the U.S., it is certainly one that enjoys great popularity. Dinners, Greek festivals, and almost any Greek restaurant feature this item on the menu.

Although in the U.S. *spanakopita* is usually made with spinach, this is not the only choice. This is a recipe where *horta*—weeds—comes into the spotlight. Walking through a Greek market, it is impossible to miss big bundles of leafy greens piled up on the stands, along with tomatoes, eggplant, and huge rounds of cheeses. The best *horta*, though, is wild and is foraged from the hillsides just before it is cooked. Older Greek women are experts at finding wild dandelion, fennel, nettles . . . a seemingly endless variety of free food, just waiting to be gathered, simply cooked, and brought fresh to the table. In the following recipe, feel free to substitute your own pesticide-free weeds for the spinach.

If you have not worked with phyllo dough, see the suggestions in the head notes for *bougatsa*.

Serves 12

1 lb. spinach leaves
1 large onion, chopped
2 Tbsp. unsalted butter
1 c. cottage cheese
4 oz. cream cheese
2 c. finely crumbled feta cheese
4 eggs, beaten
Salt and pepper to taste (the amount of additional salt depends upon the salt content of the feta)
½ c. dill, finely chopped
1 lb. phyllo pastry sheets
½ - ¾ lb. unsalted butter, melted

Wash spinach thoroughly—be sure that no sand clings to the leaves or stems. Dry as thoroughly as possible. A salad spinner works well for this.

Sauté onion in 2 tablespoons butter until soft. Add spinach, and sauté a few more minutes. Cool. With your hands, squeeze as much juice out as possible; and chop coarsely. (Save the juice for a stock.)

In a large bowl, mix cottage cheese, cream cheese, feta, eggs, dill, salt, and pepper. Gently incorporate spinach into cheese mixture.

Preheat oven to 350 degrees F.

Butter the bottom of a 9 x 13-inch pan. Layer a total of 12 sheets of phyllo into the pan, brushing each one with melted butter before placing the next sheet on top. Spread the spinach-cheese mixture evenly on top of the phyllo. Add 12 more phyllo sheets, brushing each with melted butter before adding the next. Tuck in the sides of the phyllo to give the pie a neat appearance.

With a sharp knife, score the top phyllo sheets into desired squares.
Bake for 45-60 minutes or until golden. Let cool slightly before cutting.

TIROPITA
(Cheese Pie)
Tiropita and *spanokopita* can be made as appetizers (*meze*) or as a main course. As appetizers, they are usually folded into small triangles and work well as finger food.

If you have not worked with phyllo dough, see the suggestions in the head notes for *bougatsa*.

Serves 12

1 lb. feta cheese
6 oz. cottage cheese
6 oz. cream cheese
4 eggs
½ c. chopped parsley or dill
½ lb. unsalted butter, melted
1 lb. phyllo sheets

Cheese Filling:
Preheat oven to 350 degrees F.

Using your fingers, crumble feta into small pieces into a mixing bowl. Add cottage cheese and cream cheese, and mix well without using mixer (hands work best!). Add eggs and parsley or dill, and mix thoroughly.

Assemble the *Tiropita*:

Melt butter over medium heat. Brush the bottom of a 9 x 13-inch pan with melted butter. Lay down a sheet of phyllo and brush it with melted butter. Continue until you have placed about 12 phyllo sheets in the pan. Add cheese mixture; and then continue to layer the remaining phyllo sheets on top of the filling, brushing each one with melted butter. Tuck in the ends of the pastry. With a sharp knife, score phyllo into serving-sized squares; and bake for 45-60 minutes or until golden. Before serving, cut through already-scored squares.

FISH PLAKI

Plaki refers to a style of cooking that uses olive oil, onions, tomatoes and parsley. Variations abound and may include potatoes and additional spices.

Plaki adds flavor to mild fish. Use a white fish, such as halibut, cod, or haddock fillets, about ½ - ¾-inch thick.

Serves 4-5

2 lbs. fish
salt and pepper
oregano

Plaki Sauce:

¼ c. olive oil
3 fresh tomatoes, chopped

2 onions, chopped
3 scallions, chopped
2 cloves garlic, finely minced
1 c. parsley, chopped
bread crumbs
butter
1 c. water

Preheat oven to 350 degrees F.

Place fish in greased baking pan; and season with salt, pepper, oregano, and several splashes of the olive oil.

In a heavy frying pan, add the remaining olive oil; and sauté the onions, scallions, and garlic until the onions are translucent. Add the tomatoes and chopped parsley. Cook for about 10 minutes until the sauce begins to thicken just a bit.

Pour the sauce over the fish, and smooth with a spoon to even it out, if necessary.

Sprinkle bread crumbs over top. Dot with butter, and add water.
Bake for 45 minutes.

PASTICHIO

Pastichio is a dish with a history. Its name comes from an Italian word, *pasticcio*, which means "pie." Before the early 1900s, various forms of *pastichio* were eaten in Greece. Then, a Greek chef who trained in France, Nikolaos Tselementes, introduced what has become a standard version of the casserole. In an effort to break away from the cooking traditions of the Ottoman Empire, he adapted traditional recipes to include French influences, in particular, the béchamel sauce. He published what became Greece's most popular cookbook, *Greek Cookery,* in 1910 and encouraged Greek cooks to incorporate new European influences into their traditional recipes.

This recipe is excellent for large, family dinners. It can be prepared ahead of time and baked a day later.

Serves 10-12

Bechamel Sauce:
¼ lb. unsalted butter
¾ c. flour
5 c. hot milk
2 tsp. salt
3 eggs, lightly beaten

Meat Sauce:
2 onions, chopped
4 Tbsp. unsalted butter
2 lbs. ground meat
Dash of cinnamon
½ c. water
2 Tbsp. tomato paste
salt and pepper to taste

Pasta:
1 lb. ziti, penne, or other tubular pasta
1 Tbsp. olive oil
Grated Parmigiano cheese
Bread crumbs

Make the Cream Sauce:

Melt butter in a saucepan over medium heat. Add flour; and cook, stirring until mixture is golden. Remove pan from heat, and gradually stir in half of the hot milk. Stir constantly as the milk is added. Then return pan to medium heat, and add the rest of the milk. Cook and stir until sauce begins to bubble and is smooth and thickened. Add salt. Set aside; and, when lukewarm, stir in eggs.

Make the Meat Sauce and Assemble:

Preheat oven to 350 degrees F.

Sauté onions in butter until golden. Add meat; and cook, gradually breaking the meat apart, until meat browns. Add cinnamon, salt, and pepper. Dilute the tomato paste in ½ cup water, and add to the meat. Cook for 5 minutes.

Cook pasta according to directions on package. Drain and mix in olive oil to prevent pasta from sticking together.

Sprinkle bread crumbs on the bottom of a 9 x 13-inch buttered pan, and add half of the cooked pasta. Sprinkle generously with grated Parmigiano. Add meat mixture, and sprinkle with more cheese. Add remaining pasta, and sprinkle with Parmigiano. Stir cream sauce (be sure you have added the eggs), and pour over casserole so that the pasta is covered. Top with grated cheese and a little cinnamon.

Bake for 45 minutes to one hour until nicely browned, bubbling, and set.

STIFADO
(Beef and Onion Stew)

The Venetians, who arrived in Greece in the 13th century, around the time of the fall of Constantinople and the Ottoman invasion, introduced an early version of *stifado* to Greece. Cinnamon and other spices are often used in this stew, a reminder of the connections between Greece and the Middle East—and the Venetian spice traders. The Venetian version would not have contained tomatoes, which didn't appear in Europe until after Columbus returned from the New World.

The stew may be made with other meats. Veal and rabbit often replace beef. Choose a cut of beef that is well marbled with fat, such as a chuck. The meat will cook into tender morsels, and excess fat can easily be removed. Serve with orzo, another type of pasta, or rice.

Serves 6-8, plus leftovers

2-3 lbs. beef
4 Tbsp. unsalted butter or olive oil
2-3 cloves garlic, minced
3 oz. tomato paste (half of a 6-oz. can)
1 bay leaf
1½ tsp. wine vinegar
salt and pepper
water (heated)
2 lbs. pearl onions
feta cheese

Prepare stew:
Cut beef into 1-inch cubes. Melt butter (or warm the olive

oil) in a heavy pan, and brown the beef lightly. Remove beef from pan, and add more oil if the pan is dry.

Add garlic, stir, and sauté until fragrant. Be careful not to use high heat; the garlic should not brown. Add the tomato paste, stir again, then allow it to cook briefly. Add the bay leaf, wine vinegar, salt, pepper, and enough water to cover.

Bring to a boil, and then reduce heat to a simmer. Cook until the meat is tender, about 1-1½ hours. Remove from heat, and take the meat out of the sauce.

Prepare onions:
In a large pan, bring water to a boil. Drop onions, a cup at a time, into the water. As soon as the skins are loosened, use a slotted spoon to remove the onions. Repeat with the remaining onions. Run the onions under cold water to cool; and, using your hands, slip the skins off. Trim the root end if necessary, but don't cut it off entirely. This prevents the onion from falling apart.

Finish stew:
Add the skinned onions to the pot of sauce. Bring sauce to a boil, then reduce heat to a simmer; and cook for 20-25 minutes. When the onions are tender, return the beef to the pan; and simmer an additional 15-20 minutes, until the sauce thickens. During the last 10 minutes of cooking, add cubes of feta.

KARIDOPITA
(Nut Cake with Syrup)
Karidopita, a cinnamon-scented walnut cake, is perfect for autumn and winter when the scarcity of fresh fruit

limits dessert options. The syrup, poured over after baking, assures a moist texture. A word of caution, though: Be careful when bringing the syrup to its initial boil. It can easily boil over and require a tedious clean-up! This cake is even better made the day before serving.

Serves 12

Syrup:
3 c. water
2 c. sugar
1-2 cinnamon sticks

Cake:
½ lb. unsalted butter (at room temperature)
6 eggs, separated
1   c. sugar
2   c. flour
3   tsp. baking powder
½ tsp. baking soda
2 tsp. cinnamon
1 c. walnuts, chopped coarsely

Prepare Syrup:
In a 2-quart saucepan, combine water and sugar, bring to a boil, then reduce heat to a simmer. Add 1 or 2 cinnamon sticks, and continue to boil gently for 20 minutes. Remove from heat. Cool.

Prepare Cake:
Preheat oven to 350 degrees F.

Grease a 9 x 13-inch pan, and cover the bottom with a sheet of parchment paper. (To get the right size piece of parchment paper, set the baking pan on top of a sheet; and trace around the pan with a pencil. Cut it out with scissors.)

Beat egg whites with an electric mixer until stiff peaks form when the beaters are lifted. Place in refrigerator.

In a large bowl, beat butter until creamy, then add egg yolks, one at a time. Beat well. Add sugar, and continue beating until light and fluffy.

Add flour, baking powder, baking soda, and cinnamon. Mix until well incorporated. Stir in the walnuts; and then, using a spatula and making circular motions, gently fold in egg whites.

Pour into pan, and bake for 35-45 minutes. (To determine whether the cake is done, stick a toothpick in the center. The cake is baked when the toothpick comes out clean.) Remove from oven, and carefully pour cooled syrup over hot cake.

Cool completely in pan before serving.

About the Author

Ladine Housholder has traveled extensively to Pauline sites in Greece and Turkey. A former member of Bible Study Fellowship in Texas, she received the Certificate of Biblical Spirituality from Catholic Theological Union in Chicago. A professional pianist, she resides in the Bavarian Alps.

To order more copies of

Bus to Corinth,

go to Amazon.com.

Also available as a Kindle ebook

Karen Feb 24-2018
Regina Jun 2018

63620463R00219

Made in the USA
Middletown, DE
02 February 2018